PULPIT ROCK

KATE RHODES

**SIMON &
SCHUSTER**

London · New York · Sydney · Toronto · New Delhi

First published in Great Britain by Simon & Schuster UK Ltd, 2020

This paperback edition published 2021

1 3 5 7 9 10 8 6 4 2

Simon & Schuster UK Ltd
1st Floor
222 Gray's Inn Road
London WC1X 8HB

Simon & Schuster Australia, Sydney
Simon & Schuster India, New Delhi

www.simonandschuster.co.uk
www.simonandschuster.com.au
www.simonandschuster.co.in

A CIP catalogue record for this book
is available from the British Library

Paperback ISBN: 978-1-4711-8989-0
eBook ISBN: 978-1-4711-8988-3
Audio ISBN: 978-1-4711-8990-6

Typeset in Sabon by M Rules
Printed and bound by CPI Group (UK) Ltd, Croydon, CR0 4YY

For Teresa Chris

Round
Island

St Helens

St Martin's

Bryher

Tean

Northern Rocks

Tresco

Samson

Eastern
Isles

St Mary's

Bishop Rock

Annet

Gugh

ISLES OF
SCILLY

Western Rocks

St Agnes

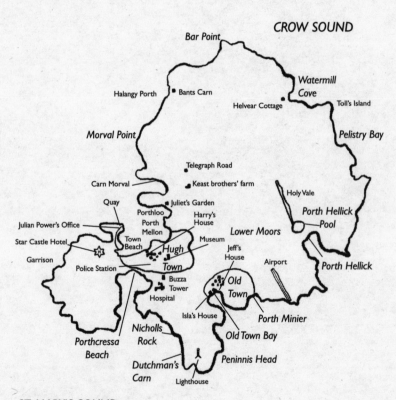

ST MARY'S

CROW SOUND

Bar Point

Watermill
Cove

Halangy Porth • Bants Carn

Toll's Island

Helvear Cottage

Morval Point

Pelistry Bay

Telegraph Road

Carn Morval ■ Keast brothers' farm

Holy Vale

Quay ■ Juliet's Garden

Porth Hellick
Pool

Porthloo
Julian Power's Office Porth
Mellon

Harry's
House

Lower Moors

Star Castle Hotel Town
Beach Museum

Jeff's
House

Garrison Hugh
Town

Airport

Porth Hellick

Police Station

■ Buzza
Tower

Old
Town

Hospital

Isla's House

Porth Minier

Nicholls
Rock

Old Town Bay

Porthcressa
Beach

Dutchman's
Carn

Peninnis Head

Lighthouse

ST MARY'S SOUND

PART 1

'If I must die,
I will encounter darkness as a bride,
And hug it in mine arms.'

Measure for Measure (Act 3, Scene 1),
William Shakespeare

Saturday 3 August

Sabine finishes her shift at midnight. She's glad to serve her last drink, leaving the hotel guests lingering over their liqueurs, while the night porter replaces her behind the bar. The young woman slips outside into air scented by roses in the walled garden, their sweetness clashing with salt rising from the sea. When she looks back at the hotel, it's easy to imagine how it looked five hundred years ago, its thick walls defending St Mary's from invasion, the castle perched high above the shore. She crosses the grounds to the staff accommodation block at a rapid pace, but disappointment hits home when she gets there. No one is waiting for her; just the bare corridor, echoing her footsteps.

Her mood lifts when she finds a note pushed under her door. It contains a message, scrawled in urgent red capitals:

MEET ME AT THE LIGHTHOUSE.

Sabine wastes no time changing into her favourite summer dress. The night is still warm when she takes one of the hotel's

3

bicycles from a rack by the entrance. Her happiness builds as she weaves through Hugh Town's narrow streets, with the breeze tugging her dark hair from its ponytail. She's imagining her university friends' reactions, back home in Riga, when she tells them about the island's beauty and her summer romances. The street lights fade as she pedals harder, her journey illuminated only by stars as she freewheels down to Peninnis Head. This part of the island has its own stark beauty, with a tumble of rocks strewn across deserted moorland, and the lighthouse blinking at the dark.

She abandons the bike on the grass then stands still, absorbing the silence. This is her first moment alone since she ate breakfast with her friend Lily and the other hotel staff. The headland is the most romantic place on St Mary's, cleansed by the Atlantic tide. Huge rock formations loom above the coast-line, resembling the outlines of giants, but the scenery will be forgotten when her new man arrives. They'll drink wine, or go skinny-dipping, then make love on the beach, like last time. She knows he's a bad choice, but the attraction is too strong to ignore. Sabine closes her eyes to imagine him holding her, while the lighthouse casts its gleam across the ocean.

Sabine is still dreaming when a voice whispers her name, in a tone she doesn't recognise. Light sears her retinas when she opens her eyes.

'Stop it,' she laughs. 'You're blinding me.'

There's no reply before something hard batters against her head, then the glare fades and her thoughts splinter into silence. She's barely conscious when her body is dragged across the moor.

Sabine can't tell how much time has passed when she comes round. There's a dull pain in her temple, but no sense of panic. She knows nothing bad could happen on such a small island, yet when she tries to open her eyes, the darkness remains. Fabric has been bound tight around her waist, making it hard to breathe. There's so little air in her lungs it feels like she's drowning. She summons all her strength, but her arms fall useless at her sides, then a muffled voice hisses in her ear.

'Keep still. You're spoiling my work.'

'Let me go, please. You're hurting me.'

'Be brave, sweetheart. Your hair needs to be beautiful for your big day.'

A comb drags through her curls, like when her mother brushed her hair each morning before school, but these movements are savage, yanking the roots until her scalp burns. Sabine's voice is shrill with pain when she cries for help, but the only reply is an ugly snarl of laughter.

1

It's 9 a.m. when I reach my uncle's boatyard on Bryher's eastern coast. I can see the island of Tresco across New Grimsby Sound, green and shimmering in the early sunlight, and my newly varnished boat, moored to the jetty, filling me with pride. Ray designed it for me last spring, but I did all the joinery and hard labour. The bowrider is cut from prime cedar, twenty feet long. It took all my savings, spare time and annual leave from my job as Deputy Commander of the island police, but the result has been worth every back-breaking minute. I used it every day last month, the scorching summer heat turning my daily commute to St Mary's into a pleasure. The boat is bobbing on the incoming tide, small and nimble, straining its mooring ropes for a new adventure.

My dog appears when I step onto the jetty. He's been missing from home since dawn, his tendency to run away just one of many bad habits. Shadow is a three-year-old Czechoslovakian wolfdog, full of restless energy, with a low boredom threshold. He chases ahead at the sight of Ray climbing on deck with a cardboard box in his hands. My uncle spent years at sea, before coming home to the Scillies to build boats. He's in his sixties now, almost as tall as me, with the athletic build of a professional sailor, his thick grey hair ruffled by the breeze.

'What are you putting in the hold?' I call out.

'Sandwiches and energy drinks; you'll need them later. Three hours of open-water swimming is a strange way to spend your day off.'

'I'm a born masochist.'

'You must be.' He straightens up to face me. 'Have you chosen a name for your boat yet?'

'I'm still thinking.'

'Don't wait forever, Ben. It's bad luck to leave a vessel unnamed.'

'I didn't know you were superstitious.'

'It's you that should worry.' He gives a slow-dawning smile. 'She's your boat, not mine.'

'Can you steer while I put on my wetsuit?'

Ray leans down to start the engine. Shadow is already standing on deck, sniffing the sea air. The dog's glacial blue eyes give me a long stare, blaming me for the delay in casting off.

'Strong currents this morning; you'll have to swim hard around the headland.' My uncle shouts to make himself heard above the engine's noise as the boat edges into St Mary's Sound. 'How many of you are training today?'

'Six, unless you fancy joining us?'

'Not a chance in hell. You lot are gluttons for punishment.'

'At least we're getting fit.'

The short journey unfolds in amicable silence. Sunlight glitters on the water as we pass Tresco's western coast, where dinghies are moored in New Grimsby's harbour, before the pale sand of Saffron Cove comes into view. Our pace quickens as the current drags us past the deserted island of Samson, where abandoned houses stand on the hillside, their roof tiles stolen by winter gales a century ago. Shadow seems to enjoy our sudden burst of speed. He's standing on the boat's prow with his paws on the rail, tongue lolling, his grey fur ruffled by the wind.

The outline of St Mary's fills the horizon as we sail due south. It's the biggest island in Scilly, almost five miles long, and a metropolis compared to Bryher, where I was born. The island used to make its living from flower growing and fishing, but most people's jobs depend on tourism now. Day trippers arrive by the thousand in summer, to admire the island's archaeological sites and sunbathe in small coves overshadowed by granite cliffs. Its ragged coastline is closer now and I realise that my uncle was telling the truth; I must be crazy to enter the island swimathon for the first time.

The brutal competition takes place every August; its route circles St Mary's coastline, beginning with a noisy send-off from Hugh Town harbour. My small team has been training all summer, hoping to complete the circuit in less than five hours. There's plenty of camaraderie right now, but when the starter's whistle blows in two weeks' time, we'll take no prisoners.

The spray is cool on my face as the boat passes Garrison Point, where the Star Castle peers down from its rocky promontory, and I'm already itching to be in the water. I've loved wild swimming since my child-hood. I know its dangers, yet I'm still keen to dive in when we reach Porthcressa Bay. The beach is one of the prettiest on St Mary's. Its wide horseshoe of sand will soon be scattered with tourists, tanning themselves mahogany, or drinking cappuccinos in the café that overlooks the shore. Right now it's deserted apart from four other swimmers, pulling on goggles and doing warm-up routines.

'Get moving then,' Ray says. 'It's too shallow to moor.'

'Hang on to my phone, can you? My whole life's in there.'

I drop the mobile into my uncle's hand then plunge into the water. The Atlantic chill bites hard, even though this summer is shaping up to be the hottest on record; the ocean's saline tang fills my mouth, its thunder silencing every other sound. My carthorse build works to my advantage once I'm submerged. My movements are heavy and lumbering on land, but my strength proves useful as I swim for shore, enjoying the power behind each stroke. The swimmers waiting for me on the beach include two other police officers: my deputy, Sergeant Eddie Nickell, and our newest recruit, Constable Isla Tremayne. The other two men are Steve and Paul Keast, a pair of local farmers. The brothers are old friends of mine, in their thirties like me. We used to play rugby together and have met regularly for a pint since I returned to the islands. They could almost be twins, sharing the same lanky frame, messy brown hair and dark eyes, yet their personalities are chalk and cheese. Steve is two years older and a real extrovert, while Paul is dragged along in his brother's slipstream. Both men are lifeboat volunteers, but Paul's the weaker swimmer. He'll need extra training sessions to help him over the finishing line.

'Where's Sabine?' I call out. 'Isn't she coming?'

'Stuck at work, I bet,' Steve replies. 'The hotels are packed.'

The girl will be disappointed to miss our training. Sabine is only here for the summer, but she's thrown herself into preparing for the race, swimming whenever she gets free time. Eddie looks like a blond-haired sixth former as he greets me, beaming with excitement about the challenge ahead. Isla Tremayne seems less enthusiastic. The local girl is twenty-one years old, a tomboy with an athletic build, black hair cut shorter than mine, with a serious air. She has worked hard from day one, but is still finding her feet. Isla observes every procedure then takes notes, like she's cramming for an exam. I was surprised to see her name on the list of volunteers for the swimathon, but she's got plenty of stamina, and tall waves don't faze her whenever we hit a swell.

'I'm on duty later. Maybe I'll skip training and sunbathe instead,' she says, her face deadpan.

'No chance,' Eddie replies.

The young sergeant grabs her wrist, and the rest of us splash into the water behind them. At least the tide is in our favour, carrying us north as we leave the harbour's protection. When I look back at the land, the coastal path unwinds like a thread of pale brown wool, separating the trees and wildflowers from the shore. Ray is sailing fifty metres behind as a safety measure, in case anyone runs into trouble during the two-hour swim to Pelistry Bay. The rescue boat allows me to focus on my own performance without worrying about the others. I concentrate on finding my rhythm, hands slicing through the water's chill, but exhilaration only sets in when I've been swimming hard for ten minutes.

The ocean sings in my ears and endorphins flood my system as we pass the black outline of Nicholl's Rock, a stone cathedral rising from the sea. I've swum this stretch of coast so often, its inlets and crevices are imprinted on my memory. Ray knows the waters well enough to keep his distance. The seabed contains hidden spikes of basalt, sharp enough to rip a boat's hull to shreds. The shore here is beautiful but vicious, covered with car-sized granite boulders.

I concentrate on building my pace, shifting through the waves at a steady crawl, until my hamstrings burn. We're heading for Dutchman's Carn, a rocky outcrop that comes into view as the cliffs soar to my left. The rest of the team are lagging behind, except for Eddie. The sight of him thrashing through the water brings a smile to my face. My deputy would love to beat me, and he's got a ten-year advantage, but I'll use every trick in the book to stay in front. The lighthouse appears as I round Peninnis Head. Gulls are scrapping for food on the rocks below, their screams blending with the ocean's noise.

Someone is calling my name when I surface for a break. Ray waves at me from the boat, arms flailing like he's performing semaphore. One of the other swimmers must be in trouble. But when I look back, they're keeping pace. Eddie is ten metres away, followed closely by Isla and Steve, with Paul working hard to catch up. The boat is rising and falling with each breaker, but my uncle is intent on catching my attention. When he points at the shore I glimpse a pale outline against the black cliff face. It could be a kite tangled on the rocks, but when I swim closer my vision clears. The shape is swinging from left to right, slow and heavy as a pendulum. It looks like a doll dressed in white, suspended from a piece of string, with a swathe of fabric flailing in the wind.

13

'A bloody suicide.'

I hiss out the words, then yell for Eddie and Isla at the top of my voice. I cut through the water at my fastest pace, even though nothing is waiting for us, except the loneliest form of death.

Lily searches for her friend in the staff block at 10 a.m. She's been hard at work for three hours already, changing beds and scouring toilets for today's new arrivals. The hotel is so warm, a trickle of sweat runs down her backbone, but she's got no complaints. Her job at the Star Castle has freed her from the misery of her past, providing a living wage and new friends. There's a smile on the girl's face when she trots down the corridor. Sabine should be back from her swim by now; there will be time for coffee and gossip before her break ends.

The girl's movements are tentative when she taps on her friend's door. It's still hard to believe that Sabine has singled her out. The older girl is beautiful and popular, yet she's chosen Lily as her closest ally. Maybe it's because they're both outsiders. Lily moved to St Mary's from Plymouth five years ago, and Sabine is a Latvian student, only here for the summer. When she knocks again, the door swings open, taking her by surprise. Her friend always keeps it locked, even though no one would steal anything here. Sabine says old habits die hard – burglaries happen often in her part of Riga.

Lily is puzzled by what she sees. It doesn't look like her friend slept in her room last night, the bed neatly made. Her uniform has been thrown across the back of a chair, her shoes abandoned in the corner. Sabine promised to meet her here, and she's never let her down before. Maybe her mysterious new boyfriend is to blame. Lily is about to leave when she spots a scrap of paper on the floor, the bright red words catching her eye. Someone must have left it for Sabine, but who would invite her to meet him at the lighthouse at midnight?

A ripple of shock runs through her when she reads the cryptic message again – the handwriting is familiar. She drops the note into her pocket in case anyone visits the room before Sabine returns. The management are obsessed by maintaining the hotel's excellent reputation; they frown on staff keeping late hours, particularly if their work suffers. Lily is about to leave when she spots her friend's bright pink phone, flashing with messages. One of the numbers on the screen belongs to Lily's brother. It looks like Harry has been lying through his teeth. He put the note under Sabine's door and sent her three texts yesterday. Her friend is probably with him now, planning to bunk off work. Anger makes her shove the phone into her pocket so she can hand it to Sabine this afternoon when her shift ends. There's still no sign of her friend, the corridor empty. Lily's heart is beating too fast when she pulls the door shut and hurries back to her room.

My eyes fix on the woman's body dangling from Pulpit Rock as I scale the narrow path to the cliff top, her face covered by a white veil. The soles of my feet are raw from climbing the wall of basalt, but the pain doesn't register. I'm more interested in why her life ended with so much drama. What kind of desperation made her leap into thin air? I've got no way of identifying her yet. My first task will be to haul her corpse back onto solid land. I stop for a moment at the top, looking around for potential witnesses. Peninnis Head is a stretch of moorland, covered in grass and heather, studded with boulders, but there are no walkers in sight. The island's automated lighthouse stands on the highest peak, fifty metres away. It's the only man-made object in sight, and its construction is basic, just a rotating lantern raised from the ground by a black metal frame. When I gaze down from the cliff's edge, the crown of the woman's head is visible, and her lace veil fluttering in the breeze. The crooked angle of her neck is so unnatural it must be broken.

I can see my boat drifting on the tide while Ray drops anchor a safe distance from a line of exposed rocks. Luckily, the shipping channel back to the mainland is clear, no vessels sailing near enough to catch sight of the victim. Eddie is scrambling up the cliff face, the others swimming ashore, but responsibility for finding out what happened to the woman rests on my shoulders alone. My decade in the Murder Squad in London never cured my squeamishness; my guts twist into a knot when I assess the scene again. We'll have to set up a cordon fast, so no dog walkers pollute the scene.

Eddie is panting for breath when he reaches my side. 'Do you know who she is?'

'We'll need photos before we find out; I should take one from up here. I'll get Lawrie to bring a camera from the station.'

'No need, I've got my phone.'

I watch in amazement as he fishes a waterproof bag from the sleeve of his wetsuit, his phone tucked inside. 'You must have been a great boy scout, Eddie.'

He looks embarrassed. 'I always carry it, in case Michelle calls about the baby.'

Eddie has been the world's most committed dad since his daughter Lottie arrived last year, greeting fatherhood with the same enthusiasm he brings to his job. He even twisted my arm into becoming her godfather, but today I'm just grateful for his vigilance. He stands close to the cliff edge, taking photographs for the coroner's report, while I walk over to the other swimmers. Isla's bent double, hands pressed against her knees, catching her breath. Steve is a few metres behind, but Paul is still struggling up the path, forcing me to wait for him. I persuaded both of my friends to become special constables so they could act as stewards during the islands' festivals and help out in emergencies.

'I need you two in Hugh Town,' I tell the brothers, once Paul arrives.

'Ray can take us back to Porthcressa,' Steve replies.

'Rest first, then swim out to the boat. I want you to guard the coastal path, please. Don't let anyone up here.'

'Do you want Ray to drop your clothes at the station?'

'Thanks, Steve, that would be great.'

He remains composed while I hand out more instructions, but his younger brother's eyes are glassy while he stares down at the woman's figure hanging from the cliff face. Paul was always sensitive when we were kids, quick to empathise with anyone in trouble. It doesn't surprise me when he turns his back abruptly, stumbling away before spewing his breakfast into the heather, the brothers' reactions at opposite ends of the spectrum. People often succumb to shock on witnessing a fatality, but I can't worry about anyone except the victim today. Steve will have to take care of his brother by himself.

Time is passing too quickly; it's mid-morning already, and everything must happen in the right sequence. When I call the pathologist, Dr Keillor, he sounds reluctant to sacrifice his golf game for such a miserable purpose. I'm lucky that my boss, DCI Madron, is on holiday in France for another ten days. The man keeps promising to retire, then changing his mind at the last minute; he seems obsessed by creating a spotless legacy. His insistence that every task be recorded in minute detail would only slow us down – there will be time for paperwork once we know why this woman died.

I realise how Pulpit Rock gained its name when I scramble over granite boulders to retrieve the victim's body. One huge rock balances on another, like a fire and brimstone preacher leaning on his lectern, delivering his sermon to a reluctant congregation. The priest seems to be addressing the Atlantic's vastness, the rock formation jutting out across the sea. I use Eddie's phone to photograph the noose that ended the woman's life, but my concerns are growing. How many suicides are composed enough to wind a rope three times around a boulder, then secure it with a double reef knot, before hurling themselves to a certain death? I try to ignore the rocks below, gaping at me like rows of broken teeth. The next gust of wind brings the rope close enough to grab, but Eddie and I need three attempts to haul the woman's dead weight up the cliff. Her form is cold and lifeless as I carry her to the nearest piece of level ground.

When I lay the body on the grass, the woman's identity remains a mystery, her face obscured by layers of thick white lace. Only her feet and hands are exposed, her nails painted a delicate shade of pink.

'Shall I lift the veil?' Eddie asks.

'I need one more photo first.'

She looks like an archetypal bride when I step back to capture the image, her slim form dressed in an ankle-length gown. Dark curls spill out from behind the opaque veil; poppies and cornflowers have been threaded through her hair, but they're already wilting.

Eddie and Isla are standing close by when I pull back the lace. The woman looks familiar, but the picture doesn't make sense. Her face has been carefully made-up, eyelids coated with pale grey shadow and lashes darkened by mascara, her twisted mouth glossy with lipstick. It's her tortured expression that makes me replace the veil fast. I'm hoping that our newest recruit hasn't seen enough to identify the victim.

'We should wait for the pathologist,' I say. 'Keep your distance, both of you.'

Eddie follows my instruction but Isla steps closer. Her face is oddly calm when she whispers a few words.

'I recognise that tattoo on her foot; the sun symbol's meant to bring good luck. It's Sabine, isn't it, boss?'

'You're right, I'm afraid.'

It goes without saying that the vivid orange design on the girl's skin has failed to do its job. Guilt washes over me when I think about her death. I've trained with her a dozen times and never spotted signs of depression, but suicide is hard to predict. My old work partner in London took her own life, after pretending to be fine right to the end.

I push my feelings about the girl's death aside before using Eddie's phone to call the station in Hugh Town. My voice resonates back from the handset while I instruct Lawrie Deane to pick me up immediately. When I straighten up, I catch sight of a distinctive yellow bicycle lying on the grass by the lighthouse. The Star Castle's name is painted on its frame. Why would Sabine dress up in full bridal regalia, then ride here in the middle of the night, instead of swallowing a handful of pills in the privacy of her own room? The sun burns the back of my neck as I return to her body, until a sudden breeze rises from the sea. It sends the veil billowing upwards, and the girl's face greets me again, her tortured stare impossible to avoid.

4

Lily has changed out of her maid's uniform, dressed now in black trousers and a crisp white blouse. It took just ten minutes to transform herself from a chambermaid into a waitress. Some of the other staff complain about having to perform many different tasks around the hotel, but Lily enjoys the variety. She will serve guests their late-morning coffee until her shift ends, then be free to look for Harry. Lily tries to focus on her work, instead of worrying about confronting her brother this afternoon.

The restaurant is her favourite place in the hotel, the ancient stones in its exposed walls revealing the Star Castle's origins. One of the porters told her that it was built by Elizabeth I; the castle has remained hidden behind its star-shaped perimeter walls for five centuries. Lily often visits the room when the last guests have gone to bed, to touch the walls and marvel at their permanence, yet she's too annoyed for the hotel's long history to give her pleasure today. Two other waiters are on duty, but Sabine still hasn't arrived.

The girl keeps busy, slipping between tables with a coffee

jug in hand. She refreshes a woman's cup and acknowledges her murmured thanks with a smile, before a male guest beckons her closer. She would rather avoid him, but it's too late. The man's name is Liam Trewin; he's in his early forties, and Lily can't explain why he makes her uncomfortable. Maybe it's the directness of his mid-blue stare; his gaze so invasive she feels like a specimen in a laboratory. Everything about him reeks of money. Even his blond hair looks expensive, falling neatly across his forehead, framing features that aren't quite handsome enough for Hollywood. His eyes are a fraction too close together, thin lips adding an edge of cruelty to his smile.

'How are you today, young lady?' His voice is a slow American drawl.

'Fine, thank you, sir.'

'What are you called again?'

'Lily.'

'Pretty name for a pretty girl.' His glossy smile looks unnaturally bright. 'Where's our friend Sabine this morning?'

'I'm not sure.'

'I thought she'd be on duty.' A frown line appears between his eyes. 'I'm hoping to tour the island with her later, if she's free.'

'Sorry, I don't know where she is.'

'Ask your manager for me, can you?'

'Yes, sir.'

Lily can feel Trewin's gaze tracking her as she hurries away. She knows Sabine would never agree to spend time alone in his company. Only yesterday she joked about the man's pathetic attempts to lure her back to his room with gifts and bottles of wine. The girl's throat goes dry when she approaches one of the hotel's managers. Lily has developed a crush on Tom Polkerris, despite him being married and almost twenty years her senior. The man has always treated her kindly, but she doesn't want to get her friend in trouble, even though she warned her that Harry's flings never last long. It's easier to tell her boss a lie than admit Sabine's probably with her brother.

'Sabine's not here, sir. Mr Trewin's asking where she is.'

'Is she in her room?'

'I don't think so.'

'Has the guy been bothering you?' Polkerris glances around the room, as if he's only just realised that a staff member is missing.

'Not really, he just wanted to know.'

'Tell him she's off duty, please, Lily. I'll find her now.'

Trewin seems irritated when she returns to his table, a muscle twitching in his jaw. 'My hire car will go to waste.' His eyes skim her body again. 'Unless you fancy taking a drive instead?'

'Sorry, I'm busy this afternoon.'

The man's gaze is sharp with anger when she backs away.

5

I'd like to guard Sabine's body until the pathologist arrives, but the luxury of honouring the dead isn't an option. I'm Commander until the DCI returns, and I can't attend a crime scene dressed in a wetsuit with a pair of goggles dangling from my hand. Eddie and Isla remain at Pulpit Rock to wait for Dr Keillor when Lawrie Deane collects me at midday in the island force's only van. The sergeant is a curmudgeon, in his mid-fifties, face set in a permanent scowl, his red hair cropped close to his skull. He gazes straight ahead as the van trundles across rutted ground to King Edward's Road, while I focus on the five-minute journey back to town, instead of imagining the girl's misery before she died.

The area's beauty is undeniable as the fields of Peninnis slip past, yellow with ripe wheat, the Atlantic unfurling in the background. The lane narrows as we near Hugh Town, edged by drystone walls. A group of tourists is clustered round Buzza Tower, photographing the old windmill from every angle. All of St Mary's hotels and holiday cottages are packed to capacity, the population swelling to over two thousand, which will make our lives more difficult.

Once we reach town, grey buildings faced with local stone press in on us. The shopping area by the quay is crawling with humanity. People are dressed in shorts and flip-flops, wandering through the narrow lanes, browsing in Mumford's for books and magazines, or buying picnic ingredients from the Co-op. The island's carefree mood will soon be broken by the announcement of Sabine's death.

'Are you okay, boss? Eddie said the girl was done up in bride's clothes.'

'None of us saw it coming. She must have been suffering in silence.'

'You're sure it was suicide?'

'I think Sabine cycled there, on a Star Castle bike. We won't know until tomorrow if anyone else was involved.'

'None of the islanders would hurt a young girl like that.'

'We've had violent crime here before, Lawrie. We can't be certain of anything till the pathologist gives his verdict. It looks like suicide, but she may have been targeted.'

'Our very own psycho killer,' Deane mutters. 'Just what we need.'

'Don't share details, even with your family. If this gets out it'll be all round the island in five minutes.'

The sergeant gives me an old-fashioned look for questioning his loyalty. Deane knows St Mary's better than any of us; he's lived here for decades. There's a difference between the people here and those on the off-islands, where there are few cars and even less amenities. Most of St Mary's inhabitants enjoy being surrounded by neighbours, with a hospital, sports centre and societies to join. They're less reserved than my neighbours on Bryher, who can avoid leaving its shores for weeks at a time. I can't forecast how a young woman's bizarre death will affect the island's upbeat personality.

We've arrived at Garrison Lane already, the pebble-dashed walls of the police house rising up to greet me. It's one of the smallest stations in the UK, with a reception area, a couple of offices and two holding cells. On days like this I yearn for the state-of-the-art building in Hammersmith where I spent a decade working as an undercover murder investigator for the Met, with every type of specialist kit under one roof, but there's no turning the clock back. Serious crime in the Scillies is so rare, anything more than the bare minimum would be a waste of resources. St Mary's is like the land that time forgot, with no CCTV, and little violent crime, except the odd drunken brawl.

'Can you ask one of our special constables to deliver the crime scene kit to Eddie and Isla at Pulpit Rock? They'll want clothes too. We can't leave them out there, sweltering.'

'I'll get it sorted.' He gives me a long-suffering look.

'Then phone the forensics lab in Penzance, please. Ask Liz Gannick to fly over straight away.' I'm living dangerously by requesting help from the county's Chief of Forensic Services. She doesn't suffer fools gladly, but I want to know every detail behind Sabine's death, before evidence is lost.

Ray must have arrived at the station before us; I spot Shadow tethered outside as we park. The clothes I left on the boat have been placed inside the porch, neatly folded, my phone in the pocket of my jeans. It's a relief to change out of the clammy neoprene of my wetsuit once we get inside, but I know it's only a matter of time before people start asking us why the coastal path is blocked.

'Answer the phone while I'm out, can you, Lawrie? I'm going to the Star Castle – I'll leave the dog with you.'

The sergeant parks himself behind the reception desk with a sour look on his face, giving me a grudging nod when I leave.

Sabine's place of work lies on the Garrison, a five-minute walk from the station. The rocky stretch of land owes its name to the British army's repeated attempts to use the island as defence against foreign invaders. The Star Castle has become a deluxe hotel and is a magnet for tourists, who flock to admire its architecture. Aerial photos make it look like a Christmas decoration, its star-shaped boundaries perfectly preserved. I pass through the town's narrow lanes, then walk up the steep hill to the archway, where soldiers on horseback once entered the compound. Sentries would have manned the lookout points centuries ago, enjoying a long view over land and sea. St Mary's was vital territory back then, but when I look east now, there's little to defend except an unspoiled landscape, shaped by centuries of farming. Hugh Town's picturesque jumble of fishermen's cottages would be called a village back on the mainland.

I'm still struggling to process Sabine's death when I enter the hotel's foyer, the quiet hitting me immediately. The castle's metre-thick walls block every external noise. All I can hear is a buzz of conversation drifting from the restaurant, where guests are gathering for an early lunch, the air scented by a huge floral display. The receptionist offers a serene smile, as if nothing could disturb her inner calm, before summoning her manager. Tom Polkerris arrives soon after she drops the phone back onto its cradle. I have to quell my dislike when he shakes my hand. He was the class bully in my year at Five Islands School, devoted to making other kids' lives miserable. I remember getting a detention for slamming him against a wall, after he yelled taunts at a friend of mine. He was an overweight teenager, using his bulk to intimidate, with rampant acne and frizzy brown hair. Today his appearance matches his role as joint manager of a high-class hotel. He seems unsettled by my arrival, but that goes with the territory: there's no escaping your past on an island this small.

Polkerris is six inches shorter than me, but must be following a rigorous exercise regime, his sharp suit revealing a lean physique. His hair is carefully styled, jaw covered with designer stubble. There's a note of concern in his voice when he finally greets me.

'This is unexpected, Ben. How can I help?'

'I need to see you and Rhianna in private, please.'

'Come this way. She's in our office doing paperwork.'

I follow him down a windowless corridor that cuts through the heart of the castle, until we enter a well-lit room with a view of the gardens. Two desks face each other across metres of plush grey carpet. Polkerris's wife is staring at her laptop. Rhianna is a native islander too, but we didn't socialise as kids. Her parents sent her to an exclusive boarding school on the mainland, and I've never seen her slumming it in the local pubs. Rhianna's appearance is even more stylish than her husband's when she rises to her feet: blonde hair flows over her shoulders in a sleek ripple, a tight grey dress accentuating her slimness. Her features remind me of a china doll with porcelain skin, green eyes open a fraction too wide. Tom Polkerris has met his match: there's no way this ice maiden would allow anyone to bully her. She barely raises a smile before pointing at a seat by the window, as if I'm being sent to the naughty step.

'I've got some news about Sabine Bertans,' I tell them.

'Not in trouble, is she?' Rhianna looks surprised. 'She's got the right paperwork. We've hired plenty of Latvian girls over the years; they're hard workers, nice manners too.'

'When's the last time you saw her?'

'Sabine was serving in the bar last night,' Tom replies. 'She volunteered for an extra shift this morning, but never showed up.'

'Why didn't you say?' his wife snaps. 'I'm in charge of staff.'

The couple glare at each other with such animosity it looks like a war might erupt at any moment, but domestic squabbles are irrelevant now.

'We know Sabine left the hotel after her shift ended.'

'That's hard to believe,' Rhianna says. 'She didn't finish till midnight. Please just tell us what's wrong.'

'Her body's been found by Pulpit Rock. I can't reveal any details, but we're certain it's Sabine. I'll do a formal identification later today for the records.'

'Are you saying she was killed?' Tom Polkerris's voice vibrates with shock.

'I can't share anything at this stage, I'm afraid.'

His face drains of colour, before he drops into a chair, collapsing like a house of cards. There's no sign now of the kid who loved to goad his classmates. Polkerris is open-mouthed with shock, but his wife's calmness remains intact.

'When did it happen?' Her tone is irritable, as if the girl's death is a minor disruption to her plans.

'We don't have a clear picture yet; I'll need to search her room before I leave. Did she seem distressed in the last few days?'

'Not at all, she was loving her time here,' Tom Polkerris replies.

His wife's composure vanishes suddenly. 'Our guests can't hear about this. They come here for peace and quiet.'

'Shut up, Rhianna,' Polkerris mutters. 'Didn't you hear what Ben said? One of our staff's been killed; nothing else matters.'

'Tell that to our shareholders if we get bad reviews on TripAdvisor.' Her lips purse into a tight line, making me question what emotions exist inside that glossy shell.

'Would it be okay to hold a public meeting here later? I want to announce Sabine's death before gossip takes hold. Your restaurant would be ideal.'

'It's busy,' Rhianna snaps. 'The church hall's your best option.'

Tom looks set to argue, but keeps his mouth shut. Our conversation has revealed the couple's differences: they seem to be falling apart in the face of this crisis instead of pulling together. Polkerris's walk is unsteady as he leads me through the hotel's internal garden to the staff accommodation block. It looks like he's spent the morning knocking back booze, but fresh air seems to help. By the time we reach the single-storey building his gait has steadied.

'Sabine was in room eleven,' he mutters. 'It was unlocked when I looked for her earlier.'

I pull on sterile gloves before touching the door handle. If anyone else turns out to be involved in Sabine's death, I could be trampling all over primary evidence, so it pays to take care. The air carries the synthetic odour of cheap perfume when I enter. A narrow bed is shoved against the wall, and the room could belong to any young woman, with hairclips, sunglasses and loose change scattered across the dressing table. She must have left in a hurry: her uniform lies in a crumpled heap, as if she was desperate to escape. If she left a suicide note, there's no sign of it here. My eyes catch on a red dress hanging inside her wardrobe. Sabine will miss out on a lifetime of parties for reasons I can't explain. I ignore the anger swilling around in my gut; there's no place for it on an investigation. Regrets are fine in your down time, but while you're on duty, they only trip you up.

It doesn't take me long to check under the mattress, behind furniture and in the pockets of her clothes, with no luck at all. I need her phone urgently to understand the context of her death, but all I find is a plastic wallet containing some letters, Sabine's passport and travel documents, which I drop into an evidence bag. Polkerris is still leaning against the wall outside, his head sagging as if the weight of his skull is a heavy burden.

'Are you okay, Tom?'

The man's eyes blink shut. 'Do you think she suffered?'

'It's too soon to tell.'

'She was nineteen years old.' A sheen of perspiration has erupted on his pale skin.

'Let's focus on tasks, shall we? I have to find Sabine's

phone. I saw her using it recently; the case is bright pink, decorated with flowers. Can you ask your staff to look for it in the hotel?'

'Of course.'

'Did Sabine have a boyfriend?'

'I wouldn't know, I'm afraid.'

'What about close friends? Who did she hang out with on her days off?'

'I can't say.' He hesitates before speaking again. 'We don't pry into our staff's private lives.'

'How did she seem to you last night?'

'Relaxed, as usual, joking with the waiters. I was on duty from six till after midnight, circulating between the restaurant, bar and reception desk. We said good night when her shift ended.'

'Do you know any personal details?'

'Only that she was Catholic; she asked if there was a church nearby.'

'I'll check that out. My team may need to come back, today or tomorrow.'

'Any time, one of us is always here.'

I close the door to Sabine's room, then ask Polkerris to lock it and hand over the key, so no one tampers with her belongings. Just as we're leaving I spy a figure at the end of the corridor, little more than a shadow, vanishing before her face is exposed. It's a reminder that rumours will already be flying around St Mary's, unless we provide accurate information.

Polkerris is too preoccupied to notice our eavesdropper

as we cross the gardens, my gaze scanning the flower-beds. The roses make an ideal backdrop for the lavish weddings that form the mainstay of the hotel's business, with couples paying thousands to say their vows in such a historic setting. My old classmate's calm has returned when we finally reach the exit, making me wonder where he's buried the aggression that fuelled him as a boy. His expression is sober as I tell him not to inform his staff of Sabine's death until after the public briefing at 3 p.m.

Lawrie Deane is still trapped behind the reception desk when I get back to the station, but Shadow jumps to his feet, clearly hoping for a run along the beach. Lawrie is on the phone to the airport, which brings the day's first good news: Liz Gannick's flight from Penzance will touch down soon. I'll accept all help on offer, if it gets us nearer the truth.

I'm about to head for the airport when I spot a brown line under the doormat. A manila envelope has got stuck there and been overlooked until now; my name and title are written on the front in ragged black capitals: DI BEN KITTO. I consider chucking it on my desk to deal with later, but instinct makes me peer inside. The envelope contains a single Polaroid photo, and the image tightens the knot in my stomach. Sabine stares back at me, her face framed by the veil she wore this morning. This time she's very much alive. No make-up has been applied to her face yet – she's still the natural beauty I remember – but the expression in her eyes is one of abject terror. If she took the picture just before committing suicide, it's a macabre type of selfie. It's possible she delivered the envelope last night, before cycling out to Peninnis Head.

Suddenly it hits home that the girl I swam with has been wrenched from this world, no matter how she died. When I stare at the photo again, it gives no clues about timing or location. I can't tell whether it was taken minutes or hours before her death. When I turn it over, someone has used a white marker to scrawl *The bride in her glory will ever be fair* on the black plastic. I don't know where the phrase comes from, but I need to find out. Sabine could have written it herself, certain that dying young would preserve her beauty forever, but she never struck me as vain. If she was murdered, the words have a different meaning. The killer wasn't content with the brutal murder of a vibrant young woman: he's taunting us, and the bastard may be less than a mile away, already planning his next attack.

6

I drive east to the airport at one o'clock with Shadow on the back seat, the photo burning a hole in my pocket. I'll need to get the handwriting identified, depending on the pathologist's news. I follow the coast road north, past Town Beach, where fishing boats lie stranded by the low tide. When I reach Porth Mellon, tourists are dawdling along the pavement with cameras slung from their shoulders, ice creams in hand. They look like members of a parallel universe, oblivious to all forms of danger. I drive through farmland on the Lower Moors, where sheep are sheltering from the sun's glare below tall elm trees. Flower fields line the airport's approach road, currently lying fallow, the soil a dull brown. It's easy to forget that the entire landscape glittered with daffodils and narcissi just a few months ago.

I reach the car park in time to watch Liz Gannick's ten-seater plane taxi down the airstrip after a perfect landing. Once it's stationary, the site manager lets me walk across the landing strip. The pilot, Jade Finbury, jumps down onto the runway, leaving her passenger locked inside. The brunette is in her early-thirties, with a round, appealing face that seems designed to smile. She moved here from London five or six years ago, straight after qualifying as a pilot. Jade has adapted well to island life, finding a partner and making friends among the community. I don't know her well but she's good at her job. I've been her passenger plenty of times, when I fly to the mainland for training events.

'Your guest's got plenty of luggage, Ben. Shall I get one of the porters?'

'That would be great, thanks.'

'Has something happened while I've been away?'

'A young woman died. You've just flown Cornwall's chief forensics officer over to help us.'

Her smile vanishes. 'Is it someone from St Mary's?'

'We're holding a public meeting at the church hall at three this afternoon to announce the news.'

She shakes her head in denial. 'Nothing bad ever happens here.'

'Come to the briefing, Jade. We'll have a better picture by then.'

'I'll be there.'

The pilot's professional manner returns when she grabs her flight manual and heads for the airport building at a brisk march, leaving me to welcome Gannick. A small mountain of boxes and crates fill the front seats, hiding the chief forensics officer from view. Her loud northern voice starts yelling instructions before we've even said hello.

'I've brought our mobile lab with me. Don't just stand there, this kit weighs a ton.'

'Great to see you too, Liz. Thanks for coming over.'

'Why in God's name do you need help with a suicide?'

'The girl was nineteen. Her parents will want every detail, and I need to know if anyone else was involved.'

Gannick scans my face for signs of panic, already making assessments. I fight my impulse to help her down the steps, watching as she manoeuvres onto the airstrip with ease, wielding her crutches like an acrobat. She told me about having spina bifida, but her condition rarely seems to slow her down. She looks more like a student than a senior crime scene investigator, her petite form clad in tight jeans and a scarlet T-shirt. The last time we met her short hair was peroxide blonde, but now it's raven black, with a few neon pink spikes for added interest. Her pixie-like features are so small and angular, they could belong to a twelve-year-old, but her gaze is world-weary.

'Let's hope it's worth my while.' She's already twitching with impatience. 'What are we waiting for? The scene's getting corrupted as we speak.'

'It's only five minutes away.'

'Have you got that bloody dog in the van?'

'He'll be overjoyed to see you.'

Gannick's loathing for Shadow is part of her act. She grumbles about him, yet slips him expensive dog treats when she thinks no one's looking. I've only worked with the chief forensics officer on one previous investigation, but her style is unchanged. She's good company off-duty, but works at breakneck speed, her brusque communication style harsh enough to terrify the faint-hearted. She scowls with irritation while the porter helps me load her equipment into the police van, as if the boxes should transport themselves.

The forensics officer sits in the back with Shadow, firing out questions during our short drive around the island's western coast, past Old Town's horseshoe bay, but she falls silent as we approach Peninnis Head. The area has been cordoned off with crime scene tape, a sterile white tent erected over Sabine's body. Gannick makes me put on a white Tyvek suit, and overshoes, even though my footprints are already scattered liberally across the grass. The synthetic fabric is punishing on a hot day – sunlight blasts the rocky landscape, bleaching the granite from grey to white. I catch sight of the pathologist walking back to his car, just as Gannick reappears at my side.

'I'm glad you're working with us, Liz. The victim was an acquaintance of mine.'

'Don't worry, I know what I'm doing. They gave me the top job for a reason.'

I'd forgotten Gannick's tendency to turn compliments into insults. She ducks under the cordon while I walk over to speak to the pathologist. Gareth Keillor retired from Home Office duties several years ago, but is still licensed to act as the islands' consultant. His small eyes observe me through tortoiseshell glasses, scant grey hair unsettled by the breeze. He slings his medical case into the boot of his car, as if he can't wait to escape.

'Thank God we don't see that type of death often,' he says. 'It's a horrible way for a young woman's life to end.'

'If she was killed, I'll need to put the island on lockdown.'

'She didn't commit suicide, that's certain. The abrasions round her wrists are rope burns: she was tied up, then murdered, within the last twelve hours.' His hands rest on the boot of his car. 'I can't tell whether she was dressed in that bride's outfit before or after the flowers were woven through her hair, but it was a labour of love for someone.'

'You're sure she didn't jump from Pulpit Rock?'

'One hundred per cent.'

'What about other injuries?'

'I've taken swabs for the lab, but there's no sign of sexual assault, if that's what you mean.'

'Do you think she was tortured?'

His face is regretful. 'Let's hope not. We'll find out more when I examine the body again.'

'Thanks for your help, Gareth. Sorry to interrupt your game.'

Keillor gives a dry laugh. 'I was winning hands down, but all I want now is a stiff drink.'

The pathologist gives a quick salute before folding his neat frame into his brand-new Audi. St Mary's is just five miles long, but the luxury vehicle must compensate for his grisly duties whenever there's an unexplained death. Gareth Keillor is the only pathologist I know who views the murder victims he examines as humans, rather than biological specimens, and he's confirmed my suspicions. I make a quick phone call to Lawrie Deane, telling him to block travel to and from the island with immediate effect.

Liz Gannick's shadow is moving around inside the tent that shields Sabine's body, a box of specimen bottles lying open on the grass. Eddie and Isla are sitting on a rock nearby, their wetsuits piled at their feet. They must be keen to cool down, after guarding the site all morning in the blazing sun.

'We can go back to the station once I've spoken to Liz,' I tell them.

Gannick seems unmoved by the sight of a young woman's corpse. She's poring over the wedding gown, her gloved hands adjusting the fabric with small, patient movements.

'Keillor says she was murdered, Liz.'

'That makes sense; I've never seen a suicide do this much staging. You can take her jewellery,' she says, pointing at a white plastic case. 'Apart from a ring that's been jammed onto her finger. I'll try and prise it off later.'

When I look inside the case, a pair of transparent

evidence bags contain items I don't recognise. I never saw Sabine wearing the small gold locket. Its engraved casing is deeply scratched, while the hoop earrings in the other bag look brand new. I can't tell whether they're solid gold, but the yellow metal glitters as I take photos with my phone.

Gannick looks up at me. 'It's like the old wedding rhyme.'

'Something old and something new?'

'If there's anything borrowed or blue, you'll be first to know.'

I want to say that I appreciate her attention to detail, but she'd only reject the compliment with a flick of her hand. It will take her an hour or two to prepare Sabine's body to be carried to the hospital's mortuary by the island's only ambulance. The transfer must be made without losing a single hair or fibre that could reveal the killer's identity. Gannick is so busy toiling over the crime scene, she doesn't notice my departure.

The Keast brothers have arrived to guard the scene. Steve appears relaxed, while Paul is shifting his weight from foot to foot. I've watched my friend grow more fragile over the years, but the emotional fallout from the murder case isn't my top priority. I can only feel grateful that the brothers have agreed to put their lives on hold while I take Eddie and Isla back to the station to review the evidence. I scan the scene again before we get into the van. Why would a killer risk choosing a renowned beauty spot to display a victim's body?

Apart from the tent concealing Sabine's body, the rest of the landscape looks pristine. Acres of wild grass and moorland flowers end abruptly when the cliff pitches into the sea, the lighthouse overlooking two thousand miles of clear ocean.

Lawrie Deane is busy typing messages when we get back, reluctant to leave his computer when I call him into Madron's office for a briefing, but at least he's had the foresight to order lunch; a tray of sandwiches and cold drinks is waiting for us. The team's faces are serious as we gather around the table. Two sergeants and one inexperienced constable are the full extent of my workforce while the DCI's away on holiday and another officer is on long-term sick leave. Under normal circumstances four full-timers can easily enforce law and order among the islands' peaceful communities, with less than two thousand permanent residents, but I may need more staff to solve a vicious murder at the height of tourist season. I could request extra officers from the mainland, but that might cause more harm than good. No one talks here until they're ready, and our biggest job will be containing the islanders' panic until the killer's found.

My three officers wait expectantly; I'm the only one with experience of leading a serious crime investigation, and hierarchy dictates that every key decision is mine. Isla's face is paler than before, her expression tense when I explain that the case has just become a murder hunt. I pull the polaroid photo from my pocket, still wrapped in an evidence bag, then pass it round.

'The sick bastard,' Isla hisses, as she reads the words scribbled on the back.

'A nutjob, obviously,' Eddie agrees. 'Who'd do that to a young girl?'

It's Lawrie Deane's reaction that surprises me. The sergeant normally plays the hardman, but his eyes are glossy when he returns the photo. His daughter is around Sabine's age, so it's not surprising he's affected on a personal level.

'We're looking for someone mentally ill,' I say. 'Only a sadist would abduct a young woman, dress her in a bride's costume, complete with make-up and flowers, then push her off a cliff. We can't tell if it's a man or a woman yet, but the killer must be a risk-taker. It took daring to hand-deliver a photo to the police station then display her body in the open. It could have been done quietly, by dropping her corpse into the sea at high tide, but the killer had a point to prove. Does anyone recognise the phrase "The bride in her glory will ever be fair?" It rings a bell, but I can't place it.'

Eddie pores over his phone. 'It's not mentioned any-where on the web.'

'It means something to the killer, but our first task is to find out who Sabine knew. She arrived on St Mary's in mid-June; I want to hear about any short flings or one-night stands during that time. We all know that ninety per cent of violent crime against women is carried out by men they know intimately, but this could be an exception. It may be a man with a fetish, or a woman strong enough to overpower someone as fit as Sabine.'

Isla looks paler than before, making me wonder if shock is affecting her. 'Do you think the killer's still here, boss?'

'It looks that way. No ferries have sailed since last night, and the harbourmaster has checked local boats to make sure he didn't leave by sea.' I scan the team's faces again. 'I want to know everything about Sabine. How did she spend her spare time? Where did that dress come from, and the jewellery? Small details could expose the killer. We also need to do an urgent trace on her phone. Lawrie has arranged an emergency public briefing at three o'clock in the church hall. Can one of you get it announced on local radio, please?'

I give each officer duties to perform but Isla still looks frail; she seems to be holding herself together by keeping busy. After I've tacked Sabine's photo to a pinboard I study her face again, trying to channel my anger towards the murderer into achieving the justice she deserves. She was a bold spirit, brave enough to trek across Europe alone, and work all summer in a foreign country, yet her killer set out to humiliate her, covering her face in layers of make-up she never wore while she was alive. I still don't know what other indignities she suffered before her death.

I lock myself into Madron's office to complete the

worst task of the day. The air carries his old-fashioned smell of Brylcreem and boot polish. It feels wrong to commandeer his room, but it's the only place at the station with guaranteed privacy. I rearrange objects on his desk, procrastinating, until I'm ready to call Sabine's home in Riga. Her mother sounds relaxed at first, curious to know why someone is phoning from the UK. I give her the news as gently as possible. There's a five-second delay before I hear a gasp. The sound is followed by a grating scream, shrill enough to make me grit my teeth, then a man's voice takes over. He speaks in broken English, begging me to explain, and I have to describe his daughter's death all over again.

7

Lily's mouth is dry with panic as she escapes the hotel compound at 2 p.m. She senses that something's wrong, because DI Kitto left Sabine's room with a frown on his face. She must talk to her brother, even though she fears him. An odd atmosphere fills the air as she walks through Hugh Town. The lanes are clogged with holidaymakers, and a queue of people runs the length of the quay, snaking back from the ferry's ticket kiosk. A red-faced woman almost barges her off the pavement, complaining loudly that today's ferry service has been cancelled. Lily hurries towards the low stone buildings that line the Strand. She pauses outside the fisherman's cottage that became her home on St Mary's five years ago, still hoping her mother might appear at the window, but the pane of glass is empty. No one answers when she unlocks the door and yells her brother's name.

Lily continues her search, passing the squat outline of the community centre then following the path to Porth Mellon Beach. She remembers her excitement on moving to the island at thirteen. It seemed magical to hear the waves greeting the land all day long after living in a high-rise flat, but even the open shorelines fail to lift her spirits today. A dozen boats stand on raised blocks behind the old chandlery, and there's no one around. The early afternoon sun is so hot, Lily raises her hand to shade her face, wishing she'd worn sunglasses. Harry has found a summer job carrying visitors round the coastline in an old speedboat owned by Paul Keast. It's resting on its trailer, and there's no sign of her brother. She expected him to be out on the water, with Sabine, soaking up the sun. Keast seems prepared to overlook Harry's flirtations and his temper, provided he makes a profit.

Lily props her back against the shady side of the boat, protecting her fair skin from the sun's glare. Half an hour passes before footsteps crunch across the sand, the sound bringing her to her feet: Harry is swigging from a can of beer, with half a dozen more inside the plastic bag dangling from his hand. It would be wise to back away, but her questions need answers. Shame crosses her brother's features before his defences rise again.

'What have I done wrong this time?' He swallows another gulp of beer.

'I need your help, Harry.'

'Why?' He steps closer, his expression softening. 'You're upset, I can see it in your face.'

Lily studies him under the screen of her hand. Harry will soon be twenty, her senior by eighteen months, tall and good-looking. The sun has picked out blond streaks in his light brown hair, his skin deeply tanned. He still looks like the swaggering show-off she worshipped as a child, but their relationship has changed. He used to confide in her, but he's spent three months in jail since then, and his drinking's growing worse. Harry is her only relative on St Mary's, yet she no longer trusts him.

'Sabine never came back to the hotel last night. I thought she'd be with you.'

'I haven't seen her.' The tenderness on Harry's face vanishes.

Lily pulls her friend's phone from her pocket, brandishing it at him. 'You've been texting her all week, arranging to meet up.'

Harry stares at her. 'Why did you take her phone?'

'You're lucky I pocketed it before the police searched her room.' Lily steps closer even though instinct tells her to run. 'You promised not to lay a finger on her.'

'I gave her a few free rides on the boat, that's all.' He offers a narrow smile.

'You said you'd leave my friends alone.'

'It just happened, Lily. It didn't mean anything, to either of us.'

'Why are you talking about her in the past tense?'

'Because it's over, that's all.'

Lily pulls the scrap of paper from her pocket and brandishes it at him. 'You put this under her door last night, didn't you? It's your handwriting.'

He shrugs. 'I was at the pub with some mates, so I got to the lighthouse late, and a bit pissed. No one was there – I saw a car drive past on the lane but she wouldn't have got a lift, she'd have cycled. I lay down on the grass to wait for her, but I fell asleep. I woke up a few hours later, and walked home alone.'

'Why are the police hunting for her?'

'How should I know? I never saw her and she hasn't messaged me.' His forehead gathers into a frown.

'You were too rat-arsed to care if she got home safe, as usual.'

'No lectures, I'm not in the mood.'

'Tell me she's safe, Harry, please.'

Pain shoots through Lily's system when he grabs her arm and gives it a vicious twist. She holds her breath, waiting for a blow that never arrives.

'You're just like all the others. I made one mistake, and now I'm the island's scapegoat.' Her brother yanks her wrist again until she winces with pain. 'Why don't you fuck off and leave me alone?'

Lily's other questions will have to wait; it only takes a few cans of lager to sour Harry's personality. She retraces her steps along the path, and when she looks back, he's slumped beside the boat, guzzling his next beer, already sinking into self-pity. Lily's mother pleaded with her to try and get him back on the straight and narrow before she died, but his temper drove her from their rented house weeks after the funeral. His violent reaction makes her believe he's hiding something about Sabine's disappearance.

Dozens of islanders are heading for Hugh Town when Lily reaches the road. An odd feeling crawls inside her gut when she hears one of them say that the police have called an emergency meeting at three o'clock, but no one can explain why.

8

Under normal circumstances, St Andrew's church hall is an oasis of calm. It lies at the heart of Hugh Town, the barn-like space used for choir practice, yoga classes and Tai Chi, but there's no chance of relaxing today. Volunteer stewards are corralling locals and tourists inside. My team has placed a hundred chairs in neat rows, but they're all taken, with more people queuing to be admitted. One of the realities of working on such small islands is that news travel fast, be it good or bad.

I wait in silence as the hall fills. My undercover work with the Murder Squad taught me that killers like to watch events unfold: I scan the crowd for scratched arms, bruised faces – signs of a recent struggle – but see only people I've known all my adult life, plus a sprinkling of tourists. The visitors' faces are burnished to a healthy glow from hours outdoors. The locals are pale by comparison, from labouring inside cafés, pubs and shops, capitalising on the money that boosts the islands' economy during holiday season. The Keast brothers are in the front row, fresh from guarding the crime scene. There's no sign of Tom and Rhianna Polkerris from the Star Castle, but Jade Finbury is in the middle of the crowd. The pilot's expression is sunny while she chats with the woman to her right. My uncle Ray is standing at the back, his features unreadable, as if nothing could surprise him. Shadow is at his side, releasing a high-pitched whine. Thank God Ray is gripping his lead or he'd bound onto the stage to join me.

I walk to the front of the platform that serves many different purposes during the year. Torch singers croon love songs on Valentine's night, and comedians perform stand-up routines. The crowd watches expectantly, as if they're hoping for a decent joke, but their faces darken when I announce Sabine Bertans' death, then share details from the crime scene.

'We need to know if she went to Pulpit Rock voluntarily, or someone forced her there. It was a brutal, premeditated attack, and we're certain the killer is still on St Mary's. I need every detail about how Sabine spent her last hours. Her phone's still missing; it's got a bright pink case, covered in a floral design. If you find it, please bring it to the station immediately. I can't stress highly enough that you all need to keep safe. Don't spend time alone, and keep your doors locked. No one can leave or visit St Mary's without our permission until her killer's found.'

My final statement prompts a hiss of irritation, which is understandable. Hundreds of tourists will be unable to return to work on Monday, while the next influx of visitors will be barred from travelling to the islands.

'Can I assume that everyone here will let us search their homes, if necessary? It would save a lot of time applying for individual search warrants.'

The sea of faces nods back at me, as I expected. I ask them to pass on the news about property searches to their neighbours, before hitting a button on my computer. A photo appears on the wall, of the gold locket and earrings the girl was wearing.

'The jewellery may belong to the victim, or to someone local. If anyone recognises it, please talk to me today.'

There's a buzz of voices as people study Sabine's photo. I show them an image of the phrase scribbled on the back, but no one recognises it, or the killer's handwriting. It crosses my mind to explain that she was wearing a bridal gown, but the grotesque detail might trigger panic. It's important to find the right balance. I need the islanders to keep functioning normally, while accepting the dangers they're facing. It requires a delicate balancing act to answer each question in turn, without revealing the violence of the attack. When the meeting ends everyone has agreed to provide alibis, to be verified before they can get permission to travel.

People are already forming queues to speak to my team. Eddie Nickell is running the operation, making sure that Lawrie and Isla collect the right details. Ploughing through the alibis will take hours, even

KATE RHODES

though the islands' six special constables have volunteered their services. They help out as stewards during the islands' festivals and gig races, but have no experience of other aspects of policing. We'll need to do most of the basic work ourselves, and I'm keen to return to the Star Castle, where Sabine worked long shifts to send money home to her family and fund her studies. I know too little about her life, except that she loved to swim, and her manner was warm and outgoing. I should have spent more time with her, to learn about any threats she was facing.

I'm still kicking myself for missing clues in the girl's behaviour when a familiar figure hurries across the room. Elaine Rawle is a slim woman of average height; her walk is so nimble, she looks like a retired tennis player, with smooth grey hair swept back from her face. Her elegant summer dress stands out among the crowd's neon-bright T-shirts and Bermuda shorts. Elaine is married to the former headmaster of Five Islands School. She has run the Isles of Scilly Museum for decades, with quiet efficiency. Her voice is usually a genteel murmur, but words spill from her mouth in a garbled rush today.

'That locket's from the museum, Ben. We had some items stolen about a year ago. I can't remember the exact date, but you'll have a record at the station, won't you?'

'Slow down, please, Elaine. I heard about some items going missing, but you need to start at the beginning.'

'The thief took a handful of jewellery from one of

56

our cabinets. The piece you showed is made of Cornish gold. I don't know much about its history, but I'd recognise it anywhere.'

'Someone just walked into the museum and grabbed it?'

'Our security was hopeless back then; DCI Madron made us install better locks after it happened. The odd thing is that the thief could have emptied the whole cabinet, but more valuable pieces were left behind.'

'Do you have any idea who did it?'

'That's the frustrating thing. It was the middle of summer, when the island was flooded with visitors. This might sound unfair, but I wondered if Harry Jago might be involved. The boy's always in trouble. I can't imagine any of the other islanders doing something so stupid.'

'Can I drop by the museum tomorrow for a tour?'

'Any time,' she replies. 'I'm not exactly rushed off my feet, but if you want to know more about the locket, Julian Power's our expert. He's collects local jewellery, and he's writing a catalogue for the museum, so people can see items online.'

Julian Power runs the Isles of Scilly Travel Company; a middle-aged bachelor with a solemn manner, who takes his responsibility for ferrying passengers seriously. He strikes me as an unlikely collector of women's jewellery, but when I scan the room again, he's nowhere in sight. Elaine Rawle disappears into the crowd, while I digest the fact that our culprit is a thief as well as a murderer. I'll have to check out her theory that Harry Jago was involved, although the boy strikes me as lost, rather than dangerous. Whoever killed Sabine must have been planning the attack all year, but my most pressing task is to find out who was close to the victim. The attack wasn't a piece of random violence. It would have taken rigorous preparation at each stage to avoid drawing attention.

I slip out of the hall to pay a visit to Sabine's priest. The street outside is packed with people, discussing the girl's death like a hot piece of gossip. At the edge of the crowd I see a woman with back turned, her glossy hair a rich shade of chocolate. I blink rapidly to clear her image away; stress must be getting to me if I'm conjuring ghosts from the past. But when my eyes open again, Nina Jackson is still standing there, perfectly real. It's the first time I've seen my ex-girlfriend in almost two years – although 'ex-girlfriend' is pushing it. We'd barely got past the fling stage before she left Bryher, but that hasn't stopped my thoughts drifting back to her countless times since. She's wearing a turquoise shirt that accentuates her tan, and a pair of faded jeans. Shadow has noticed her too. He must have given Ray the slip, his lead trailing as he bounds in her direction. The dog's enthusiastic greeting gives me time to wipe the shock from my face before saying hello. She's wearing opaque sunglasses that mask her expression, but Shadow is too busy licking her hands to notice the tense atmosphere.

'Long time no see, Nina.'

'I was planning to contact you. I'm sorry to hear about the girl that died.'

I give a slow nod. 'You picked a bad time to visit the islands. Excuse me, I need to get moving. We've got plenty to do.'

Shadow looks torn when I walk away, dashing back and forth between us, unable to decide where his loyalties lie, which makes me feel like grabbing his collar. I could tether him to a tree for the rest of the afternoon, but his howling would cause a public nuisance. He catches up with me eventually, but seeing Nina has put me on edge. She could have chosen a thousand holiday destinations instead of coming back to haunt me. By now Shadow is fifty metres ahead, always certain that he knows my destination better than I do myself, and this time he's correct. I follow him along the Strand, where the Church of Our Lady Star of the Sea is set back from the road. It looks more like a modest Victorian home than a place of worship, but the whitewashed building houses the island's only Catholic place of worship. It overlooks Town Beach, where St Mary's gig-racing boats line the road on trailers, and two old men are sitting on a bench, watching the sea in amicable silence.

Shadow sets off to pester the OAPs for food, while I try to banish thoughts of Nina from my head. The odours of candlewax and incense waft down the stairwell when I open the church door. A pinboard on the wall is crammed with notices, inviting people to join the choir, or do a sponsored walk for the Red Cross. The building is unnaturally silent, making me assume that Father Michael Trevellyan is elsewhere, tending his flock. He's the only Catholic priest in Scilly, spreading his time between the five inhabited islands.

I only catch sight of Father Michael when I reach the top of the stairs. He's kneeling by the altar, head bowed in prayer, so I drop onto a pew to wait. A murmur of Latin words streams from his lips. The attic space only contains a simple altar, and enough seating for around thirty worshippers. Two stained-glass windows provide a reminder of the islands' relationship with the sea. One depicts rowers in a lifeboat, thrashing through the waves, from the days before rescue boats were equipped with powerful engines. The other shows Christ's disciples hauling a weighty fishing net from the ocean. I don't have a religious bone in my body, yet the images still resonate. I came here sometimes as a boy to watch light flooding through the coloured glass, after my father drowned. The designs are perfect for a community that has lost more than it's gained from the ocean over the centuries.

Father Michael looks exhausted as he rises to his feet, and it's clear he's heard about the murder. The priest is dressed for his next mass in a plain white chasuble. Up close it's easy to see evidence of the varied life he led on St Mary's before training for the priesthood. People say that he loved to fight before finding religion; his broken nose and uneven jaw are relics from an earlier time. He's in his forties, with the wiry build of a long-distance runner, pepper and salt hair, and features that only come alive when he smiles. The priest has given the island police plenty of help in the past, and I may need his support again. He's a special constable like the Keast brothers, always ready to assist whenever a crisis hits.

'There you are, Ben. I've been expecting you.' The man's voice is a low Cornish burr, with sadness resonating behind each syllable.

'Is it okay to talk here, Father?'

'God won't evict us, whatever we say.' His smile quickly fades. 'I imagine you're here about Sabine.'

'I'm hoping for some background information.'

'She was a lovely, kind-spirited girl.' His gaze drops to the floor, as if he's trying to recall every detail. 'Sabine was honest to a fault. She told me she doubted her faith; I think she attended mass purely for the comfort it gave, while she was away from home.'

'Did you talk much, one to one?'

'Sabine only came to confession twice.' His lips close tightly, like a book shutting.

'You can't keep her secrets now, Father. I need details, before someone else gets hurt.'

His frown deepens. 'She seemed fine the first time we spoke, then something changed.'

'How do you mean?'

'She'd met someone new. The girl seemed frightened by the strength of her feelings; she'd kept it secret, even from her closest friend.'

'Was the bloke married?'

'I'm afraid she never mentioned a name.' The priest shivers slightly, as if a cold breeze has rushed in through the window, even though the place is stifling. 'I hope you find the killer soon. Sabine's an unquiet soul. I can feel her presence, even though I've prayed for a peaceful transition. She must have suffered terribly.'

'We'll catch whoever did it, don't worry. Do you remember anything else from her confession?'

'Only that the relationship troubled her. I told her to avoid doing anything she might regret.'

'Nothing else?'

'Sabine seemed to believe that having a few short affairs was liberating. Life at home had been stifling her.'

'She had more than one partner while she was here?'

'I think she was learning about herself, before returning to her parent's strict rules.' He holds up his hands, in a gesture of defeat. 'My bishop takes a hard line on young people with active sex lives, but times are changing. I could only advise her to take care and pray for forgiveness.'

'Can I ask how you spent last night? We're checking everyone's whereabouts.'

'The answer's not very exciting, Ben. I led our weekly prayer meeting, which ended around half past nine. After that I went home for an early night.'

When the priest reaches out to shake my hand, his skin is clammy against my palm. There's a haunted look in his eyes when he turns away, as if Sabine's death has left him too upset to face his parishioners. Shadow's high-pitched bark summons me downstairs, but when I pause in the doorway Father Michael is on his knees again, eyes closed, sending up a fresh prayer for Sabine Bertans' soul.

9

Lily has collapsed on her bed at the Star Castle, her pillow wet with tears. Her room has been her sanctuary until now, but since the briefing at the church hall nowhere feels safe. Harry's black temper lingers in her mind; it makes him punch walls and go·on the attack for the smallest of reasons. No one was surprised when their father went to prison for manslaughter, after injuring a man so badly in a fight that he died of his wounds. Their mother brought them to St Mary's for a fresh start but Harry's anger has worsened over the years. Lily can't understand why girls still adore him, despite his recklessness. The note he left for Sabine is still on her dressing table, and she's read the texts they exchanged. Why didn't her friend admit that they had been stealing moments together for several weeks? Now she'll never know why. Lily can't believe that Harry would attack Sabine, but he's out of reach while his temper runs so near the surface.

The girl splashes her face with cold water, and when she checks her reflection in the bathroom mirror, her skin is blotchy, hazel eyes bloodshot, her mousy hair in need of restyling. Suddenly a loud noise makes her jump out of her skin. Someone is rapping on her door, and Rhianna Polkerris is waiting outside when she opens it. The manager's appearance is perfectly groomed, her face expressionless.

'It's six o'clock, Lily. Why aren't you in the bar?'

'Sorry, I went to the meeting about Sabine ...'

The manager silences her with a quick shake of her head. 'It's sad news of course, but she was a risk-taker. She probably stumbled into danger.'

'Sabine wasn't like that.'

'I happen to know better, but let's not argue. Guests are waiting to be served.' She drums her long fingernails against the door surround. 'Can I come inside for a minute?'

Lily is embarrassed by her cluttered room, but her manager doesn't seem to notice.

'Stand over here, Lily.' Rhianna positions her directly in front of the mirror, appraising her appearance. 'I checked your CV the other day; you got good A levels. Why didn't you apply to university?'

'The student loan put me off,' the girl mumbles.

'You could climb the ladder without a degree, but your appearance needs work.' The older woman brushes Lily's hair back from her forehead. 'You've got decent bone structure. Put on some make-up and get some highlights, so people will give you a chance. It's important to make the best of ourselves, isn't it?'

Lily nods her head in miserable silence. Rhianna's glossy hair looks golden in the mirror, her own a lifeless beige.

'Good girl, now get ready for work. You need some blusher,

you're awfully pale.' Rhianna's cupid's bow mouth curves into a smile. 'I'm glad we had our little chat.'

Lily hears the door click shut before crumpling back onto her bed. The manager's critique of her appearance was a slap in the face, hard enough to dry her tears. She gazes at a photo on Sabine's phone to give herself courage before leaving her room. It shows her friend, young and carefree on the beach, her smile inviting everyone to share her happiness.

'What should I do?' Lily whispers, but Sabine's face only lingers on the screen, unchanged.

She drops the phone back into her pocket, like a good luck charm, before confronting the mirror again.

10

Shadow settles under my desk back at the station, ignoring the frenzy of activity, his tail folded neatly against his body. Madron's office feels packed when my trio of officers arrive for the day's final updates at 7 p.m. Eddie's eagerness shows in every movement, even though he's worked flat out since we found Sabine's corpse this morning. He spent the afternoon doing a satellite trace on her phone, while Lawrie and Isla cross names off our list of potential suspects. Statistics tell us that murders are normally committed by men between eighteen and forty-five, with previous convictions for violence, but there are few obvious candidates on St Mary's. If Sabine had a boyfriend, as Father Michael claimed, the relationship was well-concealed. The way her body was presented as a bride, with make-up applied to her face, makes me wonder if the killer is female, with a passion for detail. The attack was highly organised and intricate. Whoever committed the crime risked stealing from a tiny museum on 3 August last year – as confirmed by our slim file on the theft – then waited exactly a year to murder Sabine. The date must be significant, but I can't figure out why.

Excitement shows on Eddie's face when he shows us a map on his laptop. He's used the mobile networks' satellite software to hunt for the signal from Sabine's phone, the details triangulated from masts at either end of the island.

'It must be switched on, or we couldn't pick it up. Her phone's definitely on the Garrison, but the location finder's not pinpoint-accurate. It could be in the hotel or the grounds; she may have dropped it when she left the building. We need to find it before the battery goes flat.'

The young sergeant sounds elated as he reels off details, as if the murder hunt is an all-time career high. I ask him to gather some trusted helpers to search the Garrison area tonight, before the light fades. It's a task we can't delay: once the phone's battery fails, it's beyond our reach.

Lawrie Deane's speech sounds leaden when he gives his update. He delivers each sentence at a snail's pace, his Cornish accent so thick it sounds like he's been gargling clotted cream. The guy took twenty years to achieve the rank of sergeant, his physical movements as slow-moving as his career, but Deane has a gift for logistics. He's already found accommodation for me, Eddie and Liz Gannick. Tom and Rhianna Polkerris have plenty of vacancies at the Star Castle due to a cancelled wedding party, and they're providing rooms free of charge. I'm glad we'll be based at Sabine's place of work; I still need to find out exactly how she spent her time there.

Isla has brought a sheaf of papers to the meeting, as if she's spent the whole day scribbling notes. She joined the force straight after finishing a law degree, opting to return to Scilly rather than completing her training, even though it meant sacrificing bigger wages as a solicitor in future. She observes the proceedings in silence, like she's attending a masterclass. The day's events seem to have taken their toll; her face looks strained when I request an update.

'The dress is from a shop called Bridal Harmony in Truro. It was made three years ago, so the killer must have bought it second-hand. If it was from eBay, I should be able to track the buyer down.' She skims through her papers. 'I had more luck with the earrings. They're plate gold – a man called Liam Trewin paid for them by credit card at the Abbey Gardens giftshop on Tresco, three days ago.'

'Is he still here?'

She nods in reply. 'Staying at the Star Castle. A bit of an idiot, by all accounts.'

'Says who?'

'The manager at the gift shop described him as a sleazebag. He was all over the waitresses in the café, bragging about his island blood.'

'Good work, Isla. I'll track him down today. You and Sabine were close, weren't you?'

Her gaze drops to the polished surface of Madron's

desk. 'We met up a few times at the Atlantic for a drink; her suggestion, not mine. She was studying languages at uni in Riga, so she liked practising her English with native speakers.'

'What about boyfriends?'

'She wasn't looking,' Isla's voice falters. 'Sabine just wanted to have fun.'

'Didn't she open up to you at all?'

'Some guy was hassling her at the hotel, but she never said his name.'

'Maybe it was Trewin. Tom Polkerris didn't know about her friends. Was she close to anyone at work?'

'Sabine really liked Lily Jago, even though they're opposites. Sabine was the life and soul, but Lily wouldn't say boo to a goose.'

I've had to deal with Lily's brother Harry plenty of times. The boy has few fans on the island; he's often in trouble for drunk and disorderly, but his sister seems more mature. Isla's posture is still stiff with tension, convincing me that she knows something that might emerge in private, so I ask her to stay behind after the briefing. She shifts uneasily in her chair, while I wait for the door to close.

'You and Sabine must have talked about personal stuff, Isla. Can't you remember what she said?'

'It was mainly chit-chat about life back home, and places she'd been. She wanted the low down on jobs in the UK too.'

'She never seemed scared?'

Isla shakes her head vehemently. 'Sabine was happy-go-lucky; I think she made friends easily, wherever she went.'

'If anything comes to mind, let's talk in the morning. It's time you went home. You've worked twelve hours straight.'

The constable rises to her feet reluctantly, as if she'd like to carry on hunting for her friend's killer, but the evening light is fading outside the window.

'How are you getting back to Old Town?'

Isla's family lives half a mile further up the coast, but she gives me a puzzled look. 'On foot, as usual.'

'I'll give you a lift.'

'No thanks, sir. I could use the exercise.'

'It's an instruction, not an offer. Sabine's killer is still out there, and it'll soon be dark.'

'I've done three self-defence courses.' She's looking at me like I'm the worst dad ever.

'Great, but we're still going in the van. You can drive, if that helps.'

She gives a reluctant nod. 'You think it'll happen again, don't you, sir?'

Sabine's terrified face in the Polaroid photo is etched on my memory, like a bad tattoo. 'It's possible, if we don't figure it out soon. For all we know, the killer's looking for a groom, to match his bride.'

'So men are at risk too?'

'Everyone needs to watch their back till we find the killer.'

Isla still looks uneasy when we leave the building. I'd feel the same in her shoes, but allowing a young female officer to walk home alone after a brutal murder would be negligent. She stays silent while we follow the lane towards Old Town, and I resist asking more questions. I'll have to wait until she chooses to share whatever's on her mind. Stubbornness is an island trait; old habits of self-reliance make us reluctant to give up secrets before we're ready.

I feel a pang of envy when she pulls up outside her home. Isla's parents own a beautiful semi-detached house by Old Town beach. It's a typical piece of Scillonian architecture, built from local stone, with painted shutters and a slate roof, in far better repair than my home on Bryher. Their front garden is a cascade of flowers, spilling down to the footpath. The bench beside Isla's front door is an ideal place for gazing at the ocean and people-watching in summer, when hundreds of walkers stop for lunch at the local café, before following the coastline north.

Isla mutters a terse goodbye and I'm about to drive away when her mother appears on the steps. I should head back to the station to plan tomorrow's workload, but good manners force me out of the van. Ginny Tremayne looks puzzled when her daughter barges past without saying a word, but Isla is sure to talk to her mother tonight. Ginny's good at comforting people, not just in her job as a doctor, but everyone she meets. She looks far more relaxed than her daughter, a plump figure with greying hair pinned back from her face, wearing a faded sundress, her skin tanned from hours of gardening. Her expression is apologetic when she asks about the case.

'Sorry I missed your meeting, I was stuck at the hospital.' Ginny has led the island's small team of medics ever since I can remember.

I mention that Isla is doing well. She takes the job seriously, her attention to detail making her an ideal police officer. Ginny looks proud to hear that her daughter is coping well with her new duties. Her engineer husband is working away for the next few weeks, but she plans to call him later to share the news. I'm about to say goodbye when a familiar face peers at me from a downstairs window in the house next door. Jeff Pendelow has lived there for decades, alone since his wife went to the mainland for hospital care three months ago; he was a consultant psychologist until he retired earlier this year, and a lifelong friend of my father's. The man raises his hand to wave, then returns to scribbling in his notebook.

'Jeff would love to see you,' Ginny says. 'The poor soul's stuck at home; he can't even drive himself about. He's been low since his wife's illness, and now he's got the worst kind of back pain.'

'When's Val coming home?'

There's a pause before she replies. 'She's got early onset Alzheimer's. Jeff fought to keep her with him, but she needs specialist care. Val will stay in a residential centre in Penzance permanently.'

I'd rather not pay sick calls tonight, but the news makes it hard to walk away. Courtesy is the islands' lifeblood, keeping neighbourly relationships functional ninety per cent of the time. I cross the path between the two properties after saying goodbye to Ginny, noticing that Jeff's front garden is overrun with weeds, a line of tamarisk bushes turning into trees. When I tap on his door it swings open immediately. Like most islanders, he never bothers with security, because burglary here is practically non-existent. Pendelow's hallway reveals the schism between his personal and professional lives. Academic certificates hang on the wall, proving his credentials as a psychologist, beside a cluster of photos taken on sea-fishing trips. The man has been a keen angler ever since I was a boy. He spent years commuting to the mainland, where he worked at Plymouth Hospital, spending weekdays away from home. The largest photos are of his wife, and memories of the house engulf me suddenly. Valerie Pendelow was a favourite of mine as a kid. She worked as a chef at Old Town Inn and spoiled me and my brother rotten, always producing the best cakes and biscuits. I spent plenty of afternoons here with my father. The two men would drink beer and play chess while my brother and I flew kites on the beach, or booted a football around their garden. I feel a stab of guilt that I didn't even know Val had left the island for good.

Jeff is a native of St Mary's, his roots deep in island soil. He's a member of the community choir, but his voice quavers today when he calls out from the living room. I find him lying back on the settee, with his note-book on his lap. The man has aged since we last met. I remember Jeff as a big, strapping bloke, always taking long walks, but pain has drawn deep lines on his face, his hair and beard completely white, even though he can't be much more than sixty. My father often spoke about his brilliant sense of humour, but there's no sign of it now. The half-moon glasses perched on his nose make him look like a retired librarian.

'No need to get up, Jeff. It's just a quick hello.'

'Did Ginny send you on a sympathy call? You'd laugh if you could see me going up the stairs. It takes me ten minutes to reach the landing.' There's a tired smile on his face, as if his condition is no more than a sick joke.

'I hear you've been stuck at home.'

'Val was the driver, not me; I don't even have a license.' He winces as he shifts position.

'Have you got anything for the pain?'

'Ginny's given me three different types of tablets, but it's probably psychosomatic.'

'Because you're missing Val?'

'I can't even travel to the mainland to see her until this sciatica improves.' His eyes grow misty, but he blinks the moisture away. 'At least there's plenty for me to do. I've got to rest here for a month, so I can finish my book.'

'What's it about?'

'Psychosis. I spent years treating patients with

complex personality disorders and delusions. The NHS gave me a parting gift when I retired; they've commissioned me to write a manual for mental health professionals dealing with psychotic illnesses for the first time.'

'Do those patients ever recover?'

'The conditions are pretty intractable, but they can learn to regulate their symptoms, with the right support and medication.' His tone is sober when he speaks again. 'I heard the announcement on the radio, about a young girl being killed. Was it you that found her this morning?'

'My team were with me.'

'That must have been tough, for all of you.' The psychologist's calm gaze assesses me for signs of nervous strain.

'I saw worse during my time in London.'

'You're good at denying your feelings, like all the Kitto family.' He laughs, then studies me again. 'It's uncanny how much you resemble your dad. He's been in my thoughts often recently.'

We spend the next ten minutes exchanging news. Jeff manages to conceal his sadness about Val's absence, and his quiet wisdom undoes some of the day's tension. When my gaze wanders to his open window, the sun is setting. The arc of Old Town bay gives way to miles of open sea, with nothing to obstruct the waves until they reach Land's End. The view allows Pendelow to study every tide, but the sea's beauty must seem hollow, now he's alone. When I glance through a window on the far side of the room, his back garden is thick with shoulder-high brambles, the space reclaimed by wild nature. He must have been too busy caring for his wife to spend time outside.

'I'd better go, Jeff. There's stuff to wrap up before I can stop tonight.'

'Don't work too hard,' he says. 'Remember I'm here, if anyone on your team needs support.'

'Thanks, Jeff. I may take you up on that.'

'Even full-grown men like you can buckle without proper counselling. Plenty of police and servicemen experience work-related stress.'

'I'll take care, don't worry.'

His worn face finally relaxes. 'Your dad would be proud of you, Ben. You know that, don't you?'

The man's praise catches me off guard, silencing me for a moment. My gaze settles on a wooden crucifix above the mantelpiece. I never noticed it as a kid but the symbol makes perfect sense: Pendelow's faith must lie behind his desire to help people in desperate circumstances. I feel calmer after our conversation, but reality catches up with me when I see some holidaymakers on the sandy beach, as the sun drops behind the horizon. The island's peace is illusory. Any of the day's sunbathers who are currently packing away towels and flip-flops could become the killer's next victim, if I fail to do my job.

11

It's fully dark by the time I lock the station door and walk uphill to the Star Castle. I haven't eaten much since grabbing a few sandwiches at lunchtime, but I need to see Liz Gannick before getting dinner. The forensics chief has spent hours working alone and will have news from the crime scene. Shadow races ahead, coming to a halt by the castle's entrance. I leave him tethered to a post outside, hoping he won't howl in protest all night long.

The hotel staff must have heard about Sabine's death, but it looks like they've been told to put on a brave face, in case the murder spooks their guests. The porter greets me with a relaxed smile. He asks about luggage but I don't even have a toothbrush, let alone fresh clothes. Ray has promised to bring the basics over for me and Eddie tomorrow, as neither of us can leave St Mary's until the killer's found. The porter says little as he leads me down a stone-walled corridor. My room on the first floor is decorated in grand style, with a four-poster bed, antique furniture, and miles of ocean outside the window, already glinting with starlight. Guards would have slept under these rafters centuries ago, on bare stone floors. They were paid to defend the island from external threats, but my job involves a different kind of navigation. It won't be easy to make the islanders share their secrets, but I'll have to break through their reticence to expose the killer. When I look through the window again, Hugh Town's harbour lights are shining, a dozen lobster boats adrift on the tide. People pay high prices to enjoy such perfect views of the picturesque fishing town, yet someone is hellbent on destroying the island's calm.

A blast of Motown bursts through the wall, reminding me that Liz Gannick is next door, paying no respect whatsoever to the hotel's peaceful atmosphere. I often play music when I'm at home, from the nineties rock I grew up with, to jazz and classical, but Gannick's got good taste. Stevie Wonder is belting out 'Uptight', which seems fitting when she appears in the doorway. She's leaning heavily on her crutches, but her gaze is still bright with questions. The forensics chief has converted her suite into a science lab, complete with workbench, microscope and vials full of powder and liquids. The smell of chemicals permeates the air, reminding me of school chemistry lessons that always bored me to tears.

'You like your music loud, Liz. I bet you're a Northern Soul fan.'

'Isn't everyone?' She gives me an arch look, before turning down the volume. 'I can name every obscure backing singer Motown ever exploited.'

'That's quite a skill.'

'Where have you been all day? Behind your desk, smoking cigars?'

'The small matter of a murder investigation has kept me busy. It's been slow going. Eddie spent the whole afternoon with a band of volunteers scouring the Garrison for the missing phone, but they had no luck.' I drop into a chair by the window. 'What did you find?'

She passes me an evidence bag. 'It took me a while to get this off the girl's wedding ring finger; her knuckle was badly swollen.'

The bag contains a gold wedding band, with hallmarks stamped inside.

'It must be old, like the locket,' Gannick says. 'It's covered in scratches and dents. He's been a clever boy and kept his operation clean. I've gone over every centimetre of the dress with UV light and found nothing. It's drenched in dry cleaning chemicals, and there's no hair, or stray fibres from his clothes. He probably wore overalls and a mask when he went to work. I need the lab in Penzance to check that the blood on the sleeves of the wedding dress belongs to Sabine, from friction burns, but there are hardly any other marks.'

'Was there much evidence at the crime scene?'

She shakes her head. 'I'm hoping the lab will get more from my samples. I want the dress flown over for analysis tomorrow; we can pick up fingerprints on fabric these days, but not with the basic kit I've got here.'

'How does that work?'

'We use iodine fuming. The chemical's heated to form a vapour that sticks to the oily residue of finger-prints, so we can photograph them.'

'If the killer's that careful there won't be any, will there?'

'No one's that neat and tidy.'

I look out at the night sky, glittering above us. 'The bastard's determined to stay out of reach, and I bet Sabine's phone has been buried somewhere.'

Gannick is too preoccupied to respond. 'There's one other stain on the dress. It's a solid line of car oil.'

'Meaning what?'

'She was put in the boot of a vehicle. I imagine it was lined with plastic, but the hem got caught under the lid.'

'He was waiting for her by the lighthouse?'

'I can't prove that yet. It looks like the killer worked on her in a clean environment – I couldn't find any soil or grass stains on the dress.'

Now there's a new element to Sabine's suffering. Was she dead or alive when that lid slammed down, inches from her face? She may have screamed for help for hours. I piece details together as Gannick shows me some blurred footprints photographed at the scene, which could be valuable evidence, or from tourists following the coastal path during the last few days. It looks like the murderer captured Sabine, then found somewhere clean and tidy to dress her in bridal clothes. Whoever did it is working hard to keep their identity secret, but aspects of their personality are already clear. The killer is skilled at eradicating every clue. No one has reported any suspicious behaviour among islanders or hotel guests. I can't tell whether the murderer was fixated with Sabine, or happy to use any female victim to perform the warped ritual.

Gannick is hunched over her microscope again, examining specks of soil from the crime scene. Her teeth are gritted with determination while the Supremes belt out another tune. The music's tempo normally makes me want to lumber to my feet and dance, preferably while no one's looking, but tonight it's just a reminder that Sabine Bertans has missed out on a lifetime of celebrations.

It's 10 p.m. when I walk back downstairs to the bar in the hotel's basement. The low-ceilinged space bears little resemblance to a dungeon today, but prisoners would have languished here in Elizabethan times, waiting for summary justice. The underground space feels cooler than the oppressive heat outside. It's filled with sofas and armchairs, and about twenty guests are clustered around tables, drinking nightcaps. Their chatter drops in volume when they catch sight of me. I recognise faces from my briefing, their expressions wary, as if they expect more bad news. The restaurant stopped serving dinner an hour ago, but a barmaid brings me ciabatta, olives, and slices of cold meat, neatly arranged on a platter. It's a far cry from the fish and chips served at the Mermaid, my normal haunt on St Mary's, but once I'm settled at a corner table, my camouflage is complete. I'm just another punter enjoying a late-night meal, free to eavesdrop on conversations. The murder is mentioned a few times, but most guests seem content to have their stay extended, apart from a few whose insurance companies are dragging their feet to cover their costs. They're all blissfully unaware of the violence that ended Sabine's life.

My gaze catches on a blond guy of around forty, on the far side of bar. He's pretending to read a newspaper, to disguise his interest in the waitresses. The man strikes up a conversation with one young girl, who soon hurries back to the kitchen, but rejection doesn't faze him. He makes another attempt with the next waitress to approach his table, delivering a glass of brandy. My technique is the opposite of his. I'm confident with women, but prefer to be genuinely attracted before making a move, while he believes every girl that crosses his path is fair game. I'm willing to bet that he's the sleazeball Isla mentioned, so I pick up my beer and head for his table.

'Mind if I join you?' I ask. 'I hate drinking alone.'

'Feel free, my friend, but I'm about to call it a night.'

His accent is a refined American drawl, with a British inflection, as if he's got divided loyalties. The man's short hair lacks any sign of grey, so clean it glistens. It's only when I glance at him again that his plastic surgery shows; his skin is pulled taut over his cheekbones, no lines visible on his forehead.

'I'm DI Ben Kitto, and you're Mr Trewin, aren't you?'

He looks startled. 'Liam, please. I was very sorry to hear about Sabine's death.'

'But you didn't attend my meeting?'

'I was driving round the island. Another guest gave me the news this afternoon.'

'How well did you know Sabine?'

'No better than the rest.' The man's grip on his brandy glass tightens, his fingertips turning white. 'I'm on first name terms with most of the staff. I stayed here this time last year too – love the place.'

'She was wearing the earrings you gave her when her body was found.'

'What a horrible image.' His eyes blink rapidly. 'She mentioned it was her birthday soon after I arrived. I like to leave gifts instead of tips sometimes – it feels more personal.'

'Did you give her anything else?'

'Nothing of value.' He looks even more uncomfortable when he speaks again. 'Just some flowers and a bottle of champagne.'

'Are you married, Liam?'

'Why do you ask?'

'I can easily check.'

His face grows sullen. 'I got divorced last year.'

'I'm sorry to hear that. Just one more question,

then I'll leave you in peace. When did you collect your hire car?'

'Yesterday, I took it back this afternoon.' His gaze finally meets mine. 'This might sound callous, but do you know when I can fly home? Business is waiting for me back in Florida.'

'A young woman you showered with gifts just got murdered, Mr Trewin. I'm afraid I can't give you a specific timeframe.'

The man keeps his mouth shut, but a line of perspiration has gathered on his upper lip. He barely responds when I say goodnight, and his body language has changed when I look back. Trewin is keeping his head down, no longer bothering the waitresses. I can't guess why a relatively young man would have a facelift, unless he hates his appearance. Too many rejections may have triggered a fit of violence, but how would a tourist carry out a ritualised murder, without leaving clues?

I catch sight of Lily Jago when I leave the bar. She's sitting on a low wall outside the hotel's entrance, dressed in her uniform, her face illuminated by the light of her mobile phone. The girl's thin shoulders are hunched, light brown hair hanging down in a messy bob. There's a look of misery on her face while she checks her messages. Lily almost drops her phone when she sees me, but manages to fumble it back into her pocket. I remember how anxious she seemed when her brother attended his first probation meeting, after leaving prison. She seemed so concerned about his welfare, I asked the island's only full-time social worker to visit the pair's home, but she still looks vulnerable. Her tense body language fills me with pity. She's had a bad year since losing her mother to cancer: her father is serving a long jail sentence on the mainland, Harry can't be trusted, and now a close friend has been killed. She rises to her feet in a hurry when she sees me, like a startled deer.

'No need to run, Lily. I'm not here to arrest you.'

'My break's over; I should get back to work.'

'Stay, just for a minute, please. I understand you were friends with Sabine Bertans. Can you think of anyone who wanted to harm her?'

'She had no enemies here.'

'What about boyfriends?'

The girl pushes a stray lock of hair back behind her ear, her hand trembling. 'Sabine was single. She knew she'd be flying home soon.'

I hand her my card. 'Call me if you remember anything. You want your friend's killer found, don't you?'

'More than anything.' The girl's eyes are cloudy with tears as she turns away.

Lily vanishes back inside the building, leaving the scent of anxiety and cheap shampoo lingering on the air. I'm almost certain that she was hiding in the corridor when I searched Sabine's room. Her nervousness could mean she's concealing something, or too distressed to discuss her friend's death. I got the feeling that she'd break into a hundred pieces if I pushed too hard.

My computer screen is flashing when I get back to my room, and my boss's face appears when I hit the Skype button. DCI Madron's one concession to holiday relaxation is to swap his formal jacket and tie for a Polo shirt, tightly buttoned around his throat. The man's grey hair is so neatly combed, his parting could have been drawn with a slide rule. I don't want to share the news of Sabine's death, but it will be reported in the papers tomorrow. Anger resonates in his voice when he finally reacts.

'Why did you let the whole day pass before calling me, Kitto?'

'We've been busy, sir. I meant to ring this morning.'

'I should be kept informed at every stage.'

'We're following procedure, I promise.'

'Don't forget our special constables if you need extra help.' Alan Madron peers at me again. 'Lose that stubble before you start work tomorrow, for God's sake. Why should people place their trust in someone who looks like a tramp?'

The DCI has complained about my refusal to wear uniform ever since appointing me as his deputy last year. He spends the next ten minutes grilling me about procedural matters, before finally relenting.

'I don't want any shortcuts, Kitto, and above all, keep the islanders safe.'

I'm still fuming when I turn off my computer. It annoys the hell out of me that my boss turns critical whenever danger strikes. Liz Gannick's music has lowered to a steady heartbeat, with stray bass notes pulsing through the wall. I'm willing to bet she's still peering down her microscope at midnight, hunting for any stray molecule to identify the killer. I'm about to crawl into bed when another unwelcome sound reaches me. Shadow is baying at the top of his voice, a wolf-like scream that should only be heard in the forests of Wyoming, under a full moon. I'm forced to go downstairs and sneak him through the fire exit, cursing under my breath.

The creature gives me an innocent look before curling up, content, on a blanket in the corner, soon beginning to snore. When I put out the light the building has fallen silent, but my eyes stay open. My loneliness only surfaces at times like this. It's easy to ignore on relaxed days, when solitude can feel like a luxury, but tonight it's an unwelcome guest. It hung over me for months after Nina left, and now she's back, just when I'd almost forgotten her. I've been enjoying life alone, but tonight I could use someone to listen to my fears. Needles of starlight push through the curtains, and the knowledge that Sabine's killer is still roaming around the island rests on the centre of my chest like a lead weight.

12

Monday 5 August

It's 3 a.m., but Lily still can't sleep. The air feels stifling, even with the window ajar, her thoughts refusing to settle. Guilt nags at her for failing to tell Ben Kitto that she took Sabine's phone, but when she switches the mobile on again, new texts have arrived from Latvia. One picture shows a group of young people in a bar, raising their beer glasses to the camera. The words WE MISS YOU! are written below the image in English. Sabine's friends don't yet know that she'll never return. Lily scrolls through the messages again, until she reaches Harry's texts. Their intimate tone makes her uneasy. He invited Sabine out on the boat again, promising to show her the whole island, then the messages end abruptly the night she died.

Lily drops the phone on her bed. She ought to hand it to the police tomorrow, but that would get Harry into trouble. She still can't be sure her brother played no part in Sabine's death. When he's drunk, he becomes another person, prone to terrible mood swings. Everyone on the island knows he's unreliable. He picks arguments after he's been to the pub, and even though he apologises later, the cycle keeps repeating itself. She'd love to turn the clock back to a simpler time, but their childhood is over. Tomorrow she must find out why Sabine died, no matter how many challenges she faces.

13

I give myself a clean shave soon after dawn. My hotel bathroom comes equipped with spare toiletries, including a razor, but my reflection still looks angry. Sabine's death and the DCI's criticisms have put a scowl on my face, my green eyes giving me a hard stare, as if the black-haired giant in the mirror might punch through the glass at any minute. I make myself do a quick workout, with enough push-ups to make my muscles burn, aware that exercise breaks will be limited until the killer's found.

When I fling open the curtains, the sun is shining on Round Island in the distance, the sky picture-postcard blue. Hugh Town's cottages run in grey seams down to the harbour, where crab boats are unloading their catch. In an ideal world I could linger here, watching the tide retreat, but Shadow is desperate for fresh air. I could use a long run too, but there's no time to burn off any more of the adrenaline that's flooded my system since Sabine died. I need to reach the station early, to make plans before the team arrives.

There's little sound from the other hotel bedrooms as Shadow races down the fire escape. Once we're outside, the dog streaks ahead with his usual gusto. I take a quick detour down to the quay, where fishermen have piled creels and lobster pots, the air already warm. There's a stench of fish guts, brine and seaweed, and Shadow is in his element. He only materialises again when I unlock the station door, whining for food. His muzzle wrinkles in disgust when I pour dry biscuits into his bowl in the backyard.

'You're not human, remember? Don't hold out for sirloin steak,' I advise him, before walking back inside.

The incident board is covered in photos from yesterday's crime scene, but the bigger picture refuses to materialise. Someone on the island hated Sabine enough to subject her to a bizarre, ritualised death, photographing her, then forcing her into a bridal costume. I can't understand why the people she knew best are refusing to talk. She told her priest that she was seeing someone new, but didn't disclose his identity. It's not yet clear whether the killer was someone she'd slept with, or a psychopath with a weird obsession. Her fearless independence could be the feature her killer hated most, if he's always been trapped on the islands. The only evidence left behind is her jewellery, a single Polaroid photo, and a line of obscure poetry. When I stare at her image again the camera's flashlight has bleached most of the colour from her skin. The killer must have spent ages applying lipstick and

eye shadow to her face, like a mortician beautify-
ing a corpse.

I shuffle through the papers I collected from Sabine's
room. The details of her flight home from London are
scrawled in blue ink, and a list of places she wanted
to visit during her final week in the UK, including the
Tate Gallery and Buckingham Palace. At the bottom
of the pile there's a postcard for her parents in Riga.
Her words are breezy and upbeat, followed by a row
of kisses, but something about the message makes me
uneasy. When I compare Sabine's handwriting with the
envelope from the killer and the Polaroid, the styles
match. A graphologist will have to decide, but the writing looks identical. She may have been forced to copy
out the phrase 'The bride in her glory will ever be fair'
then address the envelope in bright-red felt tip, as if the
pen was dipped in blood.

'You sick bastard,' I mutter under my breath.

Shadow is whimpering, his head cocked to one side,
studying me intently. I don't know whether to be glad
or unnerved that he always reads my mood so accurately, but I motion for him to settle, while I look at
the jewellery found on Sabine's body. I already know
she was wearing the earrings Liam Trewin gave her,
and a locket stolen from the local museum, but the gold
band forced onto her wedding ring finger remains a
mystery. The items could have a symbolic meaning that
relates to the macabre wedding ceremony. I've asked
Lawrie Deane to search the island's register of births,

marriages and deaths, to see if 3 August is significant for any of the islanders, but so far he's found nothing. It's too soon to guess whether the killer was intending to target a young woman when he stole the locket, but I need to know more about the theft.

The Isles of Scilly Museum lies on Church Street, a short walk inland from the police station. The dog runs ahead, making forays into people's front gardens whenever he finds an interesting scent. The street is lined with typical Scillonian terraced cottages, low-roofed, and faced with grey stone. They would have belonged to fishermen in the old days, but now sell for high prices to retirees from the mainland. Elaine Rawle and her husband Frank have lived opposite the museum for decades. Their detached property is larger than its neighbours, separated from the road by a tidy front garden. The front door gleams with fresh paint when I press the bell.

The man who opens the door once struck terror into the hearts of every local child, including me: Frank Rawle was headteacher at Five Islands School until his retirement two years ago. He presided over the school during my time there, an austere presence, ruling the establishment with a rod of iron. The man had a reputation for using his cane liberally until it was banned, but pupils still feared him. I remember being sent to his office, for lack of effort in all lessons except English and PE. He gave me a stern warning, before advising me to play more rugby, which turned out to be sound advice. My old headmaster appears in good health, his tall form unbending, grey hair swept back from his forehead in the cropped style he's worn for decades, but these days the power is mine. He and his wife are both special constables, required to follow my instructions at the island's public events. Rawle no longer towers over me, but his craggy features are still imposing. He scrutinises me closely, as if I've been playing truant, before shaking my hand. When his black Labrador appears at his side our dogs sniff each other with equal caution.

'Good to see you, young man. Bring Shadow inside, if you like.'

'Not today, thanks, Frank, it's your wife I need. She promised me a tour of the museum.'

'Elaine's over there now. Is this about the girl's death?'

'I'm hoping for information about the stolen jewellery.'

Rawle doesn't seem to hear my comment. 'What kind of lunatic would hurt a young woman like that? If you need help, I'll gladly volunteer.'

'Thanks, Frank, I may well call you.'

'I helped Eddie search for the girl's phone, but the Star Castle's grounds were clean as a whistle. We must have looked under every bush.'

'Thanks, Frank. We'll be checking the hotel's interior today.'

'Want me to come to the museum? I know the place like the back of my hand.'

He's already stepping outside, taking charge like the old days, but I give a polite refusal. 'Elaine can show me round, thanks. It won't take long.'

Frank Rawle looks disappointed, as if boredom nags at him while his wife is out. It still feels odd to use his first name, after calling him 'sir' for so long, but his manner has softened since then. He's still standing in his porch when I cross the road to the museum. The building looks anonymous from the outside, with an advert pasted to the door, offering to help anyone with local roots to trace their family trees. There's no sign of Elaine and security measures remain lax, despite last year's theft. The museum's trustees haven't shelled out for a burglar alarm.

The ground floor of the museum appears deserted. It smells of dust, wet sailcloth and cleaning fluid, like the deck of a yacht that's just been swabbed down. The islands' marine history adorns every wall. Glass cabinets contain items salvaged from wrecks, including coins, flint boxes and rusting muskets. A wall display provides a history of St Mary's lifeboat, from the days when rescuers rowed out to stranded vessels in force nine gales. But the most impressive exhibit is a full-sized replica of a Victorian sailing gig, housed in the museum's basement, its mast and sail rising through the empty core of the building. When I lean over the rail to admire it, Elaine is polishing one of the cabinets on the floor below. She looks startled by my arrival, but her smile revives when I walk downstairs.

'You're bright and early,' she says. 'We don't open till nine.'

'Frank sent me over. Can you show me where the jewellery came from, Elaine?'

'Of course, the cabinet's over here.'

Elaine leads me past displays that have changed little since I was a boy, her pace rapid for a woman in her sixties. She doesn't pause as we march past an assortment of items charting life in Scilly since records began. Hand axes and knives from the Bronze Age fight for space alongside Roman scabbards. A collection of stuffed seabirds watch with beady glass eyes as we come to a halt by a small glass case.

'The thief must have known exactly what to pick,' Elaine says. 'I still don't understand why only six pieces were taken. Why not swipe the lot?'

'Do you remember what was stolen?'

'Three lockets and three gold rings. I think they were made locally, but Julian Power will know more about them. We're lucky to have such an expert as a trustee.'

'Can you show me some of the pieces the thief left behind?'

She picks up a small gold pendant etched with the outline of a sailing ship, and a man's name inscribed on the back.

'Lovely, isn't it?' Elaine murmurs. 'The engraving's so delicate.'

'Why would a killer steal something with all that history?'

'It doesn't make sense.'

'Sorry, I was thinking aloud.'

Her eyes are glossy when her gaze connects with mine. 'Frank and I met Sabine several times when we had dinner at the Star Castle. Such a lovely girl, wasn't she?'

'It's tragic for her family.'

'She was even younger than our Leah.' Elaine's voice fades to a whisper.

'Is that your daughter?'

'That's right; we lost her years ago.'

'Sorry, I had no idea.'

'Don't apologise, Ben, you were a child back then. She was twenty when she died. One minute she seemed fine, then suddenly she was gone.'

When I touch her shoulder Elaine manages a smile, but her face soon blanks again, as if so much loss still leaves her mystified. Sabine's death seems to have rekindled her grief, and I expect many of the islanders feel the same. Lives are so tightly connected in a small community, neighbours feel like relatives, because you cross paths every day.

I spend a few more minutes searching the basement floor, imagining the killer browsing through displays. He would have stood where I am now, inhaling the odour of old books, polish and cleaning fluid. There's not much to check, apart from a storeroom which contains mops, brooms and shelves loaded with back issues of *The Cornishman*. My eyes catch on a pile of cardboard boxes in a corner of the museum's ground floor, stacked almost to the ceiling. A label explains that they hold items donated for a forthcoming exhibition on island life, yet they're so thick with dust, the heap may have been there when the killer stole the jewellery. The small scale of the place means that whoever stole it was taking a huge risk, and must have been highly motivated.

I check the museum log for 3 August last year, and find that dozens of people visited, the place constantly busy. Elaine kept a tally of the number of visitors, but not their names. The killer probably dropped in several times, to plan the theft, but she can't remember specific details. She was writing a press release that day, about a new exhibition of local photographs. Elaine only noticed the cabinet's lock was broken when she closed the place at five o'clock.

'Julian loves talking about the exhibits,' she says, as I prepare to leave. 'He'll be glad to see you.'

I thank her before saying goodbye a little before 10 a.m.; the woman's sadness is still visible when I leave, but her advice to seek expert help is sound. The killer placed the stolen locket around Sabine's neck for a reason, and its history could provide new insights. It still nags at me that the theft occurred on 3 August, then Sabine died exactly a year later, but the date has no obvious significance. Shadow trips along the pavement beside me, oblivious to the thoughts whirling around my head.

Julian Power's house is a stone's throw from Hugh Town quay. The tall Georgian building has an air of faded grandeur; it looks far more sombre than Tregarthen's Hotel next door, which has welcomed paying guests for two hundred years, ever since a retired sea captain turned his home into a business. Power appears dubious when he finally answers his doorbell, and Shadow's reaction doesn't help. The dog takes an instant dislike to him, his jaws snapping, making me grab his collar. I can't see why Power has triggered so much aggression. The man's straight-backed posture makes me assume he's ex-army; he's around fifty, with a compact build, dark hair cut short, and a neat moustache. He stands his ground while Shadow barks at the top of his voice, grey eyes observing me steadily. Power's expression only softens when I ask for help to identify the items stolen from the museum.

'I'm happy to talk if the dog stays outside. But I won't be able to add much to what Elaine told you, I'm afraid. There's no record of the pieces being donated. All I know for certain is that they were crafted locally, towards the end of the nineteenth century.'

'Any new information would be useful.'

Shadow is still misbehaving when I tie him to a railing; the creature howling with outrage for no obvious reason. I know little about Power, except that he's a second-generation islander, and one of the island's richest men. He bought the Isles of Scilly Travel Company a decade ago, acting as broker for all mainland ferry and flight services. I can tell immediately that his interest in collecting extends beyond local jewellery. Antique seascapes fill the walls of his hallway, all painted in the same realist style, galleons fighting to stay afloat in harsh typhoons. His living room has shelves loaded with glassware, and decorative plates cover his French dresser.

'How long have you been collecting?'

He gives an awkward smile. 'Ever since I can remember. It started with stamps and coins, then spiralled out of control. It's my only addiction.'

'It beats drugs or booze.'

'True, but it can be expensive. A Roman coin I bought last week cost me eight hundred pounds.'

'Is it made of gold?'

'Good Lord, no. Most of those are in the British Museum. It's a bronze aureus; I've wanted one for years.'

The man's new purchase animates him at last, his eyes glowing with pleasure. He produces a wooden box then hands it to me. It contains a dozen pieces of jewellery, glittering against their black velvet lining.

'These are Cornish gold like the ones taken from the museum. Fishermen bought them here on St Mary's over a hundred years ago, as talismans for their new brides. Jewellers called them "sailors' charms", but they didn't always bring good luck.'

I pick out a locket with a date engraved on the back, a lock of hair pressed behind the glass. I can see why fishermen gave such intimate mementoes to their wives as wedding gifts, in case they perished at sea.

'Was much gold mined in Cornwall?'

Power shakes his head. 'Mostly tin and copper; it's very scarce. It's a shame that the thief took some of the museum's most important pieces. I can't understand why there's no mention of them in the record book, but they could have been donated a hundred years ago. Heirlooms like that rarely come up for sale. I only know from hearsay that the locket you found at Pulpit Rock has a tragic history. Apparently the man who gave it to his wife drowned soon after they married.'

His words silence me for a moment. Many families in Scilly have lost relatives to the sea, including mine. My father often gave my mother flowers before his fishing trips, until his trawler went down on the Atlantic Strait. The same storm killed the Keast brothers' father too, making us members of a club that no one wants to join.

'We found the locket on the victim's body,' I say.

Power shakes his head, frowning. 'The sailors' charms contain so much hope and tenderness; it's a pity the killer's tarnished them.'

'Three rings went missing too, didn't they?'

'I think they were just simple Cornish gold wedding bands made locally, but they're not listed in the museum's record book either.'

'Elaine mentioned that you're creating an online catalogue.'

He winces. 'It won't be easy; the record book

goes back a hundred and fifty years. I wish I'd never volunteered.'

'Would you check the record again, to see if there's any mention at all of which family left the stolen pieces to the museum? I think they have a special meaning for the killer.'

'When do you need to know?'

'As soon as possible, please.'

'I'll do my best.'

'How long will you need?'

'I can't promise miracles. The records are pretty impenetrable, but I'll start today.'

'Can you call me when you find out?'

I show Power the wedding band found on Sabine's finger, and he confirms from the hallmark that it's likely to be one of the stolen items. The man's solemn manner strikes me as odd; his face is so expressionless, he seems to believe that smiling might cause him pain.

'Would you mind telling me how you spent yesterday, Julian?'

He looks puzzled. 'I never met the young girl that died. You realise that, don't you?'

'It's my job to ask questions anyway, I'm afraid.'

'I was wrestling with my computer at home. Our booking system broke down last week, so I was trying to fix it. Then I went to the museum in the evening; I borrowed the key from Elaine Rawle at about 8 p.m. I got home in time for the ten o'clock news.'

'You were alone?'

'I've lived by myself for years.'

'Do you mind saying why?'

He folds his arms tighter across his chest. 'I got divorced five years ago, but the local gossip mill never stops churning, especially in winter when there's little to keep people busy. I prefer being alone to having my love life dissected in the pub.'

'You must get lonely sometimes.'

'Not at all. My house is peaceful, and I never have to placate anyone. I can do as I please.'

The man's precise speech reminds me of the killer's systematic approach, despite finding no concrete evidence to link him to Sabine's death. He seems determined to put collecting at the centre of his life, instead of other human beings. I remember the make-up so carefully applied to Sabine's face, and flowers threaded through her hair, before thanking him for his help. There seem to be two sides to the killer's personality. Whoever completed the crime is capable of the delicacy Power showed when handling his rare items, yet Sabine's body was hoisted from the ground with brutal strength, then displayed like a broken doll. My mind circles back to the sailors' charms, aware that the killer stole more than one item for a reason. I'm already braced for a phone call, telling me another victim's been taken.

14

My next visit will be a lot more challenging than a lesson on antique jewellery. I have to be present at 11 a.m. when Dr Keillor examines Sabine's body in the mortuary. Despite my long stint in the Murder Squad, corpses bother me more than I care to admit. Shadow bares his teeth when I untie his leash, clearly in no mood to forget being held captive for the past half hour. The morning heat is rising to boiling point when I follow Church Road towards the hospital, and Shadow vanishes from sight, filling me with envy. This is one duty I would happily skip, in favour of sunbathing with a cold drink in my hand.

High Town is so small that its amenities all lie close together, but it's home to half of St Mary's permanent residents. The hospital looks like a couple of modest dwellings, carefully whitewashed, with a garden area outside. It stands at the top of Carn Gwaval, where Hugh Town gives way to the untamed moors of Peninnis Head, giving patients a long view over the island's allotment site to the pale sand of Porthcressa Beach. I cut across the car park to the mortuary behind the hospital. The pre-fabricated building has frosted glass windows, to protect the privacy of the dead. Gareth Keillor has arrived already, and is dressed in blue surgical scrubs, arranging scalpels, surgical knives and bowls on a trolley. He gives me a nod of greeting before turning on his recorder, then announcing the start of his examination to the microphone that hangs over the operating table.

When he pulls back the sheet, the air is tainted with chemicals and decay. Sabine's neck is circled by dark red bruising, yet her make-up is still intact, grey shadow marking her closed eyelids, lips still frosted with pale pink lipstick. The garland in her hair has shrivelled; only the cornflowers have retained their colour. They could have been picked from any hedgerow on St Mary's. When I glance at the rest of her body, there are few visible injuries. It feels wrong to stare at her exposed breasts and hips, but her physique is athletic, the muscles she developed from distance swimming still in evidence. Keillor takes his time, using a pin to scrape dirt from under her nails into plastic specimen tubes. His voice is measured when he murmurs his findings into the recorder. Sabine's family haven't agreed to a full post-mortem yet, but he inserts a suction tube into her mouth, then eases her onto her side to examine her neck.

'Cervical vertebrae fracture, between C6 and C7,

oedema around ruptured spinal column,' he tells the microphone, then turns to face me. 'You need to see this, Ben.'

When I step forward, new odours hit me; ammonia and something sharper and more acidic, emanating from the girl's body.

'What do you make of the discoloration, above her collarbone?' he asks. 'See anything odd about it?'

A line of scarlet rope burns circles her throat, but some smaller purple marks don't make sense.

'Where do the round bruises come from?'

'They're consistent with strangulation; the killer's fingertips press so hard, they often leave a bruise. It only takes light pressure on the carotid artery to prevent blood reaching the brain, but most stranglers don't realise. They aim to cut off their victim's air supply through the windpipe.'

The pathologist completes his work without further conversation, until he strips off his surgical gloves fifteen minutes later, then lathers his hands with soap that turns his skin a virulent yellow. His expression is weary when he speaks again.

'I should give up my consultancy duties and retire properly, Ben. Cases like this test my faith in humanity.'

'And mine. Did you learn anything new?'

He gives a slow nod. 'The bruising at the base of her skull is from a blunt instrument. She was hit from behind, with a crowbar or a club. The blow would have knocked her out for several hours. Apart from that, her body is almost unmarked, until the strangulation.'

'You think Sabine was already dead when she was hung from Pulpit Rock?'

'She was beaten, then strangled to death. After that he took her back to Pulpit Rock. Her neck broke when he hung her body from the cliff.'

'Why not just dump her on a beach for the tide to carry away?'

'Motives are your domain, Ben.' He looks down at the girl's face again. 'But I'd say the killer's showing off. Her body was left hanging at one of our most famous beauty spots. It's always been popular for wedding photos too; my wife and I had our pictures taken there thirty years ago.'

'I still don't see why she was dressed as a bride. The killer seems to love the costume, flowers and lipstick, like a kid with a dressing-up box.'

'It could be some kind of fetish, but there's no overtly sexual element, or physical clues on the girl's body. Your best chance of a DNA match is from under her nails. She was young, fit and no doubt desperate to survive. If she fought her attacker, the lab will find skin samples.'

'Thanks for your help, Gareth.'

'Good luck hunting him down.' He studies me again. 'This one's getting to you, isn't it? When it's over, you should take up golf. A walk round the fairway is a great stress buster; I'd be happy to coach you.'

'I could use a game right now, Gareth, but it'll have to wait.'

By the time I leave the mortuary, another hour has passed, and a clean white sheet has hidden Sabine Bertans' body once more, her short life already slipping from view.

15

Lily can't decide how to spend her afternoon off. Her feelings are still so numb, the warm breeze barely registers when she leaves the staff accommodation block. She's dressed like a tourist in a T-shirt, denim cut-offs and espadrilles, but she's too upset to sunbathe on Porthcressa Beach. Sabine's phone is still tucked inside her pocket. It presses against her skin, reminding her to keep searching for her friend's killer.

The air smells of cooking oil and stale coffee as she passes the kitchen. One of the chefs is taking a cigarette break, leaning against the wall. The middle-aged man calls out as she walks past.

'Sorry to hear about your friend, Lily.'

'It doesn't seem real,' she says, coming to a halt beside him. 'I keep thinking she'll walk back through the gates.'

'How old was Sabine?'

'Nineteen a few weeks ago.'

'Jesus, she was still a kid.' He uses his heel to grind the stub of his cigarette into the gravel. 'It's always the boyfriend, isn't it? Who was she seeing?'

'No one.'

The chef's eyebrows shoot towards his hairline. 'There were several, most likely.'

Lily stares back at him. 'What do you mean?'

'She always flirted with the lads in the kitchen.' He gives an awkward shrug. 'Girls like that draw the wrong kind of attention.'

'It's wrong to judge her; she's not here to defend herself.'

'Sorry, love, but everyone thinks the same.' He holds up his hands, like she's holding a loaded gun.

'Sabine was friendly, that's all, and kinder than all of you.' She spits out the words.

The man's smile remains on his face when he gives a low whistle of admiration. 'I thought you were a mouse, but you're a tough little nut, aren't you?'

'No one knew her like me. The rest of you can shut up.'

Lily is trembling when she walks away. She exits the hotel grounds fast, before anyone else can pass judgement. The midday heat is so stifling, she's struggling to breathe. Her walk takes her past the police station, and she considers handing in Sabine's phone, but it's the last link to her friend's memory. Lily returns to the house where she once lived on the Strand; the modest two-storey building has seen better days. Its only beautiful feature now is the view through the ginnel to Porth Minick Beach, and its acres of pristine sand.

The front door is unlocked, the hallway reeking of spilled beer. When she enters the living room, Lily calls her brother's name, but gets no reply. She shakes her head in disgust. Her mother always kept the place clean and tidy, with wildflowers in a vase on the table. Harry has neglected it for months. Dishes are heaped in the kitchen sink, and stains mark the worn-out lino, discarded clothes and newspapers piled on the furniture. She sinks into an armchair, too upset to move, until she notices that something has fallen from her brother's jacket, thrown haphazardly over the arm of the chair. It's a Polaroid picture of Sabine, gazing at the camera, her expression beseeching. There's so much terror in her eyes, Lily blinks hard, to avoid seeing it again.

'What have you done, Harry?' She mutters the words, then presses her hand across her mouth.

16

The police station reeks of coffee and stress. Five take-away cups and half a dozen baguettes from Strudel's café have been left in Madron's office, the smell of espresso lifting my spirits. The DCI would be appalled to see his gleaming mahogany desk being used as a picnic table, but it's the only space large enough for the whole team. Liz Gannick is last to arrive, abandoning her crutches by the door when my briefing starts. The chief forensics officer's frown reminds me that she prefers running her own operation, and hates taking orders. Outside the window, Shadow is oblivious to internal power struggles; he's dozing in a patch of sunlight in the backyard, his muzzle resting on his paws, minding his own business for once. Eddie and Isla watch expectantly while I thumb through my notes, expecting me to unlock the case instantly. Lawrie Deane and Liz Gannick have been in the game long enough to know that murder cases take time, even on a small island, unless luck is on your side. Their expressions only become animated when they hear that Sabine was strangled to death before being hung from Pulpit Rock.

'The bastard wanted to watch her die at close range,' Gannick mutters. 'Only men commit crimes that violent; women hardly ever strangle their victims.'

'But what's the motive?' Eddie says. 'The Cornish wedding ring on her finger has to mean something. I've been asking round about the phrase on the back of the photo too, but no one recognises it. It sounds like the start of a poem to me.'

'Any luck with the date, Lawrie?'

The sergeant shakes his head. 'The registrar's records were useless. Two female islanders were born on the third of August, but they're both over seventy.'

'We'll have to use the sailors' charms. By putting that locket round Sabine's neck, she's become a true Cornish bride. Maybe the killer didn't want her to leave, even though she never intended to stay.' I look at each of them in turn. 'Let's start sending tourists home today, if their alibis are sound. We know the killer has access to a car, which rules most of them out. We need to thin the population down, so he's got nowhere to hide. The *Scillonian*'s waiting by the quay; it can take up to five hundred people back to Penzance this afternoon and sail back empty tomorrow morning to collect the rest. Remember the island's still closed to everyone except authorised visitors.'

Eddie catches my eye again. 'The rope around Sabine's neck was stolen. A coil was left outside the lifeboat house last week, and by morning it was gone. The RNLI use exactly the same gauge as the one at the murder scene.'

'So our killer gets a kick from nicking stuff. Ask around and see if people in Hugh Town saw anyone prowling round the lifeboat house at night.' I turn to Isla next. 'Any luck tracing the wedding dress?'

She looks apologetic. 'I've sent out loads of emails, but none of the second-hand shops can identify it.'

'Keep trying, you may still get a result.' I stare down at my scribbled notes. 'Liam Trewin has admitted to giving Sabine the earrings she was wearing when she died, but so far we've got nothing else against him. The killer must be feeling pretty smug. We still can't prove whether they're male or female, but they've carried out a complex murder in a small community, with an MO that's weird enough for the true crime books. We need a better understanding of our victim too. Sabine was bright enough to win a place at Latvia's top university, and arrange a summer job at the Star Castle to improve her English. Her family are Catholic, but she attended church here more out of habit than belief, according to Father Michael.'

'We still don't know if she was dragged to Pulpit Rock or lured there,' Liz Gannick snaps. 'I should be searching her room now, before more evidence is lost.'

'You can go soon, I promise.' My voice is calm when I reply. 'But this is going to need a coordinated approach. We know he used a car or van to transport her body, so let's do a vehicle check today.'

'That'll take forever,' Gannick replies.

I shake my head in reply. 'There are over four hundred privately owned cars here, but only three are for hire. I'd like those checked this afternoon. Most holidaymakers use bikes or golf buggies to get around. Can you check the car Liam Trewin hired first, Liz, to see if it was used to carry Sabine's body? We know he fancied her, but it may just have been heavy-handed flirting.' Gannick gives a hiss of disapproval. 'The killer could be hiding in a remote corner of the island, or right under our noses, but I think they'll try again. We know most violent crimes are carried out by men between eighteen and forty-five, but let's keep an open mind. I want to prioritise islanders in that group who knew Sabine first. Their names will stay on our suspect list until they're ruled out. Our killer is organised enough to steal jewellery from the museum to leave at the crime scene a whole year later. It's possible this is the start of a campaign.'

Gannick glowers with impatience as I allocate duties, then let the team know that the police graphologist has confirmed that it's Sabine's handwriting on the back of her photo. The killer was smart enough not to give us a sample of their handwriting. I want the suspect list narrowed down from over four hundred islanders with access to cars, so we can make progress.

'Eddie and I will be searching the Star Castle this afternoon. The CPS have given us an open search warrant for garages, agricultural and industrial buildings.

You only need to get permission before searching people's homes. If the householder refuses, it'll take hours to get a domestic warrant.'

I ask Deane to contact visitors with solid alibis, and advise them about travel home. Eddie's most important duty after our search is to speak to the remaining islanders, to ensure they're safe. Nina enters my mind as I issue the instruction; I never found out whether she travelled here alone or with a group during our brief conversation.

Liz Gannick is on her feet once the briefing ends. I follow her to the door, ready to escort her to the Star Castle, until Isla steps into my path.

'Can I have a quick word in private, sir?'

The constable's expression is so tense, I ask Eddie to escort Gannick to the hotel, then return to Madron's office.

'What's wrong, Isla?'

'There's something I should have told you at the start.' She seems lost for words, which surprises me. The girl's manner is normally blunt and straightforward.

'Take a seat then give it a try.'

She perches on a chair, hands clasped together like she's offering up a prayer. 'Sabine liked to party and have a few drinks on her nights off. She could be pretty wild company.'

'And?'

'We slept together once, after the pub. She invited me back to her room, and I left before dawn.' Isla's sexual preferences haven't occurred to me until now, but she looks afraid when she speaks again, as if she's facing the sack. 'It was soon after she arrived, at the end of June.'

'It never became a relationship?'

'Her choice, not mine. She didn't want complications.'

'How did that make you feel?'

'Hurt, at first, even though I knew she was straight. She probably just wanted to tick "sleeping with a girl" off her list of experiences. I don't think she'd ever fancied a woman before.' The constable's cheeks are blushing a furious red.

'Who knows about this?'

'She wouldn't have mentioned it, unless she told Lily Jago, and I don't brag about my sex life.'

'The pair of you still seemed close.'

'We didn't spend much time alone after that, but we never fell out.' Isla's intent gaze is trained on the lino under her feet. 'Will I be dropped from the investigation?'

'You know the rules on police involvement with victims. It normally means mandatory exclusion, but I might be able to get permission. Do you want to stay on the case?'

'Of course, boss.' Her expression combines anxiety with fervour.

'I'll speak to DCI Madron and the Cornish Constabulary.' I look at her again. 'How did you spend Saturday night?'

Isla drags her fingers through her razor-short hair. 'At home watching telly with Mum. I'd been for a long swim, so I was too tired to go out.'

'Ginny can verify that?'

She gives a miserable nod. 'Everyone's going to hear about this, aren't they?'

'We're looking for someone Sabine spent time with, male or female. Nothing can stay off the record.'

'My friends know I'm gay, but not colleagues or my family.' She dabs at her eyes, brushing away tears.

'It's nothing to be ashamed of, and you did fine telling me. Maybe it won't be that hard.'

'I'll speak to Lawrie now.' Isla stumbles to her feet. 'Thanks for listening, sir.'

'You were right to be honest. Don't wait so long next time.'

'Shall I get on with tracking down who bought the wedding dress?'

I give a brisk nod. 'Give it an hour, then I want you out on patrol for the rest of the afternoon. Reassure the islanders that we're making progress; some of them will be panicking. Take Shadow with you, please. It's a mistake to leave him alone indoors.'

'Why?'

'He destroys furniture, carpets and wallpaper.'

'You make him sound like a criminal.'

'My sofa's ruined. That deserves a custodial sentence, doesn't it?'

She manages a smile before disappearing. The

station's walls are so thin I listen to her explaining about her night with Sabine to Lawrie Deane. Most islanders adopt a live and let live attitude about people's sexuality, but he may be an exception. I'm braced to go out there and give Deane a formal warning if he shows any sign of disdain. The sergeant's default reaction is to criticise all new information, but on this occasion his reply is gentle. He makes a quiet joke about introducing Isla to his niece, because she's spent years searching for the right woman.

I'm glad our new recruit told me the truth, even though the case just got more complicated. Isla would be excluded instantly in London, because of her connection to the victim, but I need all the officers I can get. I'll have to work hard to keep her on my team, by persuading Madron and the Cornish force. I hope it's worth the effort. The more I know about Sabine, the more complex she appears. The girl seems to have drawn admirers of all persuasions, like moths to a flame.

17

Eddie is waiting for me in the hotel's reception area at half past two. The young sergeant looks out of place among the plush furniture and floral displays in his ill-fitting uniform, but his face brightens when I arrive. Our work together has taught me that tough challenges make his day, unlike Deane, who prefers to keep his feet warm under his desk. I catch sight of Rhianna Polkerris crossing the bar; the woman's stare is glacial before she turns away.

'She doesn't look real,' Eddie whispers.

'What do you mean?'

'Rhianna never smiles. She's like a waxwork at Madame Tussaud's.'

'She's probably angry about losing business. Half her rooms will stay empty until we lift the embargo on travelling.' I brush the hotel manager's coldness aside. 'Did you get hold of a master key?'

He produces it from his pocket. 'This one opens all the bedrooms. The last few guests have given permission for our search.'

'Let's start with Liam Trewin, he's in the West Room.'

Lookout points in the castle's star-shaped walls mark all four points of the compass. They would have been manned by sentries years ago, but now they serve as plush bedrooms. Trewin's west-facing room has an unbroken view of the Atlantic, but I can't imagine Elizabethan soldiers in such grand surroundings. The luxuries include an embroidered silk bedspread, a chaise longue, and a state-of-the-art TV. Eddie gives a low whistle as he looks around.

'Michelle would love all the high-end details. Maybe I should splash out and bring her here for her birthday.'

'Forget the furniture, Eddie. We may not find the murder weapon, but there's a chance her phone's hidden in this room. If you find it, I'll buy the pair of you a night in the honeymoon suite.'

Trewin has had twenty-four hours to remove telltale signs, but the American's pestering of Sabine makes him of special interest. I can hear Eddie searching the bathroom cabinet in the en suite, while I open the wardrobe. A waft of sickly aftershave hits me as I check the pockets of his Ralph Lauren shirts and jackets. Either the guy has money to burn, or he's obsessed by creating the right impression. I can't find a single mark on his clothes, his leather shoes gleaming. If he killed Sabine Bertans, it wasn't inside this pristine room. Even his choice of holiday reading seems designed to look innocent; a book about Cornish churches lies open on his bedside table.

'It's too clean,' I mutter to myself.

'The bathroom's spotless too,' Eddie replies. 'This is all I found.'

He hands over a pill bottle, with *Vicodin* printed on the label. My deputy searches for information about the drug on his phone.

'It's an opioid narcotic, very addictive. Doctors are being warned against prescribing such strong painkillers over here.'

'When you get back to the station, check for a criminal record in the US. The guy was here last year when the locket was stolen, and he had access to a hire car the night Sabine died. Can you call Gareth Keillor too, and check her toxicology results? Vicodin in her bloodstream would give us a direct link. We're still waiting for results from the scrapings under her nails too.'

'You're not in London now, boss,' Eddie replies with an apologetic smile. 'The lab often takes forty-eight hours for basic tests.'

We spend almost two hours searching twelve recently occupied hotel bedrooms. The cleaners have left them spotless, with nothing to implicate the guests in Sabine's death. It's possible that the killer is linked to the Star Castle in some way, but smart enough to conceal any signs of violence. Eddie seems elated, like a school prefect on an exotic day trip, even though Sabine's phone is still missing. His smile only vanishes when I give him the task of checking the staff accommodation block.

'Can I ask about something first, boss?'

'Go ahead.'

'Isla called earlier. Don't you think it's weird about her and Sabine?'

'Why?'

'She starts her job, then there's a murder, and the victim just happens to be someone she knew intimately.'

'What do you mean?'

He looks uncomfortable. 'I didn't know her that well at school but she could be a bit intense, defensive, you know? She didn't have many mates. If Sabine dumped her after a one night stand, she's got reason to be angry, hasn't she?'

'She's in the clear, Eddie. Ginny's confirmed they were at home together all evening.'

'Thank God for that, it's been bothering me since she rang. I must be getting paranoid.' Eddie's smile has revived already. 'Are we interviewing staff while we're here? I've got a print-out of employees' names.'

I scan the list before tearing it in half, splitting the workload between us, but my deputy's question lingers as I cross the hotel grounds. Isla's solemn manner can be unsettling. It will take time for our new constable to win acceptance from such a small team.

When I study my list of names, I decide to see Sally Carnforth first. She's been the Star Castle's house-keeper for so long, she's bound to have the lowdown on every employee. Sally is in the laundry, humming tune-lessly as she hauls bedsheets from an industrial drier.

A big woman with bleached blonde hair scraped back into a ponytail, she runs the hotel's domestic affairs with ruthless efficiency. She carries on working when I arrive, like nothing could break her stride. The room is sweltering, with condensation running down the windows; the housekeeper is dressed in a blue housecoat, the arduous physical work on such a hot day turning her skin florid.

'If you're asking about Sabine, you're in the wrong place. I'm sad she's dead, of course, but I don't know why it happened.' She leans down to ram more sheets into the drier.

'Did anything strike you as odd about her, Sally?'

'The foreign girls often get homesick. Plenty of them cry on my shoulder, but that one was independent, and a bit pleased with herself. I had no complaints about her work, mind you. It was her effect on the other staff that bothered me.'

'How do you mean?'

'She was so pretty and confident, she turned a few heads. The youngsters often dream of escaping the islands and travelling the world. I think some were envious.'

'Did Sabine fall out with anyone?'

'Not to my knowledge.' She turns her back to grab another armful of laundry. 'Lily Jago should know, those two were thick as thieves.'

'I saw her already, but another word might help. Is she on duty?'

'It's her afternoon off. She's probably with that use-less brother of hers.'

Sally's statement proves that many islanders have given up on Harry Jago. I hoped that his short spell in prison would act as a warning, but he's carried on causing trouble. Jago served a three-month sentence for theft earlier this year, after stealing booze repeatedly from the Co-op. He's been cautioned since for drunk and disorderly behaviour; his worst brawl left a local fisherman with two black eyes. He tried to lay the blame on someone else, so no one believes a word he says. The lad is one of a tiny number of islanders with a reputation for violence. If Lily was close friends with Sabine, I'll have to seek him out soon, to find out if she spent time in his company.

I'm about to check on Liz Gannick's progress in Sabine's room, when my phone buzzes in my pocket. Lawrie Deane's voice sounds anxious when I pick up.

'A woman's in trouble, boss. She called emergency services from the beach by Halangy Down.'

'Is she injured?'

'She wasn't making sense, but I think she's been attacked. I've called the hospital, but the ambulance won't make it down the track to the beach.'

'Tell her help's coming. I'll take the bike.'

I head back to the station at a rapid jog, passing two elderly guests sunbathing in the garden. If they're concerned by seeing a dishevelled giant race through the hotel grounds, they're too polite to comment. It only takes me a few minutes to get back to the station and grab a crash helmet. One of the perks of my job is riding a motorbike round the island, but it's never reliable. I have to kick the ancient Yamaha's starter pedal three times before it splutters into life. I take the back road, bypassing town, to avoid getting flagged down by islanders asking for news.

The lane winds through the Lower Moors, where poppies are blooming in the cracks between drystone walls. I have to slow down to let a party of twitchers cross as they follow the nature trail to an old bird hide. When I steer the bike onto Telegraph Road, late afternoon sun is burning through my shirt. There's no sign of the ambulance yet, and Lawrie was right: no four-wheeled vehicle could handle the track down to the beach. The stretch of rock and gravel twists in hairpin bends down to Halangy Porth. It takes all my patience to travel at ten miles an hour while an attack victim lies at the bottom.

The area looks deserted as I scan the trees that run down to the beach. I can see Samson's hazy outline on the horizon, and the tide coming in fast, breakers hammering boulders that lie strewn across the beach. I hear the woman moaning before catching sight of her lying near the tideline, the waves splashing her hiking boots, her phone still clutched in her hand. She's in her thirties, with a petite build. Blood is seeping through her short blonde hair, staining her T-shirt. She looks terrified, as if I might be another attacker.

'I'm Ben Kitto, Island Police.' I flash my ID card before dropping down at her side. 'What's your name?'

'Hannah. I thought no one would find me.' She's got a soft German accent. Her skin is unnaturally pale, but she's managing to keep her blue eyes open.

'You're safe, don't worry. What happened just now?'

'Someone hit me from behind.'

'A man or a woman?'

'I don't know, the sun was too bright to see.'

'Can you stand up, Hannah? We need to get you to a doctor.'

When I put my arm round her waist, she sways on her feet. I can't let her ride pillion, in case she loses consciousness again.

'I'll carry you to the ambulance, okay?'

I was wrong to imagine there would be no time for workouts while the case continues. Carrying a nine-stone victim up a steep hill with the sun beating down provides enough cardiovascular exercise to last me all week. I try to keep her talking during the journey, to stop her fainting again, but she replies in monosyllables. All I've learned is that she's travelling solo and has been staying at Juliet's Garden – a cluster of holiday cottages a little way south of here. The woman's eyelids flutter as she struggles to keep them open, shock and exhaustion defeating her. I'll have to wait until she's rested before getting more details about her attacker. The relief on her face when she spots the ambulance by the roadside is a just reward for so much physical labour.

Once the ambulance speeds back towards Hugh Town, I catch my breath. It's after five, but the afternoon's searing heat shows no sign of cooling down. I'm tempted to jump into a cattle trough by the side of the road, but settle for dousing my face and hair instead. I try to rinse the woman's blood from my sleeve, but a dark shadow remains on the fabric when I walk back down to the beach. There's still no sign of the killer, who may have trekked north from Juliet's Garden, keeping Hannah in sight, using the trees as cover. My frustration increases when I see how well the attacker's presence has been erased, by dragging driftwood across the sand, then escaping into the woods. But what piece of luck allowed Hannah to survive, while Sabine lost her battle? Maybe a boat passed close to the shore, or the sound of a car on the road above spooked him, or her, into abandoning their plans.

Hannah's body has left an imprint on the sand when I return to the tideline, and droplets of blood smeared across a piece of granite, but the next tall wave carries them away.

18

I've already asked Lawrie Deane to warn the hotels to keep their guests safe, but I'll have to be more specific. I want them to prioritise lone females, after the killer's second attempt. Whoever hurt the German tourist has enough confidence to attack a hiker in broad daylight, so the risk level is on red alert. Hannah may have been spending so much time alone she had no knowledge that a woman had been killed when she set off on her hike. I stare up at Halangy Down as I kick the motorbike's engine back into life. My brother and I played here sometimes at dusk when we were kids, pretending that the long shadows were ancient ghosts, flying down from hilltop graves to visit their old homes. The Bronze Age settlement is one of the biggest in Europe, its stone boundaries stretching as far as the eye can see.

Lawrie sounds annoyed when I call to check he's managed to inform all female visitors who are renting holiday cottages not to spend time alone.

'I've tried, boss, but people keep phoning in for news. They're blocking the line.'

'Work as fast as you can, Lawrie. I'm heading to the hospital now to check the victim's okay.'

His sigh echoes in my ear. 'I've phoned one number six times. The lady's staying in Watermill Cottage.'

'I can drop by there now. What's her name?'

'Nina Jackson.'

Irritation runs through me as I say goodbye. It's my professional duty to visit her, but I'd rather avoid it. Our last proper conversation was when she sailed back to the mainland, without giving our relationship time to develop. My teeth are gritted as I ride east along Watermill Lane at 6 p.m., hoping today's meeting will be the last time we clap eyes on each other before she goes home. The surroundings are beautiful, with elm trees forming a leafy archway over the road at Trenoweth, but even the picturesque scenery fails to improve my mood. I'm still scowling as I follow the track down to one of the island's loveliest coves.

Watermill Cottage stands alone at the end of a fishermen's track down to the shore. The traditional two-storey property is built from local stone, with storm shutters to protect it from winter gales. It would only appeal to someone who loves their own company, but its charm is obvious. I can see the Eastern Isles beyond Crow Sound, and the peaks of St Martin's and Tresco shimmering in the distance. I'm taking off my crash helmet when Nina calls out to me.

'The view's not bad, is it?'

She's standing in the porch. Her brown hair is longer than before, glinting in the sun. It skims her shoulders as she steps towards me, no trace of make-up on her olive skin. Her summer dress stops mid-thigh, exposing long tanned legs, and bare feet. Looking at her leaves me speechless. Suddenly I'm painfully aware that my clothes are dirty, my hair still wet from its recent soaking. She always wrongfoots me, like a sucker punch, arriving out of the blue. Nina assesses me calmly before speaking again.

'You still look like more like a wild Cornish smuggler than a cop.'

'I can't see why. My ancestors were law-abiding fishermen, for five generations,' I say, taking care to keep my distance. 'Were you planning to avoid me all week, Nina?'

'I knew our paths would cross sometime.' Her voice is slightly husky, as if she's just downed a glass of cognac.

'I'm surprised you came back.'

'The landscape's hard to forget. Like I said, I meant to call, but you're busy right now.'

'Another woman was attacked this afternoon. Why didn't you answer your phone?'

'I was swimming.' Her amber-coloured eyes show concern, but no sign of panic. 'Is she okay?'

'I'm going to the hospital now to check.'

'Have a cold drink first – this heat's punishing.'

My plan to keep our meeting brief founders when I enter the cottage. Large windows flood the rooms with light, and the air smells of her perfume; jasmine, sea salt and musk. It makes me keen to escape, before memories carry me in the wrong direction. Nina has made herself at home already, with a Jane Austen novel lying on her sofa, her violin case propped against the wall. I can see a single deckchair on the patio through the open window, proving that she travelled here alone, still happier with solitude than intimacy. Nina keeps her back turned when she opens the fridge and pours juice from a pitcher. I remain on my feet when she passes me a glass, the iced liquid chilling my throat. A pile of books is stacked on the kitchen table, with their titles on display: *Person Centred Counselling*; *The Drama of Childhood*; *Post Traumatic Stress Disorder*.

'Are these yours?'

She smiles before replying. 'I'm training to be a counsellor; there's an assessment coming up soon.'

'Another career change.' I set the empty glass down on her table. 'This place is too isolated, Nina. You should stay in town until the killer's found.'

'I'll be fine here, the owners have lent me their car.'

'You're still vulnerable.'

She points at the double-glazed windows. 'I can lock myself in at night. The place is like Fort Knox.'

'Nothing's changed, has it? You never accept help.'

'I'm leaving on Sunday. I'll stay safe until then, I promise.'

I'd forgotten her stubborn independence, and how unmoved she is by the idea of danger. Her strength attracted me back then, but now it only causes frustration as I head for the door.

'It's going on record that you ignored my request.'

Her expression remains neutral. 'Come back another time, Ben. If you want to catch up.'

I don't bother to say goodbye before putting on my crash helmet. Nina's straight-backed defiance used to fascinate me, but today it only worsens my bad mood. I drive away with irritation swilling around in my gut. The clock seems to be spinning backwards, when my focus should be on the present.

It's a relief to see the white outline of the hospital looming into view, but the receptionist looks distracted when she instructs me to take a seat. I wait in the corridor, checking messages from the station on my phone, until Ginny Tremayne appears. Her curly grey hair is caught in an untidy bun, a clutch of biros fighting for space in the pocket of her white coat. Isla's mother treats everyone that sets foot inside her hospital the same way, doling out kindness with each dose of medicine. I'm glad she's the duty doctor today; the attack victim is in safe hands, but her smile is slow to arrive.

'Hannah was nauseous and unresponsive when she arrived. That's a bad sign with head wounds.'

'I thought she was recovering.'

'Concussion's unpredictable, Ben. One minute the

patient's chatting to you, the next they're fighting for their life.' Ginny examines me over the top of her glasses. 'Do you know Hannah's last name? I want to check her medical records.'

'I'll find out and let you know. What happens now?'

'She's in a coma; the condition can last a long time in cases like this. If the swelling on her brain reduces we can airlift her to the trauma unit in Penzance.'

I let the bad news sink in, but another thought rises to the surface, after my conversation with Eddie. 'I meant to ask for some more details about how you and Isla spent Saturday night.'

'I told you on the phone.' She looks surprised by the sudden change of subject. 'We watched *The Notebook* on Netflix, ate too much popcorn and chilled out.'

'And after that?'

'Isla went out for a last look at the sea; it's a ritual of hers. I went to bed around eleven and fell asleep straight away.'

'Did you hear her come back?'

'I can't actually remember. Does that matter?'

'We have to account for everyone's precise movements, the night Sabine died, including my own team.' It occurs to me that Isla could have driven to the lighthouse, without her mother realising; there's no hard proof that she's innocent of attacking Sabine for failing to return her interest. Her mother seems unaware of the suspicions flitting through my mind.

'By the way, thanks for encouraging Isla to open up.

I've known she was gay for years, but she needed to say it in her own words.'

'I'm glad it helped.'

Ginny's relaxed smile makes me wonder how she would feel if she knew Isla had slept with the murder victim, and may have to be excluded from the case.

'Can I see the patient now?'

Hannah is struggling to breathe when I enter her room; her features look as fragile as spun glass behind her oxygen mask. The bleakness of her situation hits me for the first time. The killer has chosen another lone female, with no one to sit at her bedside. Instinct makes me touch her hand, until something catches my eye. He didn't have time to complete his elaborate wedding ritual, but still left his calling card. The gold band on Hannah's ring finger matches Sabine's. The woman's eyelids don't even flutter when I say her name, her hand limp in mine. I can only hope she's got the strength to pull through, or the killer will claim his second bride.

PART 2

'And so, all the night-tide, I lie down
    by the side
Of my darling – my darling – my life
    and my bride,
In her sepulchre there by the sea –
In her tomb by the sounding sea.'

'Annabel Lee', Edgar Allan Poe

19

Lily is on her hands and knees when evening comes, scrubbing the kitchen floor of her old home. She does it to honour her mother's memory, not for Harry's sake. The physical labour brings no peace, her mind still overloaded. She's on tenterhooks when her brother finally traipses through the door. He's sober, at least; there's no sign of the glint in his eye that signals danger.

'You live like a pig, Harry.'

'Don't nag, please. I can't take it today.' His voice is gentler than before. He looks exhausted, and afraid of something he won't name.

'What's got you so scared?'

'Nothing, I slept badly last night, that's all.'

She rises to her feet then hands him the Polaroid of Sabine. 'Why was this in your jacket pocket?'

'You shouldn't poke through my things.'

'I wasn't. It fell on the floor.'

Harry's expression darkens when she gives him Sabine's photo. He holds it gingerly between his fingertips, like its surface is caustic. 'I didn't take it.'

'You've got a Polaroid camera, haven't you?'

'It broke, years ago.'

Lily grabs his wrist, forcing him to meet her gaze. 'Sabine's dead, Harry. You were seeing her. Why didn't you tell me?'

'It only started a fortnight ago. She didn't want to spoil your friendship if it didn't work out. Look, I know I said yesterday it didn't mean anything, but I cared about her, Lily. I wanted to visit her in Riga.'

'Explain what's happened, then.'

'Someone posted that photo through the door, with my name on the envelope.' He gives her a look of dry-eyed misery. She hasn't seen him cry for years. He even sat through their mother's funeral without shedding a tear. 'I keep thinking about that car I saw by Pulpit Rock. Maybe it belonged to the killer. It was an SUV, but I can't remember the colour. I've been looking for it everywhere.'

'You can't go hunting for him – you might get hurt. Why not tell the police?'

'They'd arrest me. I get blamed for everything, but I'd never hurt a woman. You know that, don't you?'

'You've used your fists plenty of times outside the Mermaid.'

He gazes down at his hands. 'I'm sorry, all right? Dad's blood is in my veins. It's a problem I can't fix, but I promise you, I never harmed her.'

'You saw something at Pulpit Rock, didn't you? That's why you hit the booze again, before anyone else knew she was dead.'

'I was drunk by the time I got there, like I told you. I can't remember anything, except seeing the SUV driving away.'

Harry collapses forward in his seat, head bowed over his knees. 'I can't go to prison again. It would kill me.'

Sympathy floods Lily's system, yet she can't trust him. After so many false promises about staying sober, his innocence doesn't ring true.

20

The Cornish Constabulary's decision about Isla staying in the investigation team appears on my phone at 7 p.m., before I leave the hospital. The email states that she can serve on the case, if I provide a statement confirming her innocence. I still want to know what happened after her mother went to bed, the night Sabine died, but Isla's behaviour so far appears innocent. She was out on foot patrol when Hannah got hurt, so she can't be linked to the attack, which will give me leverage next time I speak to Madron. If it seems like a fait accompli, the DCI is more likely to give his blessing.

The sun is setting as I head off for Juliet's Garden on the motorbike. People are relaxing in deckchairs on Porth Mellon beach, kids building their final sandcastles before bedtime, as if the island were one big playground. I ride past the Keast brothers' farm in Porthloo, where one of my friends is opening the doors to their barn. It could be either Steve or Paul as the dusk thickens, the lanky figure offering a wave as I pass.

Juliet's Garden is a cluster of whitewashed cottages perched on high ground, just south of Carn Morval. Juliet May has lavished plenty of time and money on renovating the old fishermen's homes as holiday rentals, and creating a restaurant that guests flock to all summer long. One of the staff unlocks Hannah's rented cottage for me. The place is tidy, apart from the bedroom, where slippers lie abandoned on the floor, newspapers and books strewn across the dressing table. Hannah appears to be travelling light, with few clothes in her wardrobe, except shorts, jeans and T-shirts. I find her travel documents stashed inside a small suitcase. Her full name is Hannah Weber, a native German born in Berlin.

I ring the information through to the hospital, but the woman's papers give little new information. She's a journalist, marital status single. Hannah Weber's printed itinerary shows that she travelled overland through France, before touring the UK. The Isles of Scilly were meant to be her last stop before returning home. The only other item of interest is a journal, containing handwritten notes, but my German is limited to the days of the week, and how to order beer. It could be a diary or a travelogue. I take it with me, hoping someone can translate the last few pages to see if they reveal her attacker's identity.

I check the grounds carefully before leaving. The cottage has a fine view of Hugh Town beach, where lights are flicking on in the fishermen's cottages.

The deserted island of Samson lies to the west, with Tresco's hills a black outline on the horizon. I use my torch to scan the ground outside the cottage. The coastal path runs straight past it, shrouded by trees. Hannah's attacker could have hidden there unseen, free to track her movements without raising suspicion. Frustration nags at me when I kick-start the bike's engine again. The killer seems to have a problem with independent female travellers. Vicious attacks on women are normally sexual, but neither victim was molested; the only common denominator is that they're both travelling alone, with no plans to stay in Scilly permanently. The Cornish gold wedding rings forced onto each woman's hand is the killer's way of claiming them.

The station is still humming with activity when I get back. Sabine's death has galvanised the whole team; no one seems prepared to leave the building while there are tasks to complete. Isla and Eddie are busy tapping information into their laptops. Even Lawrie Deane is doing overtime: he's bowed over his desk, despite his normal tendency to exit the building on the stroke of 5 p.m. I can tell the evening's sticky heat is bothering him, beads of perspiration erupting on his pasty skin, even though the electric fan is working at full blast. The sergeant's breathing is laboured when he hands over a new batch of witness reports. His expression only comes to life when I tell him that a translator is needed, to interpret Hannah Weber's notes.

'Didn't you spend time in Germany as a kid, when your dad was in the army?' Eddie asks him.

Deane gives a slow nod. 'We lived there for five years; I was pretty fluent by the time we came home.'

'Could you take a look?' I ask.

'I'm rusty, but I'll give it a go.'

The sergeant pores over the notebook, frowning with concentration. He reads out a couple of sentences with a perfect German accent. 'She's writing about travelling alone through Europe. It's mainly about places she's visited, and whether she's made welcome. She's a freelance reporter for *Der Spiegel*.'

'Does she mention anyone hassling her?'

'Not a dicky bird.' He flicks through to the final page. 'Hang on though, she says a stranger approached her yesterday, near Toll's Island. He made her so uneasy she was glad to get away.'

'Does she say anything else about him?'

He shakes his head. 'Only that she was scared.'

'That's a good start, Lawrie. I had no idea you were a linguist.'

'I can try and translate it all if you want.'

Deane's triumphant expression makes me feel guilty. I've pigeonholed him as a jobsworth with narrow horizons until now; he may have travelled the world in a dugout canoe, but I've been too blinkered to notice. He's discovered far more than the rest of us about the day before Hannah Weber's attack.

The killer seems to make a habit of following women

to the island's margins. Toll's Island is a rocky outcrop on the north-eastern coast, with no houses in sight. It holds the ruins of an ancient battery, built during the English Civil War. Hannah may have wanted to report on the island's ancient sites, endangering herself by going there alone.

Eddie lets out a whoop of excitement when I pass his desk, then grins up at me. 'Liam Trewin's got form. He harassed a woman in Florida last year, but got off with a hefty fine, according to the Federal Investigation Service.'

'Was it his ex-wife?'

'The victim's a waitress at a café near the haulage company he runs.'

'What a scumbag,' Isla says, peering over Eddie's shoulder. 'He targets women who have to accept his shitty behaviour.'

'Is there anything else?'

'There's stuff about his family on Wikipedia. His dad's from Cornwall; the bloke made millions as a financial guru in New York, but his youngest son never joined his business. It looks like he's the black sheep of the family.'

'Liz Gannick can check Trewin's hotel room tomorrow morning. She may find evidence we missed.'

'His hire car's clean. She says there's no sign of blood anywhere.'

'I still want to interview him. Get him here by ten tomorrow morning, please. I'm going back to the hospital. Gannick can start checking vehicles owned by the islanders we haven't ruled out, but it's time the rest of you went home.' I look out of the window at the empty yard behind the station. 'Has anyone seen Shadow?'

'Sorry, boss, he slipped his lead down by the quay,' Isla says. 'I tried to catch him, but he ran off across the beach.'

'He'll come back when he's hungry.' I meet her eye again. 'Can we have a quick chat, Isla?'

The constable follows me into Madron's office. She appears relaxed when I quiz her more deeply about Saturday evening. I ask how long she spent outside after her mother went to bed, and she claims it was less than ten minutes. It's been her habit since childhood to walk down to the shore for a final glimpse of the sea before going to bed. I feel reassured when our conversation ends; her story tallies directly with her mother's, giving me another bargaining chip to use in my next phone call to Madron. She agrees to let Eddie drive her home, even though she seems to resent our attempts to keep her safe.

Shadow is nowhere in sight when I lock up the station at nine o'clock. I'll probably get a call tomorrow from one of the island's farmers, telling me he's been chasing sheep. The evening's heat has mellowed when I turn the corner into Church Street. It's hard to imagine anyone committing a crime when I pass St Mary's Hall Hotel, where half a dozen couples are sitting under an acacia tree, enjoying a late dinner and a glass of wine.

The hospital is quiet when I arrive, the evening shift winding down as my lungs fill with the odours of iodine, sickness and floor polish. I'm eager for news that Hannah Weber's condition is improving: I haven't forgiven myself for arriving too late to help Sabine, but the second victim may yet recover. When I peer through the glass panel into Hannah's room, a man is sitting beside her bed. Father Michael appears startled by my arrival, a Bible lying open on his lap. The strain on his face disappears when I greet him.

'I'm glad to see you here, Father.'

His smile reveals a set of yellowing teeth, as if endless cups of tea from his parishioners have stained the enamel. 'I drop by most evenings, to check if patients need anything. One of the nurses told me this young lady was attacked.'

'Her name's Hannah; it happened this afternoon.'

'The poor girl must have been terrified.' His expression sobers. 'When I spoke to her yesterday she seemed happy here.'

'Where did you meet her?'

'Near Toll's Island; I was taking my morning walk.'

I try to keep my expression neutral when I realise that it could have been the priest who scared Hannah. 'She mentioned visiting there in her diary. Did you talk for long?'

The priest looks confused. 'Just a few minutes.

148

I told her about our coffee morning on Saturday; it's a fundraiser for the church roof. She said that she was travelling alone, so I thought she'd enjoy some company.'

'That was a kind offer. Did you see anyone else there?'

'Not that I remember, but I had to get back. Some parishioners were expecting me to visit.' His attention has already returned to the unconscious woman, allowing me to study him more closely. Father Michael has always seemed content with his pastoral role, his manner open and friendly, but the language barrier could have made Hannah Weber misunderstand his invitation.

'I wish I could do more to help,' he murmurs.

'Company is all she needs right now. Were you saying a prayer?'

'Just reading some psalms. Patients say it brings them peace. Maybe it's hearing a calm voice that soothes them, but I think the message helps too.' He looks into my eyes more deeply. 'Would you like to hear Psalm twenty-eight?'

'I'm not a believer, Father.'

'That doesn't matter.' His shrewd gaze connects with mine again. 'It might give you comfort.'

I drop down on the seat opposite. 'Go ahead.'

The priest must know the words by heart, because his gaze drifts from his Bible to Hannah's face. '*The Lord is my strength and my shield; my heart trusted in him, and I am helped: therefore my heart greatly rejoices; and with my song I will praise him.*'

I can't tell whether Hannah Weber is listening, or too deeply unconscious to hear, but his conviction makes me envy his faith. His words stay with me as I return to the corridor, where Ginny Tremayne is waiting to give me an update. She explains that Hannah's vital signs and reflexes haven't improved since she arrived.

'It could go either way,' she says. 'I'm glad Michael's with her; patients always respond well to his kindness.'

Ginny's gone before I can ask another question, but when I peer into the room again the priest shows no sign of going home, even though it's approaching 10 p.m. He's still performing his incantation, and I can only hope that his faith will work miracles. Hannah Weber is still hovering between life and death, her skin as pale as candlewax, while his psalms fill the room.

21

I spend the first hour of my day dealing with the Cornish Constabulary. The DCI in Penzance has received a phone call from Madron, asking her to send a team of senior officers over to St Mary's to support the investigation. She explains that her patch is under-staffed with many officers taking annual leave; it won't be possible to help out. Her statement leaves me with mixed feelings: the islanders are edgy enough without a dozen uniformed officers raising the level of panic even higher. I thank her for contacting me then release a few swear words after I hang up. I could use some extra manpower, but it's my boss's intervention that leaves me gritting my teeth; I can't believe he contacted the mainland force behind my back.

I've regained my calm by the time Liam Trewin arrives at the station by 10 a.m. The temperature inside the building is rising as the sun beats down on the roof, but the American's appearance is immaculate, his navy shorts and polo shirt freshly ironed. I have to remind myself that the only hint that he could be involved in Sabine's death is his tendency to pester waitresses, and a few nasty details from his divorce case. Trewin's body language stiffens when Eddie joins us at the table and I notice again how unnatural the man's face looks, his skin stretched tight across his cheekbones. I pause before asking the first question; working as a murder investigator taught me the value of silence in interviews. It can create a gap in the conversation that suspects feel obliged to fill.

'What's this about?' he blusters. 'I should be outside enjoying my vacation.'

'Apologies, Mr Trewin. We just need to know about your movements in the last few days.'

'Don't I get to see a lawyer?'

'You're not under arrest, it's just a routine part of our inquiry. Can you tell us how you spent yesterday?'

'I had breakfast in my room at nine.' The man replies, his skin reddening. 'I left the hotel about an hour later. The sky was clear, so I took a walk to Pelistry Bay for a swim. I spent the morning there. I returned to Old Town in time for a late lunch, then strolled back to the hotel.'

'You never explored the island's east coast?'

'It was too warm. Maybe I'll do that another day.'

Pelistry lies several miles from Halangy Beach, but Trewin may have fabricated the whole story.

'Did you see anyone?'

'There was no one around when I left the hotel grounds.'

'How about photos? Did you take any on your walk?'

He hesitates before shaking his head. 'All I had with me was a bottle of water, my wallet and swimming gear.'

'That's a shame, the pictures would have proved your story. Did you speak to anyone?'

'I wasn't looking for company. I didn't notice many people on Porthcressa Beach or the coastal path.'

'Did you visit the museum in Hugh Town while you were here last year?'

'Several times, actually. I like their exhibits about the old way of life, when my ancestors lived here. It's incredible that the islanders made such a remote place thrive simply by growing flowers and catching fish.'

'And smuggling,' Eddie adds. 'It was our main trade for three centuries.'

'I hope my relatives were law-abiding.' He forces a smile.

'You've had your own brush with the law, haven't you? Can you tell us why the Federal Investigation Service took you to court last year?'

Trewin's lips flap open, like a fish gasping for air. 'A girl I was seeing blackmailed me. She even denied we'd had a relationship.'

'The court believed her, didn't they? You repeatedly followed her home from work at night. That sounds like stalking to me.'

'She's a fantasist.'

'Did you think Sabine Bertans would be easier to control?'

He rears back in his seat. 'I don't have to listen to this bullshit.'

'We found some strong painkillers in your room. Why do you use them?'

'For migraines. I get the kind that lay you out for days.'

'Three of those pills would render a woman of Sabine's build unconscious. Tell us how you spent Saturday night, please.'

'I had a nightcap in the hotel bar, then went to bed.'

I glance down at my notes. 'My colleague tell me the night porter saw you in the car park, around midnight.'

Trewin's eyes blink rapidly. 'I took one last stroll around the grounds to help me sleep.'

'It's a big coincidence that a woman in Florida accused you of harassment, then days after you pester Sabine she turns up dead.'

'I was just being courteous.'

'Your gifts didn't work, did they? She still turned you down.' He chooses to remain silent. 'That's all for today, Mr Trewin. You're free to go back to the hotel. Sorry if your room was untidy yesterday; we examined it for forensic evidence, but it may be necessary to look again.'

Trewin's voice is cold with anger. 'Sabine cleaned it most days; she must have touched every damn surface.'

'Not great, to be honest.'

My uncle hands over two carrier bags loaded with food parcels. My godmother Maggie runs the pub on Bryher, always convinced that a man of my size is in constant need of sustenance. She's sent over enough provisions for a small army.

'I can't stay long, Ray. We're working flat out.'

'Stop for a minute to clear your head.'

When Ray beckons me onto his boat, I step off the quay without argument; his quiet authority is hard to ignore, even when his instructions go against the grain. My uncle is in no hurry to talk, his gaze fixed once more on the sea. The horizon is a pale line of turquoise, waves flatlining as the ocean merges with the sky. When I tip my head back, the air is clear too, apart from a solitary tern riding a thermal far above us. After five minutes of silence, some of the day's tension drains from my system.

'Better?' Ray asks.

'Definitely,' I reply, climbing back onto the quay.

My uncle is on his feet now, shifting a few lobster creels into the hatch. 'Did you know Nina was down here on holiday?'

'Why do you ask?'

'She came by the boatyard a few days ago. I made her a bite to eat then ran her back to Watermill Cove.'

I stare at him, dumbfounded. 'How long did she stay?'

'All afternoon.'

My amazement deepens. Ray's conversations are always short and monosyllabic, unless he's with an old friend or relative. Nina must have magical powers.

'It never occurred to you to tip me off?'

'That's her business, not mine.' He coils his mooring rope, then restarts the engine. 'Keep an eye on the weather for the next few days. Heavy rain's coming.'

'The sky's clear as a bell.'

'Not for long. Don't let it catch you out.'

My uncle's slow-dawning smile arrives at last, then he casts off without another word. I stand on the quay for five minutes watching his small craft leave the harbour, heading for Bryher, across a carpet of blue. Ray's announcement is a typical piece of island behaviour. People here are secretive by nature, reminding me what I'm up against. Someone must know the killer's identity in a place this small, but they're not willing to share his name.

22

Lily returns to her room at the hotel in time for the afternoon shift, glad to escape her brother's company. She's afraid he'll take the law into his own hands, but knows there's no point in trying to stop him. Now she's standing in front of the mirror, trying to follow Rhianna Polkerris's advice, before reporting for kitchen duty at 2 p.m.

The girl has brought her mother's make-up bag back from the house, but emotions surface when she undoes the zip. The scent of lily of the valley brings her mother's image to mind, standing in the hallway, dabbing perfume behind her ears then applying dark pink lipstick. When Lily does the same, the effect is clownish. The vivid tone accentuates her pallor, making her look plainer than before.

Lily gazes down at the beauty kit her mother used every day. When she opens the old-fashioned powder compact, the make-up is crumbling. She closes her eyes and inhales deeply, hoping to picture her mother again, but Sabine appears instead. Her friend is haunting her, demanding the justice she deserves.

Suddenly the heat feels so overwhelming, Lily throws open the window, her hands clutching the sill, while she gasps for air. Her legs are still shaking when she forces herself out of the room.

23

Isla meets me by the gateway to the Star Castle Hotel at 2.30 p.m. The young constable's expression is curious when she stands beside me.

'I need your help to interview Lily Jago. She'll be back at work by now.'

Her shoulders stiffen. 'Won't that be awkward if she knows about me and Sabine, sir?'

'You're my only female officer. She'll be more open with you around, no matter what she's heard.'

The situation isn't ideal, but in a tiny community the police's lives blend with every island family through blood or friendship. Isla marches at a brisk pace as we head for the hotel. Despite her reluctance, her manner is calm under pressure.

The Star Castle's managers are both behind the reception desk when we arrive. Tom Polkerris offers a smile of welcome, but his wife's gaze remains cold, as if she'd rather ban us from the premises. When I ask where Lily's working, Tom points us towards the kitchen, but Rhianna keeps her mouth shut.

The hotel's kitchen is tucked away at the back of the building. It has the atmosphere of a dungeon, even though its metre-thick walls are whitewashed to maximise light. Staff are toiling over industrial ranges, scrubbing them until they gleam. There are so few guests left to feed, the head chef is keeping them busy, cleaning every surface.

'How should I play it, sir?' Isla murmurs.

'I'll ask the questions, don't worry. Lily's been cagey so far; we just need to put her at ease.'

I catch sight of the young woman on the far side of the room. Lily Jago's movements are mechanical as she polishes cutlery, then drops each item back into a wooden box. The girl's white coat is several sizes too big as she hunches over the counter. She seems anxious about being singled out, as if she'd rather bolt through the fire exit. It seems strange that an outgoing young woman like Sabine chose such a shy creature for her ally. Lily blinks rapidly in the sunlight when we step outside, like a mole coming up for air. There's no sound in the deserted gardens, except the hiss of a sprinkler, keeping the lawn emerald green. The girl perches on a bench, gazing down at her clasped hands. I notice that her lips are painted a vivid pink, which clashes with her girl-next-door appearance.

'Tell us more about your friendship with Sabine, please, Lily.'

'Why ask me? She was popular with everyone.'

'But someone hated her enough to want her dead.'

Lily gives an awkward shrug. 'I keep going over it, but none of it makes sense. She'd have told me if anything was wrong.'

'Can you describe Sabine for us, in your own words?'

'She was kind and funny. Sabine joked around at work, so the boring stuff felt easy. That was one of the things I liked most . . .' Her voice tails into silence.

'We know she'd begun a relationship recently. You're not in any trouble, but tell us now if you know that person's identity.'

The girl gives Isla a questioning look, then drops her gaze. 'I don't think she fancied anyone at the hotel. Mr Trewin gave her presents, but she tried to return them.'

Isla leans forward in her seat. 'We know about the earrings, but was there anything else?'

'Perfume, I think, and huge tips. She left the stuff outside his room, but he gave them back, even though she couldn't stand him.'

'How did Sabine spend her free time the day before she died?'

'I'm not sure; we were on different shifts.' Her tense body language makes her look so fragile, as if the first strong wind could carry her away.

'We've been searching for Sabine's phone. Do you know where it is?' When she shakes her head, tears pool in her eyes. 'We have to find out why she died. Did your brother get to know her at all?'

'They only met a few times.'

When Isla touches Lily's arm in a gesture of comfort, the girl collapses on her shoulder, crying silently. I'm glad my new recruit has the human touch. I don't have much skill in comforting the bereaved, always wary of overstepping the mark. The girl's face is flushed when she finally pulls back, but her emotions are back under control. She answers my next questions calmly, claiming that Sabine never discussed her love life, which is hard to believe. A young traveller so far from home would need great resilience not to confide her secrets. I want to know why Lily Jago is being so tight-lipped, but can't push her any further today. I'm about to give her permission to return to her duties when she finally speaks again.

'A man did invite Sabine out to dinner straight after she arrived. She thought he seemed angry when she said no.'

'Who was that?' I ask.

'My brother's boss.'

'Paul Keast?' I know that my friend renovated the old speedboat Harry Jago uses to ferry passengers around local bays.

Lily nods her head and I have to swallow my surprise. Paul never mentioned fancying Sabine, even though we've all spent plenty of time together, training for the swimathon. I can't remember his last serious relationship. I always assumed that he preferred his own company, but it's my job to suspect everyone, including old friends.

Isla asks questions about the case as we walk back to the station, keen to understand how murder investigation works. She absorbs my comments like litmus paper, while I explain that techniques need to adapt, according to each situation. Her hunger for information makes me certain she'll be a good cop, but I'm too preoccupied to offer much detail. I'm too busy trying to remember Paul's behaviour around Sabine, but his shyness often makes him seem ill-at-ease in female company. My concern increases as I leave Isla at the station, making phone calls to check all the islanders are safe. Interrogating Liam Trewin was easy, but quizzing an old friend about a brutal murder will take me way outside my comfort zone.

24

There's still no sign of Shadow when I set off for the Keast brothers' farm, hoping the walk will clear my thoughts. The tide's out, so I drop down onto the beach once I reach the High Street, keen to avoid questions from the islanders. I walk close to the harbour wall to avoid tripping over the mooring ropes strung out across the wet sand. I've only been walking five minutes when a tall figure jogs towards me across the shore, dressed in a smart tracksuit. My old headmaster, Frank Rawle, is taking his Labrador for an afternoon run, the dog splashing through puddles of seawater. The man is in his mid-sixties, but his vigorous pace proves that he's in great shape; the clear sunlight making his face look so craggy and weather-beaten it could have been chipped from the side of Mount Rushmore. I can tell he's hoping for information by the avid look in his eye.

'There you are, Ben,' he calls out. 'How's the investigation going?'

'Well, thanks, but don't let me slow you down.'

'I'm glad to take a breather. Are you off to interview somebody?' Curiosity burns in his eyes, or maybe he's so used to being in charge, he just wants to control the situation.

'It's a routine house call, but we're making progress.'

'My offers stands if you need help. By the way, your dog was up by Shooters' Pool earlier. Did you know he's on the loose?'

'He broke free yesterday. Shadow hates being kept indoors.'

'Training's the key.' Rawle bears down on me as if he plans to wield his cane. 'Show him who's boss or he'll undermine your authority.'

'I never had any. I inherited him, after a friend died. She encouraged his independent streak.'

'Mistakes can always be corrected. Remember I'm here if you need anything.'

He's standing so close I can see a network of broken capillaries in the whites of his eyes. There's something odd about the man's repeated offers of assistance. Maybe Sabine's death has triggered memories of losing his daughter at the same age. I acknowledge his offer before he continues his jog, but Rawle's controlling behaviour lingers in my head as I follow the coast-line north.

My walk takes me past tourist sites that are normally buzzing during the summer, but now stand deserted. No one is queuing to see Harry's Walls, the remains of a sixteenth century fort, and even the artists' studios at Porth Mellon are quiet now that summer visitors have gone. The islanders must be following my advice and seeking safety in numbers, instead of taking solitary walks; when I cross the sand there's no one in sight, even though the sun's still hot enough to burn. The Keast brothers' farmhouse stands directly above Porthloo Bay, overlooking the granite boulders that litter the shore. The farmyard looks like a storybook version of country life, complete with chickens pecking the hay-strewn ground, half a dozen pigs in a pen, and a dappled horse peering through the stable door. One of the brothers emerges from the barn as I arrive, a lanky figure with collar-length brown hair, carrying buckets of feed. I can tell them apart from the way they move after so long. Steve's confidence shows in his bold stride, while Paul's movements are slower and more tentative.

'Steve,' I call out.

He dumps the buckets by the wall and offers a grin. 'Hello, stranger. What are you doing here?'

'I need a quick chat. Is Paul about?'

'He's testing soil in the top field. The pasture needs some nitrogen.'

'That makes no sense to me whatsoever.'

'Stick to policing, mate. You'd make a crap farmer, but come in anyway.'

Steve takes his time, discarding his filthy wellingtons in the porch, and my pulse rate drops once I cross the threshold. I've spent so much time in the brothers' old-fashioned kitchen, after school rugby matches and as an adult, every item is familiar. The pine table, worn floor tiles and cast-iron range are unchanged since their mother retired to the mainland, leaving her sons to run the farm. The framed picture of their father Pat is a reminder of the worst side of our shared history. Our fathers drowned on the same fishing trip, and the Keast brothers' loss was crueller than mine because it could have been avoided. My dad was a professional trawler-man, but theirs only made occasional fishing trips when money was tight. He lost his life on the first voyage he'd taken all year. My brother and I visited the Keasts so often after it happened, they became more like cousins than friends. It helped to know that we were all trapped inside the same bubble, numb with shock for months, the grief that united us reflected in each other's faces.

Steve dumps two mugs of coffee on the table, then relaxes in the chair opposite. He's thirty-seven, only two years older than me, but outdoor work has aged his skin prematurely, with crows' feet winging from the corners of his eyes, laughter lines bracketing his mouth. Steve's default reaction is to smile at everything that comes his way, including my unexpected arrival. I've seen less of him recently, because he's started a relationship with a woman in Plymouth, but she hasn't visited St Mary's yet.

'When's the new girlfriend coming over?'

'Find one of your own, mate.' His eyes glitter with amusement. 'Want me to fix you up?'

'How do I know she's real?'

'You've seen her photo. I want her to fly over, but she doesn't get much time off her nursing job.' His face grows serious. 'If Paul knew I was considering leaving the farm to live on the mainland he'd lose the plot.'

'He's tougher than he seems.' I swallow a mouthful of coffee.

'I don't agree. He's never been the same since dad died.'

'It affected us all differently.' My brother became the man of the house, looking after mum and striving for the best grades, while I retreated into the long American novels I've been addicted to ever since.

'We're drifting apart,' Steve mutters. 'I keep saying he should see a counsellor, but he always refuses.'

'You think he's depressed?'

'God knows what's wrong. Some days he hardly speaks.'

'Maybe it's just a passing thing. Is Harry Jago doing okay, piloting his boat?'

'Is that why you're here? Paul only gave him work because his mum cleaned for us. He's a soft touch.'

'That's not the reason. I need to speak to you both about Sabine: you knew her pretty well, didn't you?'

'We trained with her, like you, but that was about it.'

'Someone must know why she died.'

'Not me, that's for sure. I can't get my head round it, but Paul's taken it worst.'

'How come?'

'Like I say, he's delicate, isn't he?'

I was closest to Paul when we were boys, but there's no denying he's withdrawn deeper into his shell as the years have passed. 'Someone told me he asked her out.'

'You're kidding? He wouldn't have the nerve.'

Paul walks through the door before Steve can elaborate. I don't know whether they wear matching clothes by instinct or design, but the trick highlights their similarities. The brothers' facial expressions mirror each other too, with smiles that bring their angular features to life. It's only when Paul sits beside his brother that differences show. His frame is thinner, making him look more like a poet than a farmer, deep-set eyes closer to black than brown. The two men sit so close together, they're almost rubbing shoulders, like they're connected by an umbilical cord.

'Ben's been asking about Sabine,' Steve says. 'He wants to know if we saw much of her.'

'Only through swimming.'

'That's what I said.'

I lean forward to catch Paul's eye. 'But you had a soft spot for her, didn't you?'

'I bet every bloke on the island did.' His skin flushes with embarrassment; he's always hated being put on the spot. 'She was too young for me.'

'But you asked her out anyway.'

'That was back in June, a lot's happened since then.' He turns his head away. 'I didn't know it was common knowledge.'

'That's a surprise, bro,' Steve interrupts. 'You never mentioned it.'

'I don't need your fucking seal of approval,' Paul snaps, anger coming off him in waves. 'It wouldn't have worked, even if she'd agreed. She was just passing through.'

'How did you take it, after she said no?'

'I kept my distance, I suppose.'

'When's the last time you had a relationship?'

'What's this about, Ben? I'm not looking for romantic advice.' Paul hates talking about himself, always happier to bat the conversation on to someone else.

'His ex is dating the island's weirdo,' says Steve. 'His heart was well and truly broken a few years back.'

'That's ancient history,' Paul replies, his voice fiercer than before. 'Let me speak for myself.'

He gives his brother a look of fury, suggesting a conflict that's lasted years, and my discomfort grows. The flipside of Paul's social anxiety might be rage at his own limitations, and the girls who stay out of reach.

The grandfather clock in the corner is ticking too loudly. It's a reminder that Hannah Weber is fighting for her life, while the killer is free to enjoy the sunshine.

'How did you both spend Saturday night?'

'Are you serious?' Steve asks. 'You can't think we hurt her.'

Paul's voice sounds bitter when he speaks again. 'You don't have much faith in us, do you?'

'I have to investigate everyone. Believe me, it's not personal.'

'You've known us since you were born, for Christ's sake.' Paul's anger burns brighter, until Steve places a restraining hand on his arm.

'We had dinner at the Atlantic on Saturday,' Steve explains. 'We walked back here around 11 p.m. I went to bed straight away; it was my turn to look after the livestock in the morning.'

'Did you see anyone on the beach?'

'No one.' Paul's voice is a sullen drone. 'I went to bed soon after Steve.'

'Can I take a look around? We're searching every property on St Mary's.'

The brothers' faces are solemn when they nod in agreement, the trust between us fraying at the edges. I feel awkward searching their home for clues; it's another reminder that islanders' lives are connected by invisible glue, whether we like it or not. I can hear them talking downstairs in lowered voices, while I poke through their bedrooms, checking cupboards and peering under beds. Old fashioned wallpaper is peeling from the walls, but there's no evidence of violence. The two men's rooms lie adjacent to each other, decorated with the same pale-blue paint I remember from our schooldays, and football memorabilia from trips to see Plymouth Argyle. I understand at last why Steve is keeping his new relationship quiet. The brothers' lives are so closely aligned, it would be cruel to parade his happiness in front of his fragile counterpart. If he left for the mainland, the farm might have to be sold.

I take my time searching their barns and outbuildings, but find only well-fed livestock, a rusting tractor, and ploughshares propped against the wall. Again there's no evidence of violence, yet my discomfort lingers. Lily Jago claimed that Paul was angry about Sabine's rejection. He's always lived on St Mary's; if he wanted to hurt someone, he knows every cave the winter winds have hollowed into the cliffs. Hannah Weber was attacked close to their farm – Paul could easily have strolled to Halangy Down and back to the farm in less than half an hour, without his absence being noticed.

25

Lily is still working in the hotel's kitchen as evening comes, preparing food for the few remaining guests. She prefers kitchen duties to waiting on tables: when the dinner service gathers speed it's like watching a ballet. Sous chefs move between the ovens, fridges and stainless-steel tables, as graceful as dancers. It's her job to make side salads, so that each plate looks fresh and tempting. She's glad to forget the police interview, but still feels guilty for lying about the phone. She can't let them find out about Harry and Sabine. Her brother's so afraid of going back to jail, she doesn't want to leave him vulnerable. No one else will protect him from the danger he chases.

Dusk is falling when Lily looks up from the chopping board. She lays down her knife for a moment, to admire the hotel gardens. Strings of coloured lights and Japanese lanterns hang from the trees, roses weeping petals onto the lawn. The grounds look like an enchanted kingdom, until she spots a man walking along the path towards her, wearing a scowl. Liam Trewin pauses outside the window, staring at her, like she's his worst enemy. Lily wants to back away, but the head chef will be angry if she stops working. She lowers her gaze and when she glances outside again, the man has gone, leaving her nerves jangling.

Lily almost jumps out of her skin when someone touches her shoulder. But when she turns around, Tom Polkerris is standing there, wearing a half-smile. She likes him so much, her skin flushes with embarrassment.

'Everything okay, Lily?'

'Fine thanks, sir.'

'The police spoke to you this afternoon, didn't they?'

'Sorry, I only missed a few minutes work.'

'Relax, I'm just checking you're all right. You had a deep friendship with Sabine, didn't you?'

She tries to catch her breath. 'I miss her so much.'

'It's hard to accept, but even worse for you. What did the police want to know?'

'They asked if she had a boyfriend.'

'Did she?'

'No, sir. I don't think so.'

The tension in his face eases. 'None of it makes sense, does it? Remember you can always talk to me, if you're upset. Come to my office, anytime.'

Polkerris's hand skims her shoulder again, his touch bringing comfort, unlike his wife's hard stare. Lily feels calmer when she sets to work again, turning each plate into a work of art.

26

At 8 p.m. I send my last team member home, and most of the cold chicken and boxes of pasta salad Maggie sent over have been eaten. Eddie looks disappointed to leave, but I need him firing on all cylinders tomorrow. I have one last duty to complete before meeting Liz Gannick at the hotel. The phone line crackles with static when I dial my boss's number in France. DCI Madron listens to my update in silence. If he's disappointed to learn that another victim has been attacked, he keeps his opinion to himself. There's a murmur of approval when I describe our efforts to protect the island community and find a common link between victims, but he's less impressed to hear about Isla's one night stand with Sabine Bertans. His position only shifts to consent when he learns that the Cornish Constabulary have endorsed her position. He offers to come back from his holiday early, but I refuse. The man's tendency to micro-manage would only slow the investigation down.

The muscles across my shoulders are aching when I say goodbye, the day's tension locked inside my body. I write a character reference, confirming Isla's right to stay on my team, then catch sight of my reflection; a scowling, black-haired goliath staring back at me from the dark window, hunched over a pile of witness reports. Sabine Bertans' murder has generated hundreds of sheets of paper in the three days since her death, but we're getting nowhere. I peer out at the houses opposite, where porch lights shine through the dark. The killer may be hiding in plain sight; he could even be married, with a psychopath's ability to lead two separate lives.

Sabine's killer waited just forty-eight hours before finding a new victim, and a lecture I attended during my Murder Squad training returns to haunt me. A forensic psychologist explained that the intervals between attacks reveal a killer's mental state. A short time span denotes confidence, and a strong compulsion to inflict pain. I rub the back of my neck to massage the tension away, but my head is pulsing with information. I can't forget that the killer is probably relaxing at home, feet up, in front of the telly.

I walk back to the hotel at speed, but the journey fails to relax me. Liz Gannick's music has changed when I tap on her door. Yesterday's Motown has been replaced by an English ballad, Scott Matthews' haunting voice echoing down the corridor. Gannick is hunched over her microscope when I push her door open, too distracted to look up. She peers at her slide for another minute before muttering a greeting.

'There's wine on the table, but leave some for me.'

'I'll try not to neck the whole bottle.'

I prefer beer, but tonight that doesn't matter. The first mouthful of Rioja is tart and acidic, but I knock it back like medicine, then sink into a chair. When Gannick finally abandons her work, she uses her crutches to swing across the room, her physical agility putting me to shame. It's almost 10 p.m. but the woman still looks wide awake, as if sleep is an activity only lesser mortals require.

'I hope you're bringing me good news,' she hisses out the words.

'Why?'

'Liam Trewin's hire car was valeted straight after it was returned. The hire company said there was nothing unusual when he dropped it off. A simple valet job wouldn't necessarily remove the kind of traces I can find, but there are hardly any stray fibres in the boot, and the interior's clean as a whistle, as you know.'

'How about his room?'

'My UV beam didn't pick up anything. But he could have killed her elsewhere, couldn't he?'

'He's only spent a few weeks here. How would he know about secluded sites? Someone took ages getting her into the wedding dress, then making up her face. It would be a struggle outdoors.'

'What about abandoned farm buildings?'

'Most of them have been turned into holiday lets. You'd need local knowledge to find an empty one.'

'Gareth Keillor gave me Sabine's toxicology results. There was nothing in her blood except trace amounts of alcohol; she probably had a glass of wine while she was serving behind the bar. There are no indicators for Vicodin. I was hoping for skin cells under her nails, but there's no sign she fought her attacker. I think she was bludgeoned from behind, then her hands were bound while she was unconscious.'

'Trewin sees women as prey to be hunted down.' I rub the back of my neck again, trying to relieve the tension. 'But that doesn't make him guilty of murder.'

'There were a couple of stray hairs on the carpet in his room. They're long and dark like Sabine's, but I'll need a DNA test to check.'

'That won't catch him. The hotel staff have different duties each day: she worked as a maid most mornings.'

She gives a loud sigh. 'The managers take their pound of flesh, don't they? I bet those kids are all on minimum wage.'

'Did you find anything else?'

'Four different sets of prints in Sabine's room. They're being checked for matches on the national database.'

'I'll take fingerprints from the hotel staff tomorrow. We already know at least one of her friends hung out there after work, but it's worth checking.' I knock back the last of my wine. 'A friend of mine asked the victim out to dinner soon after she arrived. She turned him down, so that's a new lead.'

'What are you doing about it?'

'Monitoring him, for now. Paul's respected by the islanders; he's in the lifeboat crew, and he's been a special constable for a year or so.'

'Even heroes commit crimes.' Gannick's pixie-like face looks older when she speaks again. 'There's bad news on the wedding dress too, I'm afraid. The iodine treatment exposed some prints, but they're too blurred to read. I've only had the chance to check five of the cars on your suspect list for blood traces. So far they're clean; I'll crack on with the rest tomorrow.'

'We'll get him, Liz. Your immaculate track record won't be tarnished.'

'It's on your slate, not mine.' She manages a laugh. 'Did you have any luck finding her phone?'

'The signal's dead. We've swept the Garrison area twice now, without any joy, so I'm focusing on the evidence in front of us.'

'That makes sense.' She gives an abrupt nod, before pointing at the door. 'Now bugger off and let me finish my wine. That bloody microscope's sent me cross-eyed.'

'Order some food or you'll feel like crap tomorrow.'

'Don't nag, for God's sake. You sound like my husband.'

Personal revelations from Gannick are so rare, I do a double take. 'I didn't know you were married.'

'The poor bastard's coped with me for fifteen years.'

'Where's your ring?'

'Who needs one? My marital status is no one else's sodding business.'

'You're such charming company, Liz.' I give her a parting grin. 'Your husband must thank his lucky stars.'

Scott Matthews' voice drifts through the wall that separates us, each note purer than the last. Working together has forced me and Gannick to exist in close proximity, just like the Keast brothers. They seemed to enjoy their closeness as kids, but cracks are starting to show, Paul's anger surfacing at last.

I throw open the window, hoping to release some of the day's frustrations, along with the room's odour of furniture polish and new carpet. There's no sign of Shadow when I scan the hotel grounds. The creature annoyed the hell out of me at first, after my old work partner died, but I couldn't bring myself to abandon him at the nearest shelter. He's grown on me since then; even though his high spirits can be annoying, I like his company. He's never kept his distance for so long, until now.

'Where the hell are you?'

I lean out of the window, watching the lighthouse draw a new white line across the sea every ninety seconds. Shadow may be stranded on the beach by the rising tide, after digging up fish carcasses and scrounging from picnickers all day. I pull on a sweatshirt and head back downstairs. A walk along the shore will kill two birds with one stone, releasing today's pent-up energy and hunting for Shadow at the same time.

The stairway from the hotel gardens down to the beach is lit by electric lanterns, but darkness engulfs me once I reach the shore. There's hardly any light pollution in the Scillies, giving me a clear view of the heavens. The night sky looks like a skein of dark blue velvet, pinpricked by a million stars. They cast a pale glow over the headland, where the tide has claimed most of the shore, leaving only a ribbon of shingle. There's no sound when I yell the dog's name, apart from breakers shattering on the beach and the in-drawn breath of the tide receding, but footsteps echo behind me when I come to a halt. Someone is pacing across the gravel. The hotel's lights have faded, making the darkness thicker than before. All I can see are whitecaps cresting in the distance, silvered by moonlight.

'Who's there?' I yell out.

Silence resonates back from the wall of rock overhead. I may have imagined it, my nerves on edge from making so little progress. But when the footsteps start again they're quicker than before, fleeing across the beach; they're so light and rapid, it must be someone in good shape. I can't see a thing, so there's no point in giving chase.

'You fucking coward!'

I shout the words into the black air for my own benefit. I'm certain that whoever was tracking my movements chose not to attack. My giant scale may have worked to my advantage for once: if the killer planned to knock me out, like his female victims, it would take a long reach. My eyes have adjusted to the dark by now, picking out the sharp peaks of Serica Rocks on the horizon, but my pursuer has left nothing behind, except my growing certainty that Sabine's killer knows this landscape like the back of his hand.

27

Wednesday 7 August

It's after midnight when Lily wakes from a nightmare. She saw Sabine swimming out to sea, tall waves dragging her under, while she could only stand and watch. Lily is trembling when she sits up in bed, instinct making her reach for her phone. All she needs is a familiar voice, to confirm she's safe, but her brother sounds angry when he finally picks up.

'Why are you calling this late?'

'I had a bad dream about Sabine.'

She hears him swear under his breath. 'Try counting sheep instead of bothering me.'

'Did you know another woman was attacked on Monday?'

There's a pause before he answers. 'I've got worse things to worry about, Lily.'

When she listens more carefully, the sound of waves crashing and the whine of a sea breeze accompany her brother's voice. 'Where are you?'

'At home, in bed.'

'Liar. You're looking for that car you saw, aren't you?'

'You need to stay out of it.'

'Go home, Harry, before you get hurt.'

Lily hears him swear before the line goes dead. When Lily rings again, her call is routed straight to voicemail, and the trembling in her hands is worse than before. She sits on her bed, trying to calm herself. Her loyalties are divided between her brother and her friend. In the morning she should take his note to the police station, but she knows he'd be furious, her conscience making rest impossible. When she lies down again, her eyes refuse to close. Lily is still wide awake when the first seagulls bawl outside her window.

28

I wake up with a tension headache throbbing behind my eyes. If I were back in London, my old boss would insist on a debrief with a psychologist after witnessing a bizarre murder scene, but formal support here is non-existent. Once the case finishes I'll ask Jeff Pendelow to see each of my team members individually. Right now I need to offload before work begins. There's no point phoning my brother Ian in New York, because it's night-time there, but it's mid-morning in India and my closest friend will have been awake for hours. I use my laptop to make the Skype call to Mumbai, and the tension in my shoulders loosens when Zoe appears, her carefree face relieving my worries. She looks like a young Marilyn Monroe, with the kind of smile that lights up a room. I spent my teenage years falling for her, but the infatuation has become a lifelong friendship.

'Hey, big man, you're alive. Why haven't you returned my calls?'

'Life's been too crazy.'

I used most of my holiday allowance travelling to India last month to watch her get married. Part of me wanted to hate the man who swept her off her feet while she was teaching music in Mumbai, but Dev's good-natured smile made it impossible. The elaborate Sikh wedding ritual reminded me just how far my friend has travelled from Scilly, but the smile on Zoe's face proves she made the right decision. She leans closer to the screen, studying me intently.

'What's up? You never ring this early.'

'I've got a tough case. I just wanted to hear your voice.'

'Go on then, spill the beans. What's happened?'

'One of the summer staff at the Star Castle was murdered.'

Zoe's eyes widen. 'Is the killer still on St Mary's?'

'Definitely.'

'And the pressure's all on you, as usual.'

'Yup.'

'No wonder you look wired. But there's something else, isn't there?' She leans closer, as if she's planning to dive through my computer screen.

'Work's hard at the moment, that's all.'

'It's something personal – that's why you're phoning. Tell me or I'll sing Kylie Minogue songs, very loud.'

'No, please, not that.' She belts out the first verse of a sugary pop song, forcing me to surrender. 'Nina Jackson's staying on St Mary's.'

Her smile becomes a grin. 'Did you invite her?'

'Hell no. Why would I?'

'She dented your bulletproof heart. You always walk away unscathed, but Nina got there first.'

'Forget about it. How was the honeymoon?'

'Lovely, thanks. Why not take her out to dinner?'

'God, you're relentless.'

'Book a table at Ruin Beach Café and show her your manly charm.'

'I can't. Ferries to Tresco are cancelled, and my charisma didn't have much effect last time.'

'The girl must be able to see you're a cross between Chris Hemsworth and Ryan Gosling.'

'Maybe she doesn't go to the cinema.'

'You were mad to let her go the first time. Promise to call her at least.' Zoe can still read my mind, even though we're five thousand miles apart. 'You want a family of your own, don't you?'

'One day, yeah.'

'It won't happen by magic, Ben. You have to find the right woman.'

'Really? I had no idea.'

Zoe ignores my sarcasm and applies more emotional pressure, from gentle teasing to outright blackmail, before telling me about her honeymoon in Kerala. She talks about deserted beaches, lazing in hammocks and swimming in azure sea, filling me with envy. When I peer through the curtains, wisps of cirrus cloud are strung across the dawn sky, turning the Atlantic pearl grey. The weather can change in an instant here, delivering all four seasons in one day. My spirits have lifted when the call ends, but while Zoe may be keen to sort out my love life, the murder case is my priority. Even if I had plenty of free time, why chase someone who prefers her own company?

I'm still thinking about Zoe's advice when a message arrives from the hospital. Hannah Weber's condition remains serious but stable, with no change overnight. I've given Isla the task of tracking down her relatives, but connections are proving hard to find.

I go downstairs at 7 a.m. to find the dining room empty. Pans are clattering in the kitchen, but the day's first service won't start for another hour. I'd like to scrounge some food before I leave, but Rhianna Polkerris appears before I can cadge some toast from the chef. Her green-eyed stare connects with mine for once, rather than looking straight through me. Her appearance is honed to perfection, from the blonde hair cascading down her back to her crimson lipstick, and the silk dress that fits her like a glove. It's a surprise when she bothers to speak; until now the woman has treated me like a bad smell.

'Take a seat, Ben. I'll get breakfast organised for you.'

'That would be great, thanks.'

When Rhianna sashays across the dining room, her body language announces that the hotel is her own personal empire, which must irritate Tom while they jockey for power. She returns a few minutes later, holding a coffee pot and two bone-china cups.

'You're a lifesaver,' I tell her, and it's almost true. It takes an industrial amount of caffeine to get me fully awake.

'Mind if I join you?' She slips into the seat opposite before I can reply. 'I should apologise for being so stressed when you told us about Sabine. The hotel's being judged for the British Travel Awards next month. We've all been working flat out to get the place ready.'

'I bet you'll do fine. This place is impressive.'

'Hotel work gives you tunnel vision.' Her tone is gentler than before, making me warm to her for the first time. 'I still can't really believe Sabine's gone.'

Emotions appear on the woman's face and I realise she might be brittle, not hard as nails. Tears well in her china doll eyes, before she blinks them away.

'The whole community's in shock, and it can't be easy working with Tom every day. I bet most husband and wife teams end up rowing.'

A frown appears on her face when she gazes down at the diamond engagement ring and thick gold band on her finger. 'We made it through ten years, just about.'

'Did you have a big wedding?'

'We had all the bells and whistles, flower girls and a white Rolls Royce. I worked as a wedding planner back then, but a fairy tale ceremony is no guarantee things will work out.'

'I can't see the appeal of blowing your life savings on a single day.'

'It took me years to realise.' She still looks upset as she cradles her cup in her hands; I'm amazed she's exposed the strife in her marriage to a stranger. 'I remembered something about Sabine, but it may not be relevant. She was on a motorboat in Porthloo Bay, on her afternoon off last Thursday. The boat was going so fast, I stopped to watch. She was with Harry Jago.'

'That's interesting.'

'It slipped my mind till now. I've been so thrown by it all, it's made me forgetful.' She takes a delicate sip of coffee. 'How's the investigation going?'

'We've got some strong lines of inquiry.'

'And suspects?'

'I can't reveal details yet, I'm afraid.'

A delicate flush covers her cheeks. 'Sorry, it's just that we're all desperate for news.'

'You'll have some soon, I promise. I need to take fingerprints from everyone who works here this morning. Is that okay?'

'Including me and Tom?'

'Yes, please.'

'I'll make sure everyone's informed. You're welcome to use the lounge upstairs.' She rises to her feet, brushing her dress with her hands, until the fabric falls in a perfect line.

'By the way, you haven't seen my dog, have you?'

'He was outside the kitchen on Monday night, but not since then.'

'If he comes back can you call me?'

'Of course, your number's on our system.' She glances at her watch, just as a waiter arrives with a huge platter of food. 'Enjoy your breakfast.'

The conversation gives me plenty to consider while I plough through my bacon, eggs and sausages. I need to speak to Harry Jago urgently, and my dog is avoiding me, for reasons unknown. Rhianna's motives are mysterious too. It sounds like she's falling out of love with her husband, and she was too curious about the case, but she may just be eager to know when her hotel can operate normally again.

It's still early when I leave the hotel. I scan Hugh Town's narrow streets again for signs of Shadow, but he's nowhere in sight. The place will remain quiet until the shops open at 9 a.m. The few remaining holidaymakers are likely to get up late, not leaving their hotels and guesthouses until mid-morning. My brief walk ends when I arrive at the Strand. Harry Jago lives in the last house in the terrace. The building is a rental property, and even though the mat in the porch carries the word 'welcome', there's little sign of it when I knock on the door. It's unlocked, and swings open to release a gust of warm air, thick with the stench of yesterday's food. The coffee table in his living room is littered with empty beer bottles and takeaway cartons. I'm not sure how he's paying the rent since his mother died. He spends his days ferrying tourists around the local bays, but his income will drop dramatically in winter when casual work dwindles. I yell Harry's name again, but an old man's querulous voice echoes through the wall.

'Stop that racket, will you?'

Stuart Helyer appears in the hallway a minute later. He has lived in the property next door with his wife Esme since he worked as a lobsterman, forty years ago. Helyer has been retired for my entire lifetime. He claims to be St Mary's oldest inhabitant, but looks too robust to be so ancient. He's still in his pyjamas and dressing gown, his watery eyes assessing me calmly, white hair standing out from his skull in thick clumps.

'Sorry to disturb your beauty sleep, Stuart.'

'I don't need much these days, but Esme likes her rest.'

'Have you seen Harry lately?'

He sighs loudly before replying. 'Not since yesterday. That boy's a royal pain in the arse, bringing girls home, drinking, and playing music too loud. Most people steer clear of him, but his mother was a sweetheart. I hope the landlord doesn't chuck him out.'

'Do you see much of him?'

'Harry's a decent lad when he's sober. He tidies our garden and never charges a penny; Esme gives him the odd hot meal in return. It's a pity the boy can't hold his drink.'

'There's something else I need help with, Stuart.

Have you heard this phrase before: *The bride in her glory will ever be fair?*'

The old man repeats the words to himself. 'Sounds like the start of an old wedding song from when I was young, but I doubt you'll find it written down anywhere. I wish I could remember the next line, but my memory's gone.'

'Don't worry, Stuart. Tell Harry to come to the station, please. I need to see him today.'

Helyer drops my card into the pocket of his dressing gown, but suspicion clouds his features, and I doubt he'll make use of use it. Most islanders prefer to settle disputes with no outside interference. Some see it as a personal failure if the law gets involved. I'll have to keep returning to Harry Jago's home to find out how well he knew Sabine.

My phone rings just as I walk out the front door. It's the security manager at the airport, his words emerging in a rapid stream. The latest flight to the mainland has been cancelled because one of the pilots hasn't reported for work. It's the first time Jade Finbury has ever missed a flight during six years of employment in Scilly, and she's not answering her mobile. I think about my brief chat with the pilot on Sunday, after she flew Liz Gannick over from Penzance. Her manner was warm and relaxed. Whatever's happened, I need to find her fast. When my gaze catches on the sea, its colour is changing from turquoise to cobalt for the first time in days – it looks like Ray was spot-on about the change in weather. My old headmaster enters my field of vision when I look down at Town Beach. He's taking another morning run, this time with his wife Elaine at his side, their dog trailing behind. The couple are crossing the wet sand at a pace that would put many younger joggers to shame. My own movements are much less graceful when I hurry back to the station.

29

Jade Finbury lives at Porth Minick, a few minutes' journey from Hugh Town. Eddie joins me in the van as we drive past Old Town Beach, which looks deserted today. Jade told me once that her passion for flying made her buy the house closest to the airport, and she wasn't kidding. The semi-detached villa has a direct view of the runway, which comes to an abrupt halt just before the cliff pitches into the sea. Jade's red Mini is still parked on her drive. The island's native agapanthus flowers are spilling through slats in her fence, every window gleaming with cleanliness.

There's no answer when I press the doorbell, apart from the sound of a cat mewing to be set free. My deputy looks apprehensive when he peers through her letterbox. He must have flown with Jade to the mainland dozens of times, like me. She's a chatty, popular figure, who seems to have no secrets to hide.

'How long's she been missing?' Eddie asks.

'For the past hour, it's only just been reported.'

There's no sign of trouble when I peer through the window into her lounge. The space looks homely, with an array of brightly coloured cushions piled on her sofa. 'Let's try round the back.'

Eddie is close behind as I follow the path. Jade has followed our safety advice to the letter: both doors to her property are locked, but there must be a reason why a conscientious pilot hasn't turned up for work. If an intruder caught her returning home, no one would have heard her cries for help. The holiday cottage next door has stood empty for months, in need of renovation.

'We need to get inside,' I mutter.

'She's left an upstairs window ajar. Want me to give it a try?'

'How, exactly?'

'Give me a leg up, I'll see what I can do.'

My admiration grows as he clambers across the flat roof, shins up a drainpipe, then slips through the open window. Eddie greets me at the front door moments later.

'Spider Man's got nothing on you.'

His choirboy face opens into a smile. 'Gymnastics was my best subject at school.'

My worst fear is that we'll find Jade in the same state as Sabine, but the house appears empty, her kitchen spotless. When I look out through her back window, the plane she flew over from Penzance is still parked on the runway, beside the airport building's square outline. A couple of letters lie on her desk, ready to be

posted: her handwriting is easy to read, the letters slop-
ing forwards as if they're racing to complete each line.

'She'd never just bunk off work, would she?' Panic
flickers across Eddie's face.

'If she was caught here, the MO is changing. The
other two attacks were at remote locations, not right
on the victim's doorstep, in sight of other houses.'

'Maybe the killer's gaining confidence.'

'We need to see if she's with Leo Kernick.'

Jade's boyfriend is the island's only professional
photographer. Kernick was born on St Mary's, but
spent years travelling with the paparazzi, photographing celebrities sunning themselves on faraway beaches,
before returning home. I've often seen him with Jade
over the past year, but the couple keep separate homes.
It's still only 9 a.m. when we pull up outside Kernick's
studio by Porth Mellon. The building is just a glori-
fied shed, with a corrugated iron roof, its shutters
firmly closed.

When I knock on the door a terse male voice instructs
us to stay outside. The photographer appears soon
after, releasing a stink of chemicals and a haze of red
light. His appearance reminds me why people gossip
about his relationship. He's twenty years older than
Jade and looks like an aging rock star, with a mane of
greying ringlets, tight jeans and a shirt that's spattered
with liquid, as if he's doused himself in champagne.
A smudge of black eyeliner would make him a dead-
ringer for Jack Sparrow in the *Pirates of the Caribbean*

films that keep being repeated on TV, long after their sell-by date.

'Sorry to keep you waiting, I was developing yesterday's shots.' The man's smile of greeting barely arrives, his voice roughened by a lifetime's cigarettes.

'Can we come in, Leo?'

He's still blocking the doorway. 'If this is about my car tax, you don't need to arrest me. I can renew it today.'

'You're not in trouble, we just need some information.'

The photographer flicks the light switch, turning the atmosphere inside his darkroom from red to white. Dozens of monochrome photos are hanging from a line to dry. They show local fishing boats in Hugh Town harbour, and close-ups of fishermen unloading their creels. The men look so relaxed they seem unaware that their images are being recorded.

Kernick sees me glancing at them. 'I've been taking the lobstermen's portraits all year.'

'How come?' I ask.

'It's the end of an era. Most of them are fourth or fifth generation fishermen, but their knowledge of the sea is dying. Their kids have moved away because they can't afford homes here. I could have shot the portraits digitally, but film feels more authentic for something so fragile.'

'You've caught them perfectly,' I reply, taking a step closer. 'When's the last time you saw Jade, Leo?'

'Last night.' He clears a pile of photographic paper from a bench, so we can sit down. 'We had dinner together at mine, then she went home.'

The man's body language seems relaxed. I can't tell yet if it's shyness or anxiety that makes him reluctant to meet my eye.

'Have you spoken to her today?'

'We had a minor disagreement last night; I'm letting her cool off.'

'Jade didn't turn up for work. Can you call her for us, please?'

Kernick picks up his phone without hesitation. His face is blank when he ends the call. 'She's not answering. Is that why you're here?'

'We're concerned she might be in danger.'

'Where's her car?'

'On her drive. What time did she leave yours?'

'Tennish, I think. Maybe she's ill; I should go to her place.' His body language is unchanged, but there's a tremor of panic in his voice.

'She's not there. Did you ask her to stay over last night?'

'That's why we argued. I want us to live together, but she likes her own space. I stayed at my flat after we finished exchanging insults.' He pulls a pack of cigarettes from his pocket, then drops it on the table, which fills me with relief. The air is so loaded with chemicals, a single spark might send the place up in flames.

'Who can verify that?'

201

'My neighbours would have heard her leave, as well as our shouting match.'

'Do you two often argue?'

'Hardly ever. Most of the time we get on fine.'

'Has Jade ever had trouble from anyone on St Mary's?'

'She's never mentioned it. There must be a simple explanation.'

'Do you own a Polaroid camera, Leo?'

'Not since I was a kid,' he says, looking bemused. 'My cheapest camera's a vintage Nikon.'

'Did you ever meet Sabine Bertans, at the Star Castle?'

'I never go there; it's outside my price range.'

'Can I have your keys, please? I'm afraid you can't go back to your flat until it's been searched.'

He pulls his key fob from his pocket with a show of reluctance. 'Jade and I have been together two years. Why in God's name would I hurt her?'

'We'll be in contact later. Thanks for your help.'

Eddie looks perplexed when we get back to the van. Leo Kernick's subdued manner makes him seem an unlikely killer, but the guy admitted to rowing with Jade last night. His flat will need to be checked carefully before we can establish whether his laid-back behaviour is just an act.

30

My team's faces are grave when I explain that Jade Finbury is missing, then tell them about being followed across the beach last night. I warn them to stay safe while out on patrol; the killer could target any of us for getting in their way, despite an apparent preference for young women. I mention that Stuart Helyer thought the phrase written on the back of Sabine's photo came from an old folk song, but my main priority is to find the missing pilot, and the morning is slipping away. I want to search St Mary's coastline tonight, when the killer appears at his most active.

Liz Gannick nods in agreement when I ask her to switch from searching cars to assessing Leo Kernick's flat, before doing a forensic check on Jade's property. I'm almost certain the pilot has been abducted, but it's possible she's lying ill somewhere. Lawrie and Isla will collect fingerprints at the Star Castle, then make house-to-house inquiries for recent sightings of Jade.

'If she's been taken, we don't have long. Sabine was

killed the night she went missing.' I point at her photo, pinned to the board. 'This time the killer knows we're watching, which could explain why Jade was abducted from her home. He's thrown us off track by making it different from the first two attacks.'

'Do you think we'll get another photo?' Eddie asks.

'I think so,' I reply. 'Part of the killer's buzz comes from feeling in control. We need to find the common link between the victims.'

'They're the same type of women,' says Isla.

'How do you mean?'

'They're all super-independent. Sabine and Hannah never planned to stay here, and were travelling alone; Jade's succeeding in a man's world. She flew all over the world before getting her job on St Mary's.'

'What are you saying, Isla?'

'Maybe the killer doesn't want them to leave.'

'The answer might be even simpler. Leo Kernick wants Jade to live with him, but she keeps refusing. That could have soured his view of women in general.'

'Leo can't be involved,' Lawrie Deane says, shaking his head vehemently. 'My wife got him to take photos at our anniversary bash last year. He's the gentle type – there's no way he'd hurt a woman, especially Jade. He's mad about her.'

'Forget personal loyalties, Lawrie. All of us have friends on the suspect list, until we can rule them out. For all we know, Jade ended their relationship last night and he flew off the handle. We need to look for connections between the attacks; try to find witnesses while you're doing house-to-house. Has anyone got anything else to add?'

Isla raises her hand. 'I've traced the dress Sabine was wearing. The last owner bought it in Penzance, two years ago. She hung on to it, then gave it to Oxfam last month.'

'Did the shop have the buyer's details?'

She looks frustrated. 'Only the date it was bought – in cash. The killer paid for it last Wednesday, four days before Sabine died. The volunteer running the shop is elderly and it was busy that day. She couldn't remember if it went to a man or a woman, and their CCTV was on the blink.'

'At least we know the killer was in Penzance last Wednesday. I'll check with Julian Power to see who travelled there and back in time to carry out the attack, before we search Kernick's flat.' I can feel the team's energy reviving now there's solid lead to pursue. 'If any of you suspect someone's involved, you're authorised to check their property unless you get a refusal. If that happens, call the CPS straight away for a warrant. Remember I don't want you working alone, Isla.' A flash of irritation crosses the young constable's face at being singled out, which comes as no surprise. If someone tried chaperoning me, I'd be scowling too. 'I'm changing my policy on protecting lone females. I want them all moved to hotels or guest houses in Hugh Town before nightfall. How many women are in properties by themselves?'

Deane thumbs through his notes before replying. 'Twenty-three, but some are already staying with relatives or friends.'

'Visit the rest, please, and don't take no for an answer.'

'What if they refuse?'

'Apply the protective custody law, for their own safety.'

Deane looks concerned when he and Isla prepare to leave. The islanders tend to be fiercely independent, after years of fending for themselves. Some women may argue to remain at home, but Jade Finbury's disappearance shows we can't take risks. After they've gone I glance through the window into the backyard, seeing only bare concrete, and the patch of sunlight where Shadow used to bask. It crosses my mind that the person we're looking for may have taken my dog to send me a brutal message. The creature's fate matters less than finding Jade Finbury, yet he stays in my mind. The idea that he's lost for good lodges there like a burr that can't be removed.

I call Frank Rawle to ask him to escort Liz Gannick to Kernick's flat, then keep watch outside. My old headmaster reports for duty five minutes later, a smile bringing his hard-boned features to life, his rarely used uniform immaculate. He seems overjoyed to be involved in the case at last, his assistance allowing me and Eddie to head for the quay immediately. Under normal circumstances I don't mind my deputy's constant chatter, but today I need time to think. There must be a common link between Sabine Bertans, Hannah Weber and Jade Finbury. The women are aged between nineteen and thirty-four, confident enough to travel the world and pursue their ambitions. But why would the killer target them for being independent? I need to understand why the Cornish wedding rings and gold lockets St Mary's fishermen gave to their wives are being left on the victims' bodies. I still believe his calling cards could unlock his motives. There's no way he's just an opportunist; there's always a common theme when a serial killer goes to work.

The dockside is normally full of people waiting for the small ferries that ply back and forth between the islands, taking visitors to Tresco's Abbey Gardens or the unspoiled beaches of St Martin's. But the coffee shop is empty today, only a few islanders watching the boats bobbing in the harbour. Two ferrymen approach us with scowls on their faces, protesting about sailing restrictions. They're growing restless, and there's no hiding from anyone's anger when you're six foot four with a hefty build. Many local families depend on cash from summer visitors, but inter-island ferry services can't resume until the killer's found. I keep my voice calm when I explain that the case will get solved faster if they let us work.

The men's tempers appear close to boiling point, like the summer heat, but they step back reluctantly, allowing Eddie and me to enter the Isles of Scilly

Travel Company's office. It's usually a hive of activity with passengers queuing for the three-hour journey to Penzance on the *Scillonian*, or waiting for goods from the mainland, but now the area's deserted. Julian Power is studying his computer screen intently, like he's gazing into the abyss.

'Please tell me the travel ban's lifted,' he says. 'People think I'm to blame. The last few tourists are having trouble getting their insurance companies to shell out for hotel bills.'

'Tell them things will soon be back to normal,' I reply. 'Can we see your passenger lists for last week, please? I need to know who travelled to Penzance.'

'I'm afraid my IT system's still down. I've got the numbers for each crossing, but no names and contact details. They've been deleted, along with half my mailing list.'

'You can't retrieve the information?'

'Believe me, I've tried. Most of our software's been infected.'

The guy looks uncomfortable, but I can't be certain he's telling the truth. 'How about you, Julian? Did you go over to the mainland last week?'

'I stayed at home. My assistant covered for me, while I tried to fix the IT system.'

Internet failures and computer breakdowns happen often in the Scillies, but this one is a disaster. Jade Finbury could be hidden anywhere on the island, and we've lost our best chance of tracking the killer down.

'Have you had any luck finding out which family donated the sailors' charms to the museum?'

'I've checked the whole archive and found no reference to them; the entries are as chaotic as my computer. I'll have to look again.'

'Tonight if possible, please, Julian. I need that information urgently.'

I thank Power before we leave, even though he's delivered a double helping of bad news. Eddie leans on the railing outside, powerless to do anything except wait while I phone the airport to check which islanders flew to Penzance last week. Half a dozen small planes leave St Mary's daily in summer, crossing to Land's End, Newquay or Exeter, but the passenger lists aren't definitive. If the killer sailed to the mainland to buy the wedding dress, he's beyond our reach.

My gaze takes in the glitter on the sea's surface, while the airport manager checks his records. A gaggle of walkers are admiring the lifeboat house, perched on its promontory beside the bay, while seagulls circle overhead in slow rotations. The sight is so peaceful, it looks like an illustration from a Cornish holiday brochure, but the island's beauty is being tarnished by so much violence. The airport manager reels off names, which I scribble in my notebook, before showing them to Eddie. 'These people were in Penzance when the dress was bought, and back here in time for the first attack.'

Isla Tremayne's name is first on the list, making me

question again whether I was wrong to keep our new constable on the case. Tom Polkerris is among the islanders that flew to the mainland, along with Steve and Paul Keast, and Leo Kernick. When I scan the names again there's only one more I recognise: Elaine Rawle, my old headmaster's wife. Now that we know the killer bought the dress last week, I'll have to find out why every islander on the list travelled to the mainland, but Polkerris seemed genuinely distressed to hear of Sabine's death. I feel uneasy when my gaze returns to the Keast brothers' names. I'll have to question them again, putting our friendship under even greater strain, but my main focus is on finding Jade Finbury before it's too late.

Eddie seems relieved when we set off for Leo Kernick's flat to check on Gannick's progress – it's a finite task to complete. He wears a focused look as we walk to the photographer's home on Pilot's Retreat. The street name refers to the mariners who earned their wages from piloting ships through the treacherous local waters, past hidden reefs that surround the Scillies. The pilots competed for work by rowing out to waiting vessels at top speed, the winner securing the job, making homes near the quay a necessity. Their dwellings have changed little in the past two centuries; dark stone cottages, huddled together like old women gossiping. Frank Rawle is standing outside Kernick's property, stiff-backed, like a sentry on duty. He looks crestfallen when I thank him for his help, reluctant to return to civilian life.

Leo Kernick's ground floor flat gives him an ideal vantage point for scoping out victims; his windows look out on passers-by, strolling to Old Town beach or Pulpit Rock. Eddie and I don sterile suits, even though we only need a quick look around Kernick's home. We wait outside while Gannick lays more plastic sheeting on the floors, and strange odours drift down the hallway. Cigarette smoke mingles with the same smell of chemicals from the photographer's dark room.

'Don't touch anything,' Gannick snaps, when she finally lets us inside. 'I'd work quicker if you left me alone.'

'We'll be gone in ten minutes.'

Kernick's hallway looks innocent enough, with his bicycle propped against the wall and a run of threadbare carpet. There's nothing unusual about his bedroom either, apart from its sparsity. It holds an unmade double bed, a wardrobe, and little else. It's only when we reach the living room that my jaw drops open. Photographs plaster two of the walls from floor to ceiling, hundreds of different images overlapping each other. The effect is so oppressive, I can see why Jade Finbury refuses to cohabit, even though her smiling face is the first I recognise. The pictures record every wedding and christening Kernick has been paid to photograph. Weddings shots show dozens of brides and grooms in formal poses. Some have been taken inside the island's churches, but more at beauty spots like Holy Vale and the Star Castle. I'm still staring at them when Eddie summons me to the other side of the room.

'Take a look at this, boss.'

He points at an image of Hannah Weber. The journalist is gazing straight at the camera, her expression wary, as if the portrait was taken against her will. I recognise the scenery immediately; the shot was taken near Toll's Island, but I can't tell whether Kernick spoke to her before or after she bumped into Father Michael.

'Maybe he hates taking wedding photographs because Jade keeps turning him down,' says Eddie.

'Are there any of Sabine?'

I focus my attention on the rest of the room while he studies the images. The place is shabby but clean, a bookshelf loaded with art magazines and biographies of famous photographers like Cartier-Bresson and Annie Leibovitz. I'm struck by the flat's smallness, for a man who must have earned big fees from selling pictures to the tabloids. It's hot and airless with the windows closed, but the kitchen is tidy. Kernick wiped the surfaces before heading to his studio this morning. Apart from the photos, he seems to live quietly, pursuing the craft he loves. Liz Gannick looks aggrieved when I ask what she's found.

'I'll need another hour, but it's clean so far,' she tells me.

A shout goes up from Eddie while I'm checking Kernick's bathroom. His face is jubilant when I find him in the lounge, pointing at a photo that's almost hidden by larger images. It's a shot of Sabine, taken on the beach. It's nothing like the Polaroid image I received from the killer: afternoon sunlight illuminates her face, her expression completely carefree. The only indication that Leo Kernick may be involved in the attacks is his shots of all three victims. Hannah Weber looks the most reluctant to have her likeness captured. She's got her back to the sea, short blonde hair ruffled by the breeze, wearing a forced smile.

31

Lily is serving lunch to a handful of guests in the hotel restaurant. The dining room is cooler than outside because the castle's thick walls lower the temperature, but her clothes still feel tight and uncomfortable. There's no sign of Liam Trewin, allowing her to serve each table without his intense stare tracking her movements. Time passes quickly as she hurries back and forth, but her thoughts drift beyond the castle's walls. It's a relief when the guests finish their desserts. She can speak to Tom Polkerris at last. Lily hovers outside his office, rehearsing what to say before summoning enough courage to knock.

When Polkerris's voice calls her inside, the manager looks flustered, shutting down his computer before she can see his work. His calm only returns when he rises to his feet, his expression concerned. Lily picks up the scent of his expensive aftershave when he walks towards her.

'Are you okay, Lily?'

'Fine thanks, sir, but I need a day's leave.'

He looks surprised. 'You're not due any holiday yet. Is work tiring you?'

Anxiety makes her palms sting with pins and needles. 'My brother needs my help.'

'Causing trouble again, is he?'

Her gaze drops to the floor. The island is so small, secrets can't be hidden. 'He's been struggling all year.'

'You don't have to explain.' Polkerris's voice is gentler than before. 'How many days are you talking about?'

'Until Thursday night, please.'

'Rhianna won't be happy, but you've got my permission. Can you stay here till this evening and come back for kitchen duty on Friday morning? If the ferries are running again we'll have a full house.'

Lily beams at him. 'I'll be here for the early shift, sir.'

'It's sweet that you want to help your brother, when others have written him off. It shows your kindness.' Polkerris takes a step closer, his gaze searching her face. 'I've been thinking about you, Lily.'

'Sorry?'

'Why didn't I choose someone caring, like you?' He touches a fingertip to her jaw, his gaze tracing the outline of her lips. 'You'd better go, before I do something stupid.'

Polkerris's behaviour leaves Lily confused. Despite the crush she's had on him all year, she could never break up someone's marriage, and why would he bother with her when his wife's so beautiful? She pushes his words to the back of her mind. The girl hurries back to her duties, wishing she could leave immediately. She knows her brother is trying to find Sabine's killer, and she wants to help so she can sleep peacefully again, without bad dreams.

215

32

Leo Kernick sounds defensive when I call him at his studio to ask about his photos of Sabine and Hannah Weber. He claims to be so passionate about documenting island life that he takes shots of everyone he sees on St Mary's, like a visual diary. When I ask why he flew over to the mainland last week, he claims to have visited a gallery in Penzance that's holding an exhibition of his work. The photographer still denies knowing Hannah's name or speaking to her for more than a few seconds. Frustration leaves a sour taste in my mouth; I've got no tangible proof of his involvement, it's his word against mine. He may just be an obsessive, whose photography rules his life. My second call is to Isla, her tone breezy when she states that her visit to Penzance was to see an orthodontist, which I can easily check. One of the limitations of island life is the lack of specialist health care; visiting an optician or dentist can cost hundreds of pounds in travel alone.

A drone is flying overhead when Eddie and I leave

Pilot's Retreat. It's large, and looks high-spec, making me suspect it's being piloted from another island by the press. It hovers above the roofline, red lights flashing as it buzzes past. I feel like shaking my fist at it, but turn my back instead, reluctant to see my face plastered across news websites. The drone soon flies off to its next target, leaving its motorised whine buzzing in my ears. I'm still processing our visit to Leo Kernick's flat. The man's love for his craft is obvious, but he seems too fond of his girlfriend to target other women.

While Eddie and I walk down to the coast road, I make another call to Lawrie Deane, telling him we'll need to search the island for Jade Finbury this evening, because all the attacks have been conducted at night. The sun won't set until around 9 p.m., giving us time to carry out more inquiries first.

I scan the view ahead when we reach the bottom of the hill; the off-islands are wavering behind a blur of heat haze. Members of the lifeboat crew are sailing the rescue launch past Hugh Town Beach on a practice mission, making me long for a job with such clearly defined boundaries. I'd happily swap places with any of them right now. They take huge risks to rescue stricken vessels, but are rewarded by saving lives. My own job is much less heroic, and not every murderer gets caught. Eddie looks preoccupied as we hurry down the Strand, with the air growing humid, and razorbills shrieking overhead. I come to a halt when the noise changes suddenly.

'What's that sound?' I ask.

'It's just birds, scrapping for food.' Eddie's expression changes when the moaning noise comes again.

We run towards the row of houses. The sound amplifies when we reach Harry Jago's home, making me look up at his bedroom window, but the curtains are drawn.

'It's coming from the ginnel,' Eddie says.

He races down the side passage, where a man sits hunched against the wall. Jago's face is a mess, with grazes across his cheekbone, his left eye swollen shut. I can't tell whether he's been beaten up, or drank so much last night that he fell on his face and had to crawl home.

'He stinks to high heaven,' Eddie mutters. The air is soured by raw alcohol, urine and mould clinging to the brick walls.

'Can you get up, Harry?' The boy remains motionless, forcing me and Eddie to hoist him to his feet. 'You need a doctor.'

'Fuck off, the pair of you.' He throws wild punches that fail to connect.

'Calm down or you're going in a cell. Let's get you cleaned up.'

Jago's body slumps against my shoulder before he can reply. Stuart Helyer gawps at us from his porch as Eddie and I haul the boy inside. My sympathy grows when we lay him down on the sofa. His face is as pale as bleached linen, bruises round his eye and jawline turning from red to blue. Jago hauls himself to an upright position, his gaze bleary.

'Who did this to you, Harry?'

'No one.' His words are slurred. 'Get out of my house.'

'That's a nice way to thank us for our help.' The boy sneers at me in response. 'I hear Sabine Bertans was on your boat last week. I thought you hardly knew each other?'

The boy is in no state to talk, his head lolling backwards as sleep overtakes him. It could be hours before he can answer questions. When I check my watch, the afternoon is vanishing. I can't waste time on a kid who's hellbent on self-destruction, while Jade Finbury is still missing.

I leave Jago in Eddie's care, then cross the road to the Catholic church. It's empty, apart from the smell of fresh incense, confirming that the priest has said mass at least once today. Father Michael looks like any middle-aged man when he answers the doorbell, dressed in jeans, trainers and a short-sleeved shirt, clutching a mug of coffee. His dog collar is the only sign of his calling; there's none of the fake piety that turns me off most religions. He dumps his drink on the hall table then hurries outside when I tell him that Jago needs his help.

'The boy's had a terrible year,' he says. 'His mother used to bring him and Lily to mass; but he's been lost since she died.'

'Harry won't see a doctor. Can you help Eddie to sober him up?'

'I'll do my best.'

The priest doesn't flinch when the stench of vomit and stale booze hits us in Jago's living room. The boy is swaying wildly as he yells at Eddie to leave him alone. He only stops shouting when Father Michael enters the room. It looks like he's about to faint, but Eddie grabs his arm in time, then lowers him onto the settee. Jago's face is so badly swollen I couldn't read his reaction to the priest, but at least he's more compliant. Father Michael kneels at his feet, using the flannel and soapy water Eddie has provided to clean his wounds. My deputy looks relieved to have help with such a difficult customer; the priest murmurs words of comfort as he wipes dried blood from the boy's jaw. Something about the situation leaves me unsettled. It could just be my own prejudices, because the boy is one of a tiny handful of islanders with a criminal conviction, but Rhianna Polkerris had no reason to lie about seeing Sabine on his boat. The kid may not be linked to the attacks in any way, but I need straight answers from him soon.

Liz Gannick has messaged me, saying that Isla has driven her from Pilot's Retreat to Jade Finbury's home. I decide to walk there, to clear my head, taking the direct route across open farmland, past Buzza Tower. The circular building has been converted into a camera obscura, projecting a reverse image of the surrounding scenery on the walls inside, making me wish that I could see the killer's face in such perfect focus. The land opens into a patchwork of tiny fields, hemmed in by stone walls, full of late blooming pinks and carnations, grown for the mainland's flower markets. Farmers will soon be baying for my blood, as well as the boatmen, if the killer isn't found. The island depends on exporting its produce, but the embargo on travel can't be lifted while more than forty islanders have no clear alibi for the night Sabine died.

Gannick looks irritated by my arrival at Jade Finbury's house, her diminutive form swamped by her white overalls. I put on another sterile suit and overshoes, the extra layer of fabric making me feel like a piece of shrink-wrapped meat, rotting in the afternoon sun.

'Not you again,' she snaps. 'I only just arrived.'

'It's urgent, Liz. A woman's still missing.'

'So I hear.' She glowers at me again. 'There was nothing at Kernick's flat: no blood traces, potential weapons, or evidence of harm. This place is a different matter. I'll show you the kitchen, then I'd be grateful for some time to do my job.'

Gannick clips away across the wooden floor, the tap of her crutches sounding like a scattergun. Jade's kitchen looks unchanged, with an expensive coffee machine on one of the surfaces, the breakfast bar scrubbed clean. No incriminating evidence is visible, until Gannick shines her UV beam on the lino. A dark smear suddenly appears, over a foot long, by the back door.

'The blood must be fresh to show up so clearly,' the chief SOCO says.

'How long before we know if it's Jade's?'

'Get my samples to Penzance today, so the lab can tell us tomorrow morning.'

'I'll pay a boatman to deliver it.'

Gannick runs her torch over the bloodstain again. 'The beam picks up trace evidence, but someone's tried to cover their tracks. My litmus test picked up ammonia and iron oxide.'

'The killer used bleach?'

'And a Brillo pad, to remove the stain. The sink's marked too. It must have been a deep cut; the droplets trail right back to the door.'

Gannick points the torch at the sink, revealing a diagonal line of teardrop-shaped marks, but when she switches the torch off, the wooden draining board looks clean and innocent. The forensics chief is so focused on her work, she soon forgets my presence, and I can only admire her as she runs her torch beam over the pilot's possessions. Gannick must have crawled over a thousand filthy floors in her time, but the sordid side of her profession never seems to faze her; she pursues every task with the same determination, and I could use some of her confidence today. It looks like Jade Finbury was abducted from her own home, just forty-eight hours after our last conversation.

33

A wall of sticky heat engulfs me as I leave Jade Finbury's house, and another drone passes overhead. Its camera clicks wildly as it buzzes along, making me grit my teeth. The press must be furious at being barred from the island. The death of a beautiful young Eastern European in a remote corner of the British Isles is bound to raise interest, so they'll keep on sending mechanical spies on reconnaissance flights until they get the pictures they crave.

'Blood-sucking vampires,' I hiss to myself.

The media's focus on the case is the least of my worries as I march back to Hugh Town, looking for Shadow in the fields, but finding no sign. The sea is an innocent pastel blue when I reach the coast road; a gaggle of kids are being taught how to capsize their canoes, laughing as they spill into the water and resurface again. The intense heat tempts me to wade in too, but there will be no time for swimming until the killer's found.

Lawrie is sifting through witness reports when I

get back, and Isla has returned from her foot patrol. Maybe I should have barred her from the case after she confessed to a one-night stand with Sabine, to save us both discomfort: I don't want to question her again, but I've got no choice. When I ask for her orthodontist's phone number she forwards it from her phone without batting an eye. She's still on the list of suspects I'm carrying around in my head, which doesn't quite match the printed sheet on the incident board, of three dozen islanders with no solid alibis.

The team listen in silence when I talk about Harry Jago's reluctance to name whoever injured him. The boy remains a person of interest, but only because Rhianna Polkerris has reported seeing Sabine in his company shortly before she died. Plenty of islanders seem to think he's a dangerous character, but I've got no concrete proof that he's involved.

'Harry's life is so chaotic, I doubt he could deliver such complex attacks.'

Deane shakes his head. 'I took him in for fighting back in May; he was still pissed when I released him from the holding cell the next morning.'

'What are you saying, Lawrie?'

'He's out of control. I bet he's violent enough to kill someone.'

Isla looks uncertain. 'Where would he get the money for a fancy wedding dress?'

'He's stolen before,' says Deane. 'Maybe he nicked

it. The boy's so messed up, he'd lash out for no good reason.'

'We don't have any clear proof against him.' My thoughts suddenly shift into focus. 'But you're right about Jago being our only convicted thief. Maybe the killer paid him to steal the jewellery from the museum.'

Someone like Julian Power might be so keen to increase his collection he'd pay for stolen goods, but why would such a fastidious man attack Jade Finbury, spilling her blood across her kitchen floor? I'll need to visit Power's property again soon, to lay the idea to rest. I ask Isla to finish gathering volunteers to search the coastline at 6 p.m., then carry on checking that every lone female on the island has a safe place to stay.

'There are just two names left, sir.'

My heart sinks when she gives me a piece of paper. One name belongs to an elderly widow who's lived alone since her husband died, and the second is Nina Jackson, just as I expected.

Lawrie and Isla are busy organising the search party when I climb into the police van, with a growing sense of irritation. I'm still scowling as I drive north through the well-kept fields of Trewince, with sheep fleeing from the noise of a passing vehicle. The old lady lives at the island's highest point, opposite Telegraph Tower. The building fascinated me as a kid, its round walls rising from the ground like an inland lighthouse. A hundred years ago it was the only place where telegram signals could be received, but today it houses the local radio station, where the DJs manage to dredge up enough local news to broadcast all week to Scilly's two thousand inhabitants.

It's late afternoon when I arrive at the widow's house. She comes to the door wearing a puzzled expression – her hearing aid has broken, which explains why she hasn't answered her phone. Before long she's agreed to pack an overnight bag and take a taxi to the Star Castle. Tom and Rhianna are giving islanders a night's free accommodation, and the old lady looks thrilled when the taxi arrives, as if staying in a deluxe hotel is a dream come true.

I'm unlikely to get such a positive response from Nina. She's nowhere in sight when I reach Watermill Cove, but a familiar sound greets me. Part of my tension drops away when I recognise Shadow's growl. He's standing by the back door of her cottage, barking at full volume. He bounds across the grass, paws landing on my chest, like we've been apart all year.

'Why run away if you're that glad to see me, you hellhound?'

The dog whines loudly, like he's trying to explain, until Nina appears. There's a smile on her face as she watches him fawning at my feet, rolling over to let me rub his chest.

'Shadow got here last night,' she says. 'He was behaving oddly, snarling at me if I went near the front door. He wouldn't let me go outside until this morning.'

'Why didn't you call me?'

'I left my phone in the car. He barked his head off every time I tried opening the back door.'

'Sounds like he's been on guard duty.'

Now that he's greeted me, the dog returns to Nina's side. She was his favourite during our brief relationship, but how did he track her down? The creature would make an excellent sniffer dog if his wayward streak could be controlled. I brace myself for a row when I tell Nina to stay in town until the killer's found. Her looks distract me while I talk: the pale-green sundress she's wearing highlights her tan, the sun glinting in her hair. There's a long pause while she considers my request.

'I'll need to pack my walking boots so I can join the search tonight.'

'You're not going to argue?'

'Why would I? You just told me another woman's been attacked, while she was home alone. I like my own company, but I'm not crazy. Give me five minutes to grab my stuff.'

Nina vanishes indoors with Shadow at her side. It dawns on me that they have a lot in common: both live by their own rules. The dog still seems reluctant to let her out of his sight. I wait for them on the front steps, and Shadow emerges first, checking the environment for safety. He circles the cottage before returning to the front garden, keeping his body low to the ground. His ears are pricked, but there's no one on the footpath that cuts between elm trees and tamarisk bushes down to the sea. I can see why Nina loves the solitude of the place, but Shadow isn't so keen. Something must have spooked him badly last night, even though the threat has vanished. The dog leaps into the van before Nina, sitting between us, like a canine chaperone. She's carrying a rucksack and the violin her husband gave her just months before he died. Silence presses against the windows as we rattle down the unmade road.

'Is being in my company really so hard, Ben?' she asks.

'I came to fetch you, didn't I?'

'Only because it's your duty.'

'There's no point in raking up the past.'

'I only need to say one thing. It was wrong of me to leave without having a proper conversation; that was a cowardly thing to do.'

'Your reason made perfect sense. It was too soon after losing Simon.'

'But I hoped we'd stay friends. I'd hate to stop visiting the islands.'

'You don't need my blessing to come here.' My words sound harsher than I intended, but it's too late to retract them.

'At least have a drink with me before I leave on Sunday. I'd like to hear how you've spent the last year.' Nina's direct stare undoes me all over again; her eyes are the colour of the amber I spent my childhood holidays hunting for on the beach, like buried treasure.

'You won't be able to avoid me, don't worry. We're staying at the same hotel.'

She remains silent until I park outside the Star

Castle. Shadow jumps out of the van immediately, like they're joined by an invisible thread. He stays beside her even when I call his name.

'You're stuck with him for now,' I say. 'He's your new bodyguard.'

Something shifts inside my chest while Nina walks away, her straight-backed posture like a dancer's, with my dog trailing behind like a lovesick suitor.

'Good luck figuring her out, mate. She's all yours,' I mutter, then swing the van into reverse and head back to the station.

The place is empty when I arrive, giving me time to switch on my computer. I should tackle the backlog of emails from islanders, all asking when travel restrictions will be lifted, but my mind shifts to the killer's calling cards. If I can find out why they matter, I'll be one step closer to understanding his mindset.

When I run an internet search, it's soon clear that sailors' charms are a rarity. Apart from the local museum, only the Pitt Rivers in Oxford has a collection of Cornish amulets, mostly made in Scilly, ranging from gold lockets to tiny sailing vessels for charm bracelets. I stare at the screen until my eyes ache, but can only see pretty gold trinkets that newly married sailors hoped would carry them home to their wives, through wild storms. It's hard to accept that the same person who throttled Sabine would be drawn to such delicate, sentimental objects, unless two different people are carrying out the attacks.

Liz Gannick is the first person to arrive back at the station. I can tell from her expression that she's disappointed by finding little more evidence at Jade Finbury's house, but her discovery of the bloodstain in the kitchen makes me certain the pilot's been taken. Somehow Gannick has found time in her day to look for matches with the four sets of fingerprints in Sabine's room.

'I've got three positives.' She runs her gaze over her list. 'Lily Jago and the hotel's two managers.'

'Tom and Rhianna?'

She nods in reply. 'Their prints are on her door, bed-side table and chair.'

'How about the fourth set?'

'It's not a staff member. I'll run it through the national database, but the result could take hours to arrive.'

Gannick has been working flat out, yet she's delivered more frustration. It's no surprise that Lily Jago spent time with her close friend, and the two hotel managers have legitimate reasons to visit Sabine's room; they probably inspect the staff accommodation regularly to make sure it's being kept clean. I walk into Madron's office and shut the door, before releasing silent curses into the air.

34

Lily walks to her old home at her fastest pace. Harry hasn't answered her texts and she knows something's wrong when she enters the hallway. It smells of sickness and the sharp tang of antiseptic. A male voice drifts from the lounge; she can't hear the exact words, but the speaker's anger resonates through the wall. When she bursts into the living room, her brother is cowering on the settee, and Father Michael stands over him with fists clenched. The priest's expression softens when he faces her, but Lily is staring at Harry's injuries.

'What are you doing here, Father?'

'Your brother's been in another fight; the police found him in a dreadful state.'

The priest visited often during her mother's last illness, arriving in time to administer last rites, yet Lily has never liked him. Her mother died young, despite all his prayers, and there's something weird about his manner. When she studies Harry's face again, she knows her brother's afraid.

'What were you telling Harry just now, Father?'

'That it's time to face his demons. Why don't we pray together, to help him turn over a new leaf?'

'Mum believed in God, but we don't. You're wasting your time here.'

Father Trevellyan lingers until she pulls the door wide and waits for him to go. There's something frightening about the man's desire to remain at Harry's side. He murmurs a few holy words, conferring a blessing she never requested, then lays his hand on her forearm. His touch is so clammy, she's desperate for him to leave.

'Your brother needs God's love more than ever, Lily. Don't try and stop him from coming to church. I'll pray for you both tonight.'

He issues the statement in a mild tone, but there's anger behind it. The priest's words sound more like a curse than a blessing.

35

I launch the island-wide search for Jade Finbury at 6 p.m. The search party has been split into four groups; each will cover separate parts of St Mary's coastline, the killer's favoured location for his attacks, apart from Jade Finbury's abduction. Lawrie and Isla's groups will cover the south, while Eddie and I scour the northern coastline. Splitting up will ensure that every beach and cave is checked for signs of the killer's presence, while Jade still has a chance.

The community has turned out in force, with over three hundred people keen to look for the pilot, which comes as no surprise. The islanders always unite in a crisis, sharing resources to keep everyone safe. Some people have chosen not to volunteer, including Julian Power and Rhianna Polkerris, but we have more than enough helpers to sweep the island. My own group are waiting for me by Old Town Bay, equipped with torches and lanterns in case the light fails. I forgot how dramatic dusk could be in the Scillies when I lived in London. Night arrives here like sudden blindness, with no streetlights to guide you past the islands' settlements.

I explain that the shoreline must be searched thoroughly, with half the party spreading inland from the coastal path. We will need two hours to reach Bar Point at St Mary's northern tip. The group spans a wide age range, and several pillars of the community have reported for duty, including Frank and Elaine Rawle. My old headmaster's face is grave as we pass Church Point; he stands on the path while younger group members scramble down a slope to the shoreline. I can tell the couple are glad to be involved, and their approach is vigilant, using fallen branches to peer under thickets of ground elder, and examining every inch of ground. Our walk would be enjoyable under normal circumstances, the route providing long views across Crow Sound to the Eastern Isles. Scilly's native poppies, gorse and yarrow are blooming beside the path, reminding me that the killer used similar flowers in his first attack; if we don't act fast, the same wild blossoms will be woven through Jade's hair.

The airport's landing strip up ahead looks more like a country lane than a runway, just long enough for small aircraft to take off before plummeting over the cliff's edge. If any of the local pilots misjudge their timing, their aircraft would crash onto the allotment site and the rocks below. Jade Finbury's plane is still waiting on the tarmac, pricking my conscience. I push back weeds from the path, looking for anything the killer might have dropped. Tom Polkerris is keeping his distance, his gaze scanning the ground. When he trudges closer his expression is troubled. There's no sign now of the jeering bully who threw younger kids' dinner money down toilets to amuse himself.

'Rhianna sends her apologies,' he says. 'One of us has to stay at the hotel round the clock.'

'It's okay, we've got plenty of volunteers.'

'We needed a break from each other anyway. The bloody Travel Awards inspection's been a real wind-up. Sorry, I shouldn't mention work at a time like this.' He studies me again. 'You've never liked me much, have you?'

'A woman's missing, Tom. The past isn't relevant.'

'I regret hurting people, for what it's worth. Life was shit at home; money was tight and my parents' tempers got frayed. I've tried to learn from my mistakes. I even went on an anger management course.'

'I've heard that can help.' I'm too focused on Jade to care about the guy's apology, despite the misery in his voice.

'Sabine's dad called me yesterday. The hotel owners have agreed to pay for her body to be flown home, and for the funeral in Riga.'

'Her family will appreciate that.'

'It won't bring her back.' Polkerris focuses on the path ahead. 'I still feel bad about it.'

'How do you mean?'

'Sabine was our employee and we let her down. I've had nightmares ever since.'

'She chose to leave the hotel grounds of her own accord, Tom.' The guilt on his face finally weakens my old prejudices, but a few suspicions linger. 'I've been meaning to ask why you flew over to Penzance last week.'

'For a shareholders' meeting. They're held four times a year, Rhianna and I take it in turns. They expect more from us every time; we're running just to stand still.'

'You came back that evening, didn't you?'

He nods rapidly. 'I caught the 4 p.m. flight. I'd prefer to use Skype, but they love grilling me face to face.'

Polkerris's story sounds straightforward, unlike the islanders that boarded the *Scillonian* to Penzance when the wedding dress was bought, whose names remain a mystery. I know Elaine Rawle flew over to visit her elderly mother in a care home, like she does once a fortnight, as regular as clockwork. The Keast brothers say that their day was spent ordering feed and farmyard equipment, and Leo Kernick was at an art gallery, but many others still haven't been identified thanks to the IT failure. Tom Polkerris hurries ahead to join the rest of the search party, leaving me alone with my thoughts. It sounds like his marriage is struggling, but the hotel manager's romantic problems can't be used as evidence.

Leo Kernick is at the back of the group when the footpath winds through a landscape marked by earlier inhabitants. The huge granite formations rising from the ground were christened centuries ago: Horse Rock, the Druid's Chair, and Giant's Grave. Their titles are still accurate today: Horse Rock resembles a stallion rearing, its mane splayed by the wind. I slow my pace to wait for the photographer. The guy's ageing-rock-star persona is on full display; his grey ringlets look like they haven't been combed for weeks. He's wearing a battle-scarred leather jacket despite the evening's warmth, a red bandana around his neck, and skin-tight jeans. His face is so tense it looks like he's barely holding on to his composure, the camera around his neck a safety blanket that he cradles with one hand as he walks. Before I can greet him he takes a photograph of me, his expression empty as he presses the shutter.

'You should ask for permission first, Leo.'

'I record everyone that crosses my path, but I'll delete it if you want.'

'You must have a huge collection of shots.'

'Tens of thousands, probably. The ones in my flat are a drop in the ocean.'

'But you don't remember taking one of Hannah Weber near here, by Toll's Island?'

He shakes his head. 'I never ask people's names; I'm just documenting island life. It's a hell of a lot more fulfilling than waiting outside shitty nightclubs in Ibiza for some D-list celebrity to stagger out, pissed on champagne.'

'Did you earn big wages back then?'

'I blew the lot. The lifestyle took its toll; I can't remember much of my thirties.'

'What does Jade think about your photos?'

His voice softens when her name is mentioned. 'She tells me they'll hang in museums one day.'

'How did you two meet?'

'You mean how did an old wreck like me get together with a fresh-faced young Catholic?'

'I didn't know she went to church.'

'Jade's parents are religious. I don't think it's big thing for her, she just goes to mass occasionally.'

'Do you know much about her earlier relationships?'

'She got hurt by her last boyfriend; he mucked her around. Jade keeps saying she doesn't want anything serious, but we've been together two years. I keep hoping she'll change her mind.' He grinds out the butt of his cigarette with the heel of his boot so forcefully, it's like he's stamping on the killer's face. 'Bring her back safe and sound, please. She's the only one to keep me on the straight and narrow.'

'We'll do our best.'

Kernick slips into a reverie, so I walk on alone, wondering if the man's eccentric manner is just a cover. I've investigated enough murders to know that even mild-mannered individuals can turn violent. When I look east, the sky is turning red behind Toll's Island, where the ancient fortress is crumbling into the sea. Pelistry Beach opens in front of us, as the path winds round the headland, revealing another hidden cove. Smugglers used the secluded inlets to bring contraband ashore for centuries, and it's perfect territory for a murderer to conceal a victim. I know that Jade Finbury may already be dead, her body hidden in one of the Neolithic graves that riddle the island's hills.

When Jeff Pendelow calls my name, it's a relief to put my concerns aside. The psychologist is walking with a limp; his heavy frame still looks robust, but his skin is so pale I can tell he's suffering.

'How's your back, Jeff?'

'Not great, but I couldn't stay at home while Jade's missing. She dropped in a lot after Val after got ill.' He studies me over his half-moon glasses. 'How's the investigation going?'

'We've got all the pieces. I just need to assemble them in the right order.'

'My job often felt like that, when patients didn't respond to treatment.' He pauses as the path dips down to the beach. 'I studied forensic psychology years ago, but the only advice I can give you is common knowledge.'

'What's that?'

'It's going to be someone you trust. Killers love watching an investigation unfold. They often stay close to the police, even volunteering to help.'

Jeff delivers the statement with quiet certainty, echoing my own beliefs. Serial killers see their campaigns as a game, often prepared to risk capture for the sake of gaining the upper hand. When I turn to my father's old friend again, his features are even more drawn, his pace slowing.

'Take a rest, Jeff, you don't look well.'

Ginny Tremayne is hurrying along the path towards us, her expression concerned when her friend lowers himself onto a boulder, his skin waxy.

'I told you to stay indoors, you old fool,' she says. 'Why can't you follow doctor's orders once in a while? Come on, let's get you home.'

'You're an angel, Ginny.' The psychologist looks upset when she helps him back onto his feet. 'I hope you find her, Ben. Sorry to leave early.'

I watch Jeff hobble back down the path, his hand on the medic's shoulder, with a pulse of envy. It's been years since I could lean on anyone that hard. I even put Nina in another search group to avoid complications. The thought recedes from my mind as the search takes us past Watermill Cove. The light is fading now, but it's still one of the most beautiful spots on St Mary's. The sand is pure white, full of mica and crushed shells, no buildings in sight except Nina's rented cottage, half-hidden by trees. The ocean spills across the horizon for miles, the colour of tarnished silver as the sun plummets towards the horizon.

A shout goes up as I reach the shoreline. A woman is calling my name and I see Elaine Rawle crouching by the high-tide mark. She's dressed in jeans and walking boots, clutching something in her hands.

'Jade's got a bag like this,' she says. 'I've seen her carrying it.'

I don't bother to put on sterile gloves before taking the bright red handbag; the brine will have scoured away every fingerprint. It's festooned with seaweed, but the man-made fabric is still glossy, the zip functional. When I upend its contents onto the sand, a set of keys, a phone, and a purse land at my feet. Jade Finbury's name is printed on the first credit card I see.

'It's hers, isn't it?' Elaine's voice quavers, her eyes brimming.

'You did well finding it. This could lead us to her.'

Leo Kernick lingers at the edge of the crowd, hiding from the truth, until I call his name.

'Anyone could have chucked her bag into the sea, couldn't they?' His voice is almost too quiet to hear, behind the waves beating on the sand. 'It doesn't mean she's been hurt.'

I can tell he's clutching at straws, trying to pretend his girlfriend's safe even though the returning tide has dumped her possessions at our feet.

Another shout goes up while I'm checking for more items inside the bag. Tom Polkerris jogs across the shore with a sodden jacket flapping in his hand. It's like the one Jade wore, with the Isles of Scilly Travel Company logo on the lapel, sending a hush over the search party. The killer may be so afraid of being caught he's abandoned the elaborate staging from his first attack, but this time even Kernick can't deny its significance. He stumbles away, until one of the other searchers goes to comfort him. Jade Finbury may have been killed metres away from Nina's holiday cottage, her body cast into the sea.

'Keep moving, everyone, please. Let's finish our search before it gets dark.'

Leo Kernick returns as the party continues its journey. He kneels on the sand, head bowed over his girlfriend's belongings. I expect him to raise his camera to photograph the credit cards, keys and make-up strewn across the sand, just as he records everything else he witnesses. But this time he surprises me. He gazes at his girlfriend's possessions in silence for a long time, his face a blank mask when he finally rises to his feet.

36

The search reveals nothing else, and the light has died by the time I lead my team round the headland, with Jade Finbury's possessions gathered inside an evidence bag. Eddie's team is waiting at Bar Point. The sergeant's expression announces that his search was fruitless, and phone calls to Isla and Lawrie give the same disappointing result. I send everyone home, after thanking them for their hard work, making sure the women walk in groups rather than risking the journey alone.

Eddie looks upset when he sees the items we recovered from the shore. 'Do you think she drowned, boss?'

'It doesn't fit the killer's MO, but he may be trying to fool us. He took so much more care over the first murder. Either he's got a surprise in store, or she's persuaded him to keep her alive.'

Jade Finbury's things are still tucked under my arm while we walk back to Hugh Town. If she can buy herself more time, we may yet find her alive. It surprises me that the killer is getting sloppy, taking the risk of throwing the pilot's bag into the sea at ebb-tide, knowing the returning waves might deliver it into my hands.

It's 9.30 p.m. when we reach town, and I've got one more visit to make. Eddie looks exhausted, so I send him back to the hotel, leaving me to check on Harry Jago alone. The boy will be sober by now, and I need the information he's hiding more than ever. His sister answers my knock, the girl an odd mixture of confidence and timidity. Lily keeps her head up when she finally allows me inside. There are two empty pizza boxes on the dining table, but no sign of Harry.

'I need to speak to your brother, Lily.'

'He's sleeping.'

'Wake him for me, please.'

'Harry's too weak for any more questions tonight. I'm taking tomorrow off to look after him.' The girl stands her ground, her manner transformed from the shy creature I saw at the hotel. 'He's done nothing wrong. You can't just come after him because he's got a record.'

'I got him cleaned up. That's not my idea of harassment.'

I can tell she's scared, but she'd walk through fire to defend her brother. It's a shame the pair have no older relatives on St Mary's. I remember my own anger after my father died; I could easily have come off the rails without family to keep me on track.

'Has he said who hurt him yet, Lily?'

'He fell coming home from the pub.'

'The pavement didn't give him that black eye.'

She keeps her mouth shut, her gaze averted. I don't know whether she's afraid her brother will be arrested, or hiding secrets of her own.

'Tell me about Harry and Sabine. Were they seeing each other?'

'He took her out on the boat, that's all. Harry flirts with plenty of girls; it doesn't mean anything.' Lily rises to her feet like she's planning to chase me from the property, but her shoulders are trembling, filling me with pity. She should be spreading her wings, not using all her energy to fight her brother's corner.

'I admire you for defending Harry, but he needs to be at the station bright and early tomorrow morning. If he tells me the truth he won't be in any trouble.'

Lily gives a grudging nod, then follows me down the hallway, clearly longing to see me gone. I'm still not convinced that the boy would harm anyone seriously, despite his habit of picking drunken fights, but he spent time with Sabine and may have information we've missed. I'll have to ask the right questions tomorrow to get past his defences.

My head's still buzzing when I return to the hotel, so I take a walk to settle my thoughts. The garden is at its best at night, the blossoms releasing their scent into the dark. I collapse on a bench to check the messages on my phone: another text has arrived from the hospital, letting me know that Hannah Weber's condition is unchanged. The island seems to be stuck in a continuous loop, like in *Groundhog Day*, running over the same terrain without making progress. I force my body to relax as the roses' clean scent fills my airways, but a familiar sound disturbs me. Shadow's bark is unmistakeable. My dog chases down the path, scattering gravel in a wild spray, before jumping onto my lap.

'Don't patronise me; I know she's your favourite.'

Nina appears while the dog makes desperate efforts to lick my face. 'He ran off before I could grab him.'

'That's Shadow for you. He's got a will of his own.'

When she sits beside me on the bench, half of me wants to run for cover, while the other half wishes the dog would leave us in peace. Her hair is clipped back from her face, revealing the soft curve of her jaw. The urge to reach out and touch is getting harder to resist.

'I'd better say goodnight. Tomorrow's another early start.'

'Stay, just for a minute, Ben. Did your group find any trace of the missing woman?'

'We collected some of her things from the beach.'

'That's good, isn't it? It might lead you somewhere.' She runs her hand down Shadow's back, smoothing his fur. 'Everyone's so upset. A woman was crying her eyes out on the walk back to town.'

'Who's that?'

'She told me her name's Elaine Rawle. I spoke to her for a while; the whole thing's raised bad memories about losing her daughter. She'd heard I'm training to be a counsellor and asked if she could speak to me before I leave.'

'What did you say?'

'That I'm not qualified yet, but I'd be happy to meet for a coffee tomorrow morning. I don't mind listening if someone's upset. It sounds like she never managed to release her grief.'

'The attacks have got everyone on edge.' I turn in her direction, forcing her to meet my eye. 'Why did you come back, Nina?'

'I'd forgotten you don't do small talk,' she says, smiling. 'Why not leave it for another night? You look exhausted.'

'Now suits me fine.'

'Do you want me to be honest?'

'It's better than a lie.'

She gazes down at her hands. 'I was in pieces last time I came to the islands. Simon had died a few months earlier, and I hadn't begun to accept it. The landscape helped, and the solitude, but meeting you confused everything.'

'Why?'

'It felt like being unfaithful; the guilt nagged at me. That's the only way I can describe it.' When she looks at me again she seems relieved, as if she's shifted a burden from her shoulders to mine. 'Do you still read all those old American novels? I remember your shelves were full of Steinbeck and Hemingway.'

'I've bought plenty more since then; I bet they're more fun than your heavy-duty textbooks. How come you switched from being a chiropractor to counselling?'

She shrugs. 'The mind's more interesting than the body. Emotional pain can be crippling, can't it?'

'So they say.' Her words echo Jeff Pendelow's comments about the effects of stress, and it's easy to imagine her as a counsellor, serene and reasonable while her clients vent their fears.

'I don't want any bad blood between us, Ben.'

'We'll have that drink before you leave, if the case closes in time.'

'I'd like that.'

When she rises to her feet, Shadow circles us, still uncertain where his loyalties lie.

'Keep him with you tonight,' I say. 'He snores like a trooper, but he's a decent guard dog. Which room are you in?'

She points at a ground-floor window, where a yellow light glows behind closed curtains, directly below my room. I'd love to follow her inside, even though the timing's wrong. She's only come back to lay old ghosts to rest.

Nina disappears into the building, but it takes me a while to follow suit. When I return to my room the sound of her violin drifts through the floorboards, its notes high and restless. I lie down on the bed fully clothed and stare at a stray beam of moonlight on the ceiling. The only woman I've ever struggled to forget is too close for comfort, but she's not my biggest concern. I won't forgive myself if Jade Finbury doesn't make it home alive.

37

Lily is doing her best to calm Harry down. An hour has passed since Kitto left, but he's pacing the floor of his room, refusing to get back into bed.

'They're after me, Lily, I heard what Kitto said. I should go to the mainland and start over.'

'You've done nothing wrong.'

'He won't believe anything I say, with my track record, and he knows Dad's doing time. I'll take the boat tonight.'

'You can't cross forty kilometres of rough sea in a tiny speedboat.'

'It's my best chance.'

She leans forward to touch his arm. 'Why are you so afraid?'

'I didn't deserve Sabine.' There's a look of shame on his face. 'I was too drunk to protect her.'

'Stop punishing yourself.' She gives a frustrated sigh. 'Tell me who hurt you.'

'I don't know. He put a hood over my head, then kicked me senseless. I thought I was going to die. He'd gone by the time I came round.'

'You're not going anywhere tonight. You need to rest.'

Harry gives in at last, finally returning to bed. Lily is so exhausted by worry, she falls into a dreamless sleep once her own head touches the pillow, but silence wakes her in the middle of the night. She can always hear her brother through the wall, shifting in his sleep, but now there's only the distant sound of waves retreating from the shore. When she throws back her duvet, Harry's room is empty. Instinct makes her pull on jeans and a T-shirt before going downstairs. Her brother has left the house, his blue hoodie missing from the coat stand.

She peers out of the front door at the empty street, the houses opposite in darkness. He may have gone looking for late-night drinking companions. It's only when she retreats inside that she spots a manila envelope on the hall table, bearing Harry's name. It's been opened already, another Polaroid photo dropping into her hand; a woman's terrified face stares back at her. Why has someone sent Harry a picture like the one of Sabine just before she died? Maybe he got in the killer's way and now he's being targeted.

Lily covers her mouth with her hand to stop herself crying out. A few words are scribbled on the back, but she can't concentrate well enough to read them. She shoves the photo back into the envelope then puts on trainers and rushes outside. She drops the envelope into the dustbin as a car engine further down the street chugs into life. All that matters is finding her brother before it's too late. He must have gone to his boat after all, so desperate to escape he'd risk a dangerous crossing. She sets off at a rapid pace, running to the outskirts of Hugh Town, where the streetlights end. Lily wishes she'd brought a torch, but at least the moon will guide her search.

She's out of breath by the time she reaches Porthloo Beach. Relief overtakes her at the sight of the speedboat, beached on the sand, and fragments of starlight littered across the ocean's surface. He can't sail anywhere until the tide rises again. The sea whispers to her as waves greet the shore, as quiet as a lullaby. She shouldn't have panicked. He's probably with one of his mates, making drunken jokes about his overprotective kid sister. She's still relaxed when a hand settles on her shoulder. The touch is gentle and familiar, her fear lifting at last.

'You gave me a scare, Harry.'

But when she swings round a figure in dark clothes stands there, his face hidden by shadows. She tries to run, but blows rain down on her ribs and back. Lily is only half conscious when her body is dragged across the sand. She sees a last glint of moonlight, before being pushed into a car boot, head first, too weak to scream when the lid slams down.

PART 3

'Upon the whiteness of her robe the dew
distilled, and on her veil
And on her cheek of carvéd pearl that
gleamed so pale.'

'The Dead Bride', Isabel Ecclestone Mackay

38

Thursday 8 August

Something rattles beside my ear at 7 a.m. It takes me a while to realise that the mechanical buzz is my phone, vibrating on the bedside table. Steve Keast gabbles in my ear, telling me to meet him at Porth Hellick Pool. He rings off before saying why, but the panic in his voice makes me haul myself out of bed. The hotel is silent now that so many guests have returned to the mainland. When I run across the grounds, there's no one to observe the spectacle of a hefty man trying to sprint like Usain Bolt. Hugh Town looks deserted too, apart from a few lobstermen unloading their catch onto the quay. My thoughts are still spiralling when I set off in the police van, the countryside passing in a blur of elm trees and late summer flowers.

I park on Carn Friars Lane then jog down the track to Holy Vale. The kids at Five Islands School often come here for nature lessons about birds and butterflies, but there's no time to admire the wildlife today. The lake opens in front of me, glittering with early sunlight. Steve is on the far side of the water, his hand raised in greeting; he's dressed in running gear, his face gaunt. My friend's constant smile is missing today, his movements jittery as he rubs sweat from his forehead.

'What is it, Steve?'

'Come and see for yourself.'

He leads me deeper into the woods. The area is popular for family picnics, but the atmosphere feels darker today, even though light is falling through the tangled branches, leaving a dappled pattern on the ground below. Steve comes to a halt when we reach a clearing, his face so blank with shock it looks like he's about to pass out.

'Rest for a minute,' I tell him. 'I'll take over now.'

The place looks peaceful at first, just a circle of ground ringed with saplings. But my eyes catch on a pale outline, half hidden by branches. The white shape comes into focus as I get closer. A second bride is hanging from a high branch, her bare feet level with my eyes. The skewed angle of her neck brings nausea to my throat. I've missed something vital, and another victim has paid with her life. I already know it's Jade Finbury, even though a veil obscures her face, just like Sabine. Her chestnut hair is adorned with flowers. When I touch her foot, her skin feels cool, despite the morning's warmth.

My heart is drumming an odd tattoo when I phone

Gannick and the pathologist, but anger is already sinking back into my core, where it can't do damage. My friend is sitting on a fallen tree trunk, his head resting in his hands.

'It's Jade, isn't it?' he asks.

'We'll need to do a formal identification later.'

'I know it's her.' Steve's voice is rising to a shout. 'I only saw her last week in the pub. Who the fuck's doing this, Ben?'

'I'm close to finding out.'

'How many more have to die before then?'

'None, I hope. What made you go running so early, Steve?'

'I need more stamina for the swimathon. That's not a crime, is it?' His stare is laser-sharp. 'I can't believe you were sniffing round our place. Do me and Paul seem like murderers to you?'

'No, but women are being killed. I have to treat everyone the same.'

'You're making a mistake.'

'There are procedures we have to follow, Steve. Surely you get that, don't you?'

He rubs his hand across his mouth, pulling himself together. 'Sorry, I shouldn't blame you, but this'll knock Paul sideways. He's spent two years hoping Jade would go back to him.'

'I didn't know they had a relationship.'

'You missed plenty when you fucked off to London. Their fling was pretty intense. She hated the farm taking all his time, so they started rowing. When Paul asked her to ditch Kernick, they were both too proud to compromise.'

'Where is he now?'

'At home feeding the livestock, and don't blame this on him. There's no way he'd hurt Jade.'

A shrill noise rings out before Steve can speak again. I recognise it before he pulls his RNLI bleeper from his pocket, summoning the lifeboat crew down to the harbour.

'Get moving, Steve, we can talk later.'

He seems eager to leave, jogging down the trail then breaking into a sprint to escape the murder scene. Despite his complaints, his brother has just become my chief suspect; Paul Keast is the only islander with links to both murder victims. He was rejected by Sabine, had a painful break-up with Jade, and he's Harry Jago's boss. I can't imagine Paul applying make-up to the faces of his victims, but it's possible he's found an accomplice. If he's the killer, I can't guess where he took his victims: every building on St Mary's has been searched, as well as the island's coastline. Jade's death makes me even more certain that the killer knows the landscape well enough to stay one step ahead of the investigation.

I focus my attention on the body while I wait for help. The killer's neat workmanship is in evidence again: a heavy-gauge rope has been tied around a branch, with a professional-looking knot. He must be physically strong to haul her weight so far off the ground. When

I look at the tree again, the killer has chosen a Cornish oak, which may have its own symbolism. I can't lift the veil until Gannick arrives, in case forensic evidence is lost, but I'm certain her dress is simpler than Sabine's, the plain muslin rippling in the breeze. Another gold wedding band has been placed on Jade's finger, even though she shunned permanent commitments while she was alive.

I'm still absorbing details when a car pulls up on the lane, and muffled voices drift through the trees as my helpers enter Holy Vale. Gareth Keillor arrives first, followed by Liz Gannick, and deja vu hits me while photos are taken, the body lowered to the ground.

It takes several hours for the crime scene protocol to unfold, filling me with frustration. When Keillor finally lifts the veil, Jade Finbury's carefully painted face makes a grotesque contrast with her tortured expression. There are no cuts on her exposed hands or feet to explain the blood Gannick found in her kitchen, but the wound may be concealed by her long dress.

Keillor remains silent as he scribbles details for the death certificate, only sharing a few pieces of information before he leaves. Marks on Jade's wrists prove that she was tied up, like Sabine, and there's no sign of rigor mortis, which means she died in the last four hours. The news that we missed finding her alive by such a narrow margin adds to my list of regrets. Eddie looks solemn as he winds yellow and black tape between the trees, creating a cordon around Jade's body, but it's Isla I'm worried about. The constable's first big case has become a hunt for a serial killer. Her eyes are glassy when I catch her leaning against a tree; she looks so fragile, my fear that she could be involved finally lifts.

'Go back to the station, Isla. There's plenty of work there.'

'I'm okay, boss. It just feels a bit surreal.'

'How do you mean?'

'I'd never seen a dead body before Sunday.' She's dry-eyed but her voice is cracking. 'Jade was my role model all through my GCSEs and A Levels – she started working here when I was about fifteen. I even thought about training as a pilot for a while.'

'Why not take a break, if you need one?'

'I don't want special privileges.' She lifts her chin, like a fighter heading for the ring. 'What happens now, sir?'

'We keep whittling down our list of suspects. I want to know who had the capacity and a motive to kill Jade.' The young PC appears calmer when I look at her again. 'Can you call Leo Kernick for me, please? Tell him I'm on my way.'

She pulls her phone from her pocket, even though her hands are shaking, and my admiration increases. Plenty of new recruits would crumble at the sight of another corpse, but she's coping with the worst duties policing can offer. When she addresses Kernick her voice is completely calm.

'He's waiting for you at his studio, boss.'

Under normal circumstances two officers would inform the partner of a murder victim of the bad news, but Isla and Eddie are needed at Holy Vale and Lawrie Deane is organising another public meeting. I won't have the luxury of company when Leo Kernick hears of Jade's death, forcing me to gather my thoughts as I drive across the open moorland. The sunlight has intensified while I've been in the woods, humid air cloying in my throat. The beach is deserted when I park the van, apart from a local family playing volleyball on the sand, the kids laughing uproariously at each other's mistakes.

The photographer is outside his studio when I arrive, smoking a cigarette. His thin face looks haggard, as if his rock-and-roll lifestyle has finally caught up with him, exhaustion painting dark circles under his eyes. He fires out questions before I've even crossed the car park.

'What's this about? Have you found Jade?'

'Can we talk inside, Leo? It's best if we sit down.'

Kernick's studio still looks chaotic, but fresh images have been pegged to a line. They're black and white pictures of his girlfriend, beaming for the camera, unaware of her fate. I try to deliver the news gently, but his shock looks real. Tears pour down his cheeks while he absorbs the truth. If he's bluffing, the man deserves an Oscar for the hollow-eyed misery I can see on his face.

'Last time we were together I had a meltdown. She drove off before I could apologise.'

'She'd have forgiven you eventually.'

'I was too stupid to say I loved her. Anger got in the way.'

'We've all made mistakes, Leo, it's not your fault. Is it okay to ask a few questions?'

'If it finds the bastard that killed her.'

'Where did you go after the search last night?'

He drags a crumpled hankie from his pocket. 'I couldn't face going home, so I went to the Mermaid.'

'Who did you see there?'

'Ginny Tremayne for a while, then Frank Rawle walked home with me at closing time. He's an old friend.'

'Really?'

'Photography's one of his hobbies. I let Frank develop his pictures here.'

'Have you got any more questions, Leo?'

His face is vacant. 'I can't believe it. She's only thirty-four years old.'

'Someone can stay with you for a while. Would that help?'

'Nothing will, I need time alone.'

Kernick looks broken when I say goodbye, but it could be an elaborate show. I'll need to call his neighbours and find out whether they heard him going out again, late last night.

Instinct tells me to return to the crime scene and follow every lead, no matter how trivial, but DCI Madron is waiting for news. I climb back into the van to make the call and keep my gaze focused on the beach while I wait for my boss to pick up. My throat is so dry when I describe the second fatality, it feels like I've swallowed sand. Madron normally spits out curses when he's angry, but this time the silence at the end of the line sounds ominous, his tone flat with disappointment.

'I'll take over as SIO, but I'm stuck here for now. The Eurotunnel workers are on strike, and flights are packed for the next two days. Don't do anything without consulting me.'

Madron hangs up without ceremony, but no matter how harshly he judges me, it won't match my own regret about Jade's death. It should be easy to safeguard the population of a small island, but my failure has cost another life. The pilot didn't deserve her fate any more than Sabine Bertans, and Hannah Weber remains dangerously ill. I'm certain the answer is right in front of me, if only I could see it. When I focus on the beach again the family group is still there, with their picnic basket and bottles of lemonade. Some people on St Mary's seem happy to ignore the evils we're facing. I check my phone before setting off, but there's just one message from Julian Power. He's checked the museum's records again but found no reference to the sailors' charms, shutting down another avenue to understanding the killer's mindset.

39

The weather is finally changing from endless sunshine to the threat of rain my uncle predicted, with clouds massing in the sky. The air is so loaded with humidity I feel stupefied when Isla finally comes back to the station by mid-morning. The young constable looks drained, so I give her the menial task of inputting report outcomes while I check our incident board. It's covered with photos from the first two crime scenes, but nothing yet about Jade Finbury's murder. I still can't find anyone connected to all three attacks. Paul Keast is linked to two of the victims, but I've got no proof that he met Hannah Weber. The killer has thrown us a curveball by making his first two attacks coastal, then choosing an inland location for the third, taking the pilot from her own home.

He picked another of the island's beauty spots to display Finbury's body. A friend of mine had his wedding pictures taken in Holy Vale last summer; the dappled light and woodland setting looked romantic in the pictures, but the location has lost its innocence now. I'll never forget that bridal figure swaying in the breeze. But why is he turning his victims into dead brides, while no men have been transformed into grooms? Plenty of male tourists and overseas workers visit the Scillies, without attracting his wrath. Hatred mingles with reverence when he transforms his victims, dressing them in traditional white.

I need to see Harry Jago before making any decisions. He's the only person on St Mary's with a history of stealing: he could have taken the items from the museum to sell to another islander. He's not answering his mobile, so I set off for his rented home again on foot. Hugh Town is eerily silent, like it's trapped in the eye of a storm. The only human activity I can see is a pair of canoeists paddling between vessels moored in the harbour, their movements slow and languid, like they have all the time in the world.

Jago is dressed in boxer shorts and a ripped T-shirt when he finally opens his door. The boy's face is less swollen than yesterday, but still covered in ugly scrapes and bruises, his expression groggy. His drink problem must be more serious than I thought, his hands trembling at his sides.

'You should have been at the station first thing. Didn't Lily pass on my message?'

'She's not here.'

I step past him into the hallway. 'Get dressed, please; we need a chat.'

The boy traipses upstairs with all the enthusiasm of a schoolboy being sent to do his homework. He's still sulking when he returns to his untidy kitchen. The fridge contains little except a six pack of beer, but I empty a carton of orange juice into a pint glass then shunt it across the table.

'They say Vitamin C cures hangovers.'

He swallows a mouthful, then grimaces. 'You're wasting your time. I told you, I don't know anything.'

The boy's sullen expression proves that his trust in the police expired when his dad went to jail, his own sentence providing the final nail in the coffin. He looks wary, as if another brutal beating could start at any minute.

'When did your drinking start, Harry?'

'What's it to you?'

'I'm sitting here; we may as well have a conversation.'

Jago's story arrives in broken sentences. He didn't want to leave Plymouth after his dad's conviction. His drinking began at fourteen to impress his new school-mates in Hugh Town. Knocking back cider behind the bike sheds became a badge of honour, making him seem harder than the rest. His mother tried to stop him, but it was a losing battle. He'd steal money from her purse then get older friends to buy his booze. The craving triggered his shoplifting too. When the boy finally stops talking, his expression is stunned, like he's amazed to have spilled his secrets to a policeman. I was exactly the same after my father died, lost and afraid, hiding it all behind a show of bravado. There's no way this kid's got the concentration skills to carry out such sophisticated attacks.

'School didn't work for me either,' I admit. 'Playing rugby gave me an outlet.'

'I'm shit at ball games.'

'Run or swim then; burn off some energy. It'll help you make better choices.'

The boy stares back at me, but I know he's listening. He's not stupid, just vulnerable, and his life will fall apart if he carries on drowning his sorrows.

'Another woman's been killed, Harry. It's time to explain, if you know about any threats Sabine was facing.'

'It's not my fault.' A tear rolls down his cheek. 'She was kinder than everyone here, except Lily.'

'Did you nick that jewellery from the museum?'

The boy flinches. 'Why do I get blamed for everything?'

'You're not in trouble, but I know you were seeing Sabine. I just need the truth so no one else gets hurt.'

'This is bullshit.' His voice is raw with strain, like he's been caught red-handed. 'You'd arrest me if you had any proof.'

'The bloke prefers killing women, but you're in danger too, if you know anything. Did he beat you up for getting too close?' Jago carries on studying the table's worn surface. 'Where's Lily? I thought she was taking today off to look after you.'

'My sister's given up on me. She prefers her cushy hotel job.'

'How do you pay the rent? Your wages can't cover it.'

'Some of the islanders are helping me.'

'Such as?'

His answer is slow to arrive. 'Father Michael, Julian Power and the Rawles. Mum cleaned their houses, so it's for her sake, not mine. That's why Paul Keast gives me work too.'

'What happens when their charity ends?'

'Mum left some savings.'

'And when that's gone?'

'I don't look that far ahead.'

The boy slumps in his chair, eyes closed. Instinct tells me he stole the items to cover his overheads, but there's no proof. If he's got information about the killer, he's too scared to say.

I can't waste more time on an interview that's going nowhere, so I tell him to contact me if he remembers anything relevant. Harry doesn't bother to show me to the door, and frustration makes me feel like yelling curses at the sky. It's filled with dark ridges of cloud while I've been inside, chasing in circles.

I'm about to return to the station when I spot an envelope sticking out of the dustbin. Something shifts inside my chest when I pick it up. Harry's name is scrawled across the front, in the same forward-sloping handwriting I saw in Jade Finbury's kitchen. The photo inside is nothing like the ones displayed in Leo

Kernick's studio. It's an extreme close-up, revealing terror and fury in the pilot's expression. The bastard forced Jade to address the envelope before killing her, just like Sabine. When I turn it over, Jade has scrawled another phrase on the back: *Come winter or summer, no queen can compare.* Why hand-deliver that cryptic message to the boy's home, if he's not involved? I hammer on his door again, but he must have been watching. He's locked it from the inside.

'You stupid little shit,' I mutter.

I take a few steps back then ram the door open with my bodyweight, in time to see Jago sprinting across Porth Mellon beach from the back window. The boy is already too far away to catch. There are a dozen paths he could follow, and the island's coves and woodland make ideal hiding places, but he must know more than he revealed, and his sister probably shares his secret. Anger washes over me as I leave the house, still clutching the envelope. Whoever posted it through Harry's door has scared him so badly he's running from the one person who could keep him safe.

40

Lily can't see anything when she opens her eyes. A blindfold blocks her vision, and a sharp pain is jabbing at her side. The air smells of mildew, its dampness lingering on her skin. There's blood in her mouth when she swallows, but she feels no sense of panic. Her mind is too numb to register emotions. She needs to stand upright, and stretch her aching limbs, but her arms and legs are tightly bound.

When she lifts her hands, her wrist scrapes over a rough wooden surface. Nails hold the planks together, inches above her face. The air is growing heavier with each breath. She's always hated the dark, but her fears have been imaginary until now: if no one finds her soon, she'll suffocate. Lily yells for help, but her voice is a cracked whisper. She's locked inside a home-made coffin. Panic squeezes the oxygen from her lungs, her breathing so rapid she loses consciousness.

The next time Lily comes round, there's a moment of clarity: at least she'll get to see Sabine's killer face to face. She concentrates on slowing her breathing, until her ribcage rises and falls more steadily. She wants to be fully conscious when the man returns. Her brother's name is the last word Lily whispers before blackness smothers her again.

41

Leo Kernick is outside the police station when I return at 1 p.m. I don't have time to help him, but he's in no mood to be ignored. He sways towards me, with anger glinting in his eye.

'Let me see Jade, to say goodbye.'

The photographer's voice is guttural, his body language so aggressive, I keep a space between us, despite having a four stone weight advantage. I've seen every type of grief reaction over the years, but one hundred per cent of Kernick's rage is centred on me, as if I'd killed his girlfriend with my bare hands. The man's anger intensifies when I explain that Jade's body still hasn't been brought to the mortuary. He throws a punch that fails to connect, but I grab his wrists, bracing his arms at his sides.

'Calm down, Leo. I don't want to arrest you for assault.'

The guy breaks down suddenly, sobbing on my shoulder, his fury melting into tears. He's in such a raw state, I can't send him home alone. I flick through names in my head, trying to decide which islander would provide the best support. Kernick mentioned that Frank Rawle was a friend, and my old headmaster has been offering his help since the case began. The photographer's weeping has been replaced by a whispered mantra as he repeats his girlfriend's name. Kernick appears beyond reach, but allows me to lead him to the Rawles' home.

Church Street is quiet when we arrive, the inhabitants unaware of the pilot's death. Elaine Rawle is trimming the hedges in her front garden, at home for once, instead of toiling at the museum. Her Labrador is relaxing in the sticky heat, tongue lolling. The woman's movements are graceful when she walks towards us, her expression anxious. I can see shock registering when she hears of Jade's death. It seems cruel to burden her with it, when her own painful memories have resurfaced. Elaine's movements are gentle when she touches Leo's arm.

'Come in, sweetheart. I'll call Frank. He's only gone to the shops.'

'No need,' I tell her. 'Just keep Leo here while he recovers, please.'

Elaine murmurs quiet words of comfort to the photographer, before leading him inside. The house reflects the couple's personalities perfectly. The hallway is panelled with sombre dark wood, the floorboards gleaming. Their living room contains old-fashioned

Chippendale-style furniture, and even the artworks look respectable: oil paintings of local beauty spots, so accurately drawn they could be photographs. The Rawles' kitchen is a throwback from a previous era, with a butler sink, oak table and ladder-backed chairs.

Elaine helps Leo Kernick into a seat, but he seems oblivious to his surroundings, his eyes glazed while she busies herself making tea.

'How on earth did it happen?' she asks. When I explain about Jade's death, her eyes glisten with tears. 'What kind of monster would do that?'

Her words echo every islander's opinion, except the killer, who is sure to be enjoying his latest success. I can tell it was the right decision to bring Kernick here; the peaceful atmosphere should restore his calm. I notice some framed photographs by the front door when I leave, their colours faded from long exposure to daylight: they show a fair-haired young woman smiling at the camera, sitting in a flower garden. Elaine pauses beside me, her voice calmer than before.

'That's our Leah, a few months before she died.'

'She's beautiful. It must have been tough on both of you.'

'Frank's been an amazing support, and talking to Nina helped this morning. She gave me some new insights. Would you thank her for me?'

'Of course.'

'All this violence has plunged me back into the past, but I'm sure it will fade, once it's over ...' Her speech dulls into silence, as if exposing her frailty to one of her husband's former pupils embarrasses her. 'Grief's a strange emotion. You think you've dealt with it, then it comes back to hurt you again.'

'Are you sure you don't mind taking care of Leo?'

'I want to, Ben. He's a friend of ours.'

'Don't leave him alone, please. He's still in shock.'

'Frank will be back soon. We'll both keep watch, don't worry.'

The Rawles' dog has wandered back inside, stationing himself by Kernick's chair, as if he too intends to offer comfort. Elaine looks pensive when she opens the front door for me.

'Did Julian know about the sailor's charms?' she asks.

'He tried his best, but they're not mentioned anywhere in the archive. I still don't know who donated them.'

She shakes her head. 'That's odd, when we've got details about everything else. Do you want me to do some phoning round when Frank gets back? Someone must know which family they come from.'

'That would be great.'

I can still hear Leo Kernick weeping when she hurries back to her kitchen to care for him.

Once I'm back outside I notice the hospital has left me a new message, saying that Hannah Weber has had a seizure, her condition critical. The news rocks me back on my heels. I'm not prepared for the killer to claim a third victim, my breathing ragged as I leave

Church Street and jog up the hill. Visiting Hannah Weber's bedside won't improve her chances of survival, but something forces me to see her again before continuing my search for her attacker.

Ginny Tremayne looks grave when I reach the hospital, the medical terms she uses flying over my head. All I can gather is that Hannah's life hangs in the balance. When I peer through the glass panel in the door, the priest is at her bedside once more.

'I asked Michael to come, so she's not alone,' Ginny says. 'We should know in the next twenty-four hours whether she'll survive. If there's significant brain damage, her vital functions may start shutting down.'

'Are you sure she can't be airlifted to the mainland?'

'The flight would cause more trauma. I doubt she'd survive.'

The atmosphere has changed when I enter Hannah Weber's room. This time the priest doesn't notice my presence. He's holding the woman's hand, head bowed as he whispers his incantation. I recognise enough Latin words to know he's reciting a mass. Hannah's face is as pale as her hospital-issue pillowcase, a drip feeding saline into her veins, while her oxygen mask clouds with each ragged breath. I'd like to offer up a prayer of my own, but I've always been quietly certain that God doesn't exist. All I can do is promise to catch whoever tried to kill her on Halangy Beach.

42

Eddie is at the station when I get back in the early afternoon; the others are still with Gannick, stopping walkers from entering Holy Vale. He listens in silence to my explanation of finding the envelope addressed to Harry Jago, and the boy running away, afraid to confess what he knows. My deputy studies Jade's picture at length, but the image reveals nothing about where she died. The new line of verse written on the back seems to follow on from the one on Sabine's photo:

> *The bride in her glory will ever be fair,*
> *Come winter or summer no queen*
>   *can compare.*

Stuart Helyer may have been right about the lines coming from a wedding ballad, but even the island's oldest resident can't remember all the lyrics. The song will die with him, like the lobstermen's knowledge of the sea.

'Why would the killer send Harry the photo?' Eddie asks.

'It's a reminder not to talk if he witnessed something. I think he scarpered because he's terrified of giving secrets away.'

'So it's someone Jago knows well?'

'It's time we arrested Paul Keast. He gave Harry his summer job on the boat, and two of the victims rejected him. Maybe he's angry enough to destroy lives, under that quiet surface. He's the only name on our list with links to more than one victim, except Leo Kernick, who photographed them all.'

Eddie looks relieved. 'I know he's your friend, but there's something weird about him, isn't there? Paul's always been the secretive type. Plenty of women seem to fancy him, but he's too wrapped up in his own world to notice.'

'I'll bring him in straight after the meeting.'

'The islanders are arriving at three o'clock. I don't envy you, announcing Jade's death. She was popular with everyone.'

'My job's easier when things go well, that's for sure.'

Madron's threat to replace me as SIO is still ringing in my ears, but I keep my mouth shut. The team needs to stay focused on the investigation, not be distracted by my failure to close the case.

The streets are quiet when I walk to Church Street, with just a few islanders hurrying to the meeting. St Mary's community has arrived in force, and the atmosphere inside the hall feels stifling. My audience needs to believe we're making progress, even though the killer has struck again. A sea of blank faces stares back at me. People resent the threat to their safety, and the disruption to island life, shocked whispers circulating the room when I announce Jade's death. Many of her closest friends are in the audience, although Leo Kernick and Frank Rawle are absent; I'm relieved the photographer has stayed in his friend's care. When I look for the Keast brothers, only Paul is present, his arms folded tightly across his chest. Steve and five other members of the lifeboat crew are still at sea, towing a stricken yacht back to harbour.

I'm hit by a barrage of questions when I finish speaking. Public opinion is turning against us, even when I provide clear answers. Elaine Rawle is in floods of tears. She's sitting beside Rhianna Polkerris. The hotel manager looks stunned, as if she can't believe another woman has died. The only person who appears content is Liam Trewin. The satisfaction on his face proves that the American is enjoying my discomfort. He may not have perpetrated the attacks, but our last conversation has left its mark, and he remains a suspect. Nina is at the back of the hall with Shadow at her side. The expression on her face could be sympathy or pity, but I'd rather not have her present while I battle for the community's trust.

'We need your help, now more than ever,' I tell the crowd. 'I want to speak to Harry Jago urgently. If you see him, please report it to us immediately. Take care of yourselves and your neighbours, whether it's day- or night-time. Don't go walking alone, and keep your properties secure.'

I ask for information about Jade's last movements, telling everyone to speak to my team after the meeting. The atmosphere in the hall remains hostile, raised voices criticising us for failing to find the killer. Shopkeepers and hoteliers are still furious about cancelled bookings, and the ferrymen are out of pocket, with no tourists travelling between the islands.

Eddie stands by the door when the meeting ends, placating the islanders who have remained behind. My deputy's people skills have always outstripped mine. He sends the group away reassured, his polite manner keeping everyone on side.

'Good work, Eddie. You handled that perfectly.'

He glows like he's been awarded a medal. 'Paul Keast's waiting, boss. I told him you need a word.'

'Send him in, then wait here, please. I need you as a witness.'

Most of the islanders left in a hurry, scattering chairs in their race to the exit, but Paul doesn't seem to notice the mess. His face is void of emotion when he leans against the platform's edge, facing a jumble of empty seats. My old friend's air of detachment is even stronger today. I've trusted him since childhood, but since my return to Scilly there's been a distance between us, putting the relationship under strain.

'Are you okay, Paul?'

'I should have seen she was in danger. Maybe I could have done something.'

'How come you never told me about you and Jade?'

'Getting dumped by an amazing woman isn't my favourite topic.' His eyes blink shut for a moment.

'When did it end?'

'Two and a half years ago.' There's a hard edge to his voice, as if the memory prompts anger, as well as regret. 'Steve was doing a contract farming job on the mainland to get us out of a financial hole. I was working so hard Jade got neglected. She deserved more of my time.'

'Did you try to win her back?'

'She accused me of being married to my job, and she was right.' He carries on staring into the middle distance. 'Farming can take over your existence, but I won't let it happen again.'

'The break-up must have been painful.'

'I hated bumping into her for a while, that's for sure.' The misery in his voice is mixed with the kind of anger that causes serious damage.

'Why didn't you talk to someone?'

He barks out a dry laugh. 'Can you imagine me on a therapist's couch?'

'There's no shame in it.'

He shakes his head. 'It's tragic she's dead, but my life's moved on. I've met someone else. The situation's messy, but we'll figure it out.'

Paul's tentative speech doesn't convince me. Steve

would know if he'd found a girlfriend, or the other islanders would be gossiping about an illicit romance. He seems like a different person from the good-natured lad I played rugby with twenty years ago, his brother's shy sidekick, the butt of many affectionate jokes. His face is taut with strain, but it still takes effort to set aside old loyalties, even though Paul is the only islander with a clear link to both murder victims. He's Harry Jago's boss too, which could explain why the boy's so twitchy. Paul is fit enough to deal out the brutal beating Jago received. I can't prove that he followed Hannah Weber before she was attacked, but his farm is the closest property to her rented cottage in Juliet's Garden. So many factors link him to the attacks, I have to take action, even though it will end our friendship once and for all.

'I can understand you targeting Jade and Sabine, but why Hannah Weber?' I ask.

'Sorry?'

'Why go to all that fuss with the dresses and make-up?'

His eyes widen. 'You're not making sense.'

'Paul Keast, I'm arresting you on suspicion of murdering Sabine Bertans and Jade Finbury, and attacking Hannah Weber. You do not have to say anything, but it may harm your defence if you do not mention, when questioned, something you later rely on in court.'

'Are you serious?' he says, gaping at me. 'I've never hurt anyone.'

'We'll discuss that at the station.'

My old friend's expression is chilling. I've only witnessed that much repressed fury a few times before, on the faces of convicted murderers.

43

Eddie acts as custody sergeant when I escort Paul back to the station. There's an uncomfortable wait while my deputy completes the custody paperwork, then makes our suspect empty his pockets. Paul asks a stream of questions, still protesting his innocence, but my time on the Murder Squad taught me that even prolific killers rarely confess at point of arrest. Once his possessions have been bagged and recorded, he's led to the holding cells. The station's internal walls are so thin, I know the exact moment when Paul Keast loses his liberty, the cell door clanking shut, followed by a key twisting in the lock, but he'll have a long wait before our interview, because he's entitled to legal representation. Solicitors are hard to find in such a remote place. There are just three in Scilly, and one is currently on maternity leave, the other two on holiday abroad. Keast will remain in his minute cell, with only a mattress and barred windows for company, until a lawyer can be flown over from the mainland.

I've called a team briefing for 5 p.m. this afternoon, leaving just a couple of hours to review crime scene evidence and answer messages. Dozens of islanders are reporting last sightings of Jade Finbury, while others just want to vent their frustrations. Paul Keast's arrest nags at me. Even though he fits the stereotype for a killer perfectly – quiet and obsessive, with limited social skills – we still need hard proof. The farmhouse he shares with Steve has been searched thoroughly, but no clear evidence has come to light.

Lawrie Deane looks jaded when the team file into Madron's office for the briefing at five. The sergeant seems disgruntled after chaperoning Liz Gannick at the crime scene, then organising the public meeting. Isla is still so bright-eyed it's easy to forget she's been working since dawn, while Gannick scrolls through notes on her tablet, too distracted by forensic details to pay full attention. Eddie is last to arrive, his expression pensive. The Keast brothers are respected members of the community; it will shock the entire island if Paul turns out to be the murderer.

I have the whole team's attention when I announce Keast's arrest, but other names remain on our suspect list. We need to find Harry Jago urgently. The boy may have been dragged into the killer's slipstream, stealing the items from the museum and receiving a photo of Jade Finbury as a warning to keep his mouth shut. Liam Trewin's name has been struck from the suspect list. The American has only visited St Mary's twice, and his hotel room is too pristine for a murder scene. All of the staff at the Star Castle have sound alibis, with no previous criminal records. Serial killers normally have a record of violence before embarking on a murder spree, but no one on the island has committed a serious crime.

I turn to face Liz Gannick. 'Can you give us an update?'

She abandons her tablet at last. 'I've just had a result from the lab. The blood on Jade Finbury's floor doesn't match her DNA, which explains why there's so much around her sink. If she grabbed a knife and wounded her attacker, he'd have washed the blood away.'

'You think she hurt him?' The idea makes sense; the pilot was tough and independent. She would have fought hard to defend herself.

'A flesh wound can shed plenty of blood without being life-threatening. It looks like he dressed it himself, to avoid seeking medical help, and removed the weapon from the scene.'

'So our killer's injured, and a blood sample would prove his guilt.'

'You only need a mouth swab for a DNA match.'

'Let's take one from Paul Keast now; that'll decide it for us.'

'You'll have to wait twenty-four hours for results, but there was more evidence at Jade's murder scene. I found a footprint right beside her body. It's from a size ten trainer.' Gannick drops a sheet of paper in the middle of the table. 'I used an adhesive gel sheet to lift it.'

The monochrome image shows every nick and scratch on the sole, the details as incriminating as a fingerprint.

'That's great, Liz. Can you get over to the Keasts' farm to check Paul's shoes and his van straight away?'

'Let me finish what I was saying.' Gannick gives me a withering look. 'The killer left a trail through the forest; he hauled her fifty yards to the clearing. This was on the ground near Jade's body.'

She passes me an evidence bag, which contains a small gold locket with a broken chain. It's a simpler design than the other two, bearing the engraved outline of a ship, like the others stolen from the museum. A date is inscribed on the back, from the early 1900s. It looks just like the other sailors' charms, made of Cornish gold, to remind a new bride to pray for her husband while he toiled at sea.

'The chain must have broken when he carried her into the wood,' says Eddie. 'I haven't had as much luck tracing Jade's dress. It's from the UK's biggest online bridal store.'

Isla frowns as she peers down at the locket. 'They'd be beautiful gifts if the women were alive,' she mutters. 'Why does he love and hate them at the same time?'

Our new constable blushes when the words slip from her mouth, but I've been asking myself the same question. The tenderness he shows towards his victims, by adorning their bodies with jewellery and weaving flowers through their hair, doesn't match the violence

287

of their deaths. It's possible we're looking for two killers. At least Gannick's news has dragged the case forwards: we've got the killer's DNA and his footprint, but if he's got an accomplice, it won't be long before another victim is targeted.

44

Lily's blindfold has been removed when she wakes again, and her surroundings have changed. She's inside a fisherman's shack; the air tastes of salt, decaying fish, and seaweed. It's getting dark, the gaps in the wooden walls admitting little light. Someone has lain her on her side, ribs aching with every breath. The ropes around her wrists and ankles keep her tethered in place. She's so thirsty her tongue sticks to the roof of her mouth, but her senses are working overtime. The sea must be close by, because the sound of waves hauling shingle up the beach murmurs through the walls.

The darkness is thickening, leaving only the shapes of objects behind. She can just make out a net hanging from the wall, and a pile of lobster creels. When she tries to move again, her clothes feel different; silk caresses her legs, the texture far smoother than the rough fabric of her jeans.

Something shifts in the dark, triggering a new spurt of panic. Has the killer been sitting there, watching her sleep? It's only when Lily looks again that she understands the room is empty. Her own movements have caught her eye, a mirror reflecting her attempts to squirm free: she's swathed in white from head to toe, the dress immaculate against the darkness. The killer has turned her into a ghost already, even though her heart is still beating.

45

I spend most of my evening digging through evidence forms, hunting for the missing element, until Madron calls at 9 p.m. The DCI's voice is scratchy with irritation when he explains that he's still stuck in Brittany, unable to return for twenty-four hours. My boss's negativity rings in my ears, even when I tell him about the team's hard work and Paul Keast's arrest. He reminds me to follow the murder case protocol accurately before ending our conversation. I'd love to have the kind of boss I could consult about strategies, but danger always sends Madron into a head-spin, leaving me to make every decision alone. The responsibility weighs heavily tonight, like the memory of Jade Finbury's body hanging from the oak tree. The pilot was a little younger than me; there's no knowing what she could have achieved, if she'd survived.

When I check on Paul Keast in his holding cell, he's on his feet, clearly expecting an immediate release. I explain that a solicitor will fly over from Penzance tomorrow, but Keast kicks the wall, too furious to meet my eye. Innocent or guilty, his arrest has terminated our thirty-year friendship, just as I predicted, and his brother feels the same. Steve marched into the station after the lifeboat rescue to call me every name under the sun, forcing me to caution him for abusing an officer.

I'm returning to my desk when someone knocks on the station door. Elaine Rawle is standing in the porch, giving me a tired smile.

'I thought you'd like an update on Leo. He's staying with us tonight, but he's in a wretched state. Frank's comforting him, but I needed a minute on my own. I can't bear listening to him crying his heart out.'

'Someone else can give him a bed, if you'd prefer?'

'We'll look after him. That's how things work here, isn't it? He'd do the same for us.' Her gentle gaze settles on my face. 'I've had no luck with the sailors' charms yet, but I'll keep trying.'

'Thanks so much for your help.'

Elaine's attitude echoes the rule most islanders live by, often putting others' needs above their own. The Scillies may be marooned in the Atlantic, far from the mainland, but no one gets abandoned when a crisis hits. After she's gone, I linger in the doorway, watching storm clouds race across the night sky.

I scan the incident board again when I get inside, tiredness blurring the photos and diagrams. Twenty islanders still have no watertight alibis, because they live alone, but the only ones with a clear motive to hurt any of the victims are Paul Keast, Leo Kernick and Harry Jago. I still don't understand why someone would go to such lengths to dress the women as brides. Pulpit Rock, Halangy Beach and Holy Vale are all popular sites for wedding photos. The killer must be physically fit to overpower his victims then place them in a vehicle we can't locate. I still feel certain that the sailors' charms are important, because the killer went to great lengths to get them. It's frustrating that Julian Power has had no luck finding out which family donated them to the museum.

Eddie returns to the station just before 10 p.m. He's offered to guard Keast in his holding cell tonight, because we can't leave a prisoner unsupervised on police premises. It's a relief that he's volunteered, giving me time to clear my head. Finbury's death – and my failure to find her killer – has nagged at me all day. I need time alone to consider the evidence. Lily Jago still isn't answering her phone, and I can guess why: her brother may have told her where he's hiding, leaving her reluctant to be interrogated. I'll have to track her down at the hotel first thing tomorrow.

The young sergeant settles into his chair after dumping a takeaway box from the fish and chip van by Porthcressa Beach on his desk, but he doesn't seem interested in his meal. He's already scrolling through this morning's crime scene report from Liz Gannick. His passion for his job is obvious, despite the latest murder. He barely notices me preparing to leave.

'Don't work all night, will you, Eddie?'

'I'll take breaks, don't worry.'

His statement doesn't convince me. Eddie is motivated by finishing any race first, no matter how much effort is required. He hasn't realised yet that murder investigations require time to reflect – and a helping of good luck.

The temperature is lower when I go outside, the sea's cool breath a welcome relief after weeks of oppressive heat. I'm glad to let the investigation slip to the back of my mind, but reluctant to return to the hotel. I'm heading for the quay when someone walks towards me down the hill. His back is bent over, as if he's carrying the world's burdens on his shoulders, the street light too dim to reveal his features. It's only when he crosses the street that I recognise Father Michael.

'Have you been with Hannah all this time, Father?' I call out.

He comes to a halt beside me, his face drained. 'She's so ill, I couldn't walk away.'

'Is she any better?'

'No change, but they say hearing is the last sense we lose. I hope she got comfort from my readings.'

'I'm sure she did. The words are beautiful, aren't they?'

'The psalms are my favourite. Most of them are pure poetry.'

'Are you heading home?'

'After I've had a drink at the Mermaid. I rarely indulge, but tonight's an exception.'

'Mind if I join you?'

'Please do, I'd enjoy the company.'

The priest's gaze remains locked on the pavement, oblivious to the sea widening in front of us, and the off-islands glittering like distant stars. He only seems to relax when we reach the Mermaid. It's the smallest, rowdiest pub on St Mary's and was my favourite drinking den in my teens. The bar area is tiny, with old wooden floorboards and walls lined with nautical memorabilia, including ships' compasses, sharks' teeth and scrimshaw, from the days before whaling was banned. It's packed solid at the weekends, but the place is quiet tonight, just a few old boys perched on bar stools, grumbling among themselves.

Father Michael looks grateful for the pint of bitter I place in front of him. 'That's just what I need.'

'I've never seen you drink before, Father.'

'Call me Michael, please. I don't suppose you remember my hellraising days.'

'You grew up in Scilly, didn't you?'

'My parents ran a flower farm here on St Mary's, but labouring outdoors didn't suit my ambitions. I planned to get rich quick, as a businessman on the mainland, and anyone that said different got a pasting.' He gives a wry laugh. 'You can imagine the misery I caused my poor family.'

'You seem pretty calm now.'

'Because I got it out of my system. I fought so much as a teenager people told me to take up boxing.'

'But you found God instead?'

'It was the other way round.'

'How do you mean?'

'He came for me, before I was ready. I woke up in the middle of the night and his presence filled the room. It was terrifying and beautiful at the same time.' Fervour makes the priest look young again. 'I had no faith at all, but suddenly I was lit up like a Christmas tree, glowing with certainty.'

'Like falling in love?'

'I had plenty to atone for, yet my guilt melted away. Catholics call it the divine light; it's a pity I've never seen it again.'

'Why do you stay in the priesthood?'

'I can't give up whenever my belief falters. We're all being tested, aren't we?'

'It's felt that way today.'

His gaze is so penetrating, he seems to be auditing the contents of my soul. 'Want me to pray for you, Ben?'

'I'd rather you said one to find the vicious bastard behind the attacks.'

'I'll drink to that.' He hesitates before lifting his glass. 'But I heard someone was arrested today. Haven't you caught your man?'

'An arrest isn't a conviction. I still need to understand why a killer would dress his victims as brides.'

'It makes no sense.' He stares down at his drink. 'I've conducted hundreds of marriage ceremonies during my priesthood, but it's normally the brides who fret about costumes, not the men. The grooms are so in love, their partners could walk down the aisle in jeans and they wouldn't care.'

'You think the killer's female?'

'Or a man who missed his chance.' His voice sounds wistful. 'He could be jealous of everyone who wears a wedding ring.'

'Did you ever consider marrying, before the priesthood?'

'I fell for a girl, head over heels. She was perfect as far as I could see, even though she was troubled. A music student with a passion for the islands. The only saving grace is the empathy I got from the pain of losing her, but that's a story for another night.'

Loneliness echoes behind the priest's words as I say goodnight. When I look back, Father Michael appears to be paying a high price for his faith, his shoulders hunched over the table as he nurses his beer.

46

It's 11 p.m. when I walk back to the hotel, my system still revving with nervous energy. The building is lit up like a ghost ship against the dark, its corridors empty, but the eerie quiet doesn't soothe me. I could do a few dozen press-ups or watch late-night TV to empty Jade's death from my head, but neither option appeals. I'm about to run a bath when Shadow's piercing howl echoes through the floor, steadily rising in volume. Nina must have left him alone for some reason. I know from bitter experience that the only remedy is immediate action, before he destroys the hotel's furniture.

The canine screams have become blood-curdling when I get downstairs. Nina is wearing a bathrobe when I knock on the door, her expression panicked.

'Have you been torturing him?' I ask. 'I wouldn't blame you; he can be a pain in the arse.'

'I left him alone for five minutes to take a shower.'

'He can't stand his own company.' Shadow jumps up

to greet me when I enter her room, then the howling continues. 'Have you fed him lately?'

'Half an hour ago.'

'Then he must want fresh air.' I pull up the sash window and Shadow leaps through the opening, without a backwards glance. 'Only hunger or claustrophobia upset him that much.'

'Thank God you understand him.'

Nina is keeping her distance. She's on the far side of the room, her hair still wet from her shower. It's her steady gaze that draws me, or the fact that so much of her bare skin is on display, crying out to be touched.

'Don't look at me like that, Nina.'

'Why not?'

'It got us into trouble before.'

'I've always enjoyed looking at you. Why should I stop?'

She stands her ground as I close the gap between us. When she lays her hands on my shoulders there's no going back; her eyes are wide open when I kiss her for the first time in nearly two years. She presses herself against me, pulling me close. The lines of her body are imprinted on my memory, but her skin is softer than I remembered, her touch more urgent. She fumbles with the buttons on my shirt, her breath warm against my throat. My job's easier – I only have to undo her bathrobe for it to slide to the floor. There's no need to think once she's naked in my arms, my body on autopilot. I'd forgotten how beautiful she is, those long legs that go on for miles. I try to slow down, but it's impossible. I watch her eyes blur, her head thrown back as she loses control, then it's all over, much too fast. I'm still wearing most of my clothes and we're both on our feet, her back pressed to the wall, laughing like fools. I kiss her again, then draw back to look at her. She's still smiling, her skin flushed with pleasure.

'That wasn't my best performance.'

'It worked for me,' she replies. 'Let's aim for the bed next time.'

We share some wine from her minibar and talk about the past year. Nina admits that going home to Bristol was harder than she expected; her husband's belongings filled every room, his clothes still hanging in the wardrobe. She visited her grandparents in Italy for a month, the long sunny days helping her to heal. Her stay in Rome made her decide on another career change.

'I've always been fascinated by how people think,' she says. 'Counselling seemed like the right choice.'

'You worked me out pretty fast.' I've always been daunted by how many details her pale gold eyes pick up.

'I can see the investigation's weighing on you.'

'Why would a killer set out to hurt young women, then dress them up as brides?'

'To possess them, maybe?' Her voice is growing drowsy.

'That could be it.' I watch her drifting into sleep. 'Did you come back to find me, Nina?'

Her eyes open again, suddenly wide awake. 'What do you think?'

'I'm not a mind reader, just tell me.'

Nina's reply is physical, not verbal. Moonlight streams through the open window, the air turning silver when she rises over me. She presses me back against the pillows, her hips rocking against mine. The second time is more satisfying than before, slower and more memorable. I fall asleep with her arms around my neck, waking just once in the middle of the night to see Shadow leaping through the window. He spots my discarded clothes on the floor, then turns in a circle three times, before using them as his mattress.

My eyes blink open again when morning's first light floods the room. Nina doesn't stir when I drop a kiss on her shoulder, but Shadow is bolt upright, watching my every move. His eyes are a hard, judgemental blue.

'She's not for you, mate. You're canine, she's human,' I mutter.

I scan the room again, where aspects of Nina's complex personality are on display: a copy of *Dombey and Son* lies on her bedside table, her violin propped in the corner beside a psychology textbook, and a yellow bikini drying on the radiator. The woman is impossible to categorise, because she covers so many bases, her unreadable smile just part of her charm. If she travelled here for my sake, she'd never admit it. My only certainty is that the physical connection between us is even stronger than before.

Nina is still sleeping when I ease out of bed, her breathing slow and regular while I put on the clothes Shadow has covered with dog hair. He replaces me on the bed with a look of triumph, settling in the hollow of Nina's back. I'm about to leave when I spot a small photo album by her suitcase. Curiosity makes me leaf through the pages. They're from her wedding a decade ago. I've begun to hate images of brides, but Nina looks beautiful and carefree; her husband thrilled to be marrying his Italian princess. Simon Jackson is blond and slim, just a few inches taller than his new wife. Maybe she chose me for the simple reason that my hulking build is so different. Seeing her dressed as a bride makes me so uneasy I lock the window on my way out, checking twice that it's secure.

I stand under the shower for a long time in my room. Nina's situation won't change, no matter how much time passes. I'm still competing with a ghost, and the odds are stacked against me, because memories grow glossier with time, compared to the present's gritty challenges. She'll return home to Bristol on Sunday morning, but it's the wrong time to think about the future. I can't let anything distract me from the case.

47

Friday 9 August

I visit the hotel's kitchen at 7.30 a.m. looking for Lily Jago. The staff are catching up on cleaning tasks, scrubbing the floor and cleaning fridges, while the hotel is almost empty. Just a few cooks are slicing tomatoes and grilling bacon, preparing for the small cohort of guests. The head chef looks irritable when I ask if she's on duty.

'Lily's half an hour late. I'm not thrilled, believe me.'

'Ask her to call me when she arrives, please.'

He gives a curt nod before applying all his concentration to the eggs he's whisking, as if producing a perfect omelette was a matter of global importance. It's possible that Lily has had a change of heart and returned home, but Harry sounded certain she'd written him off as a lost cause. I need to speak to her urgently now her brother's run away. It's time Lily gave up the secrets she's hiding.

The Polkerris's flat is in a remote part of the hotel that I missed while Eddie searched the staff's quarters. The castle's top floor hasn't been renovated, with plaster crumbling from the walls, leaving the original stone exposed, the air cooler than the temperature outside. Tom Polkerris looks shocked to see me when he opens his door. He's wearing a sweat-stained tracksuit, dark hair sticking to his scalp. The hotel manager stands squarely in the doorway, blocking my view of his apartment. His stance reminds me of the way he lorded it over the younger kids at school, often reducing them to tears, but his boyhood arrogance is missing today, his expression wary.

'Sorry to bother you so early Tom.' I point at his trainers. 'Have you been running?'

'I try to use the gym before our guests wake up. Is something wrong?'

'Lily Jago hasn't reported for work.'

His eyebrows rise. 'She took leave to spend time with her brother, but she should be back by now.'

'Can I check her room, please?'

Polkerris looks reluctant to comply, but manages a polite smile. 'You'll have to wait in here while I change. Our guests can't see me like this.'

The man's living room occupies one of the castle's towers, its high windows giving a view over the staff accommodation block and the off-islands on the horizon. A pile of laundry has been dumped in the corner, newspapers strewn across the furniture and used coffee cups on the table. I can't imagine Rhianna tolerating such chaos; it would clash with her flawless appearance. Tom soon returns, dressed in a sleek suit and polished brogues.

'Is Rhianna already in the office?'

His gaze wanders to the window. 'We've been working so hard, she's having a lie-in.' The man seems in a hurry to leave, his defensiveness raising my suspicions.

'I need to see her, please. She may have spoken to Lily recently.'

'I'd rather not wake her.'

'She manages your staff, doesn't she? It won't take long.'

Polkerris leaves a pause before replying. 'Rhianna's not actually here.'

'I thought not. Why did you lie, Tom?' I park myself on his sofa, unwilling to move until he gives me a convincing story.

'We're getting a divorce. She's using a guest suite that's due for refurbishment; no one knows we're splitting up.'

'Why not?'

'The staff might be distracted. We need to pass the inspection with flying colours or both our careers will suffer.'

'What went wrong between you?'

He blinks at my direct question. 'We ran out of steam soon after our wedding. Our families ploughed thousands into making it a special day, because Rhianna wanted everything perfect.'

'Was splitting up your idea?'

'I suppose so.' His words falter. 'Something was missing; I had no choice.'

The man looks crestfallen as we set off to find Lily Jago, but his manner changes once we reach the ground floor. He produces an upbeat greeting for every staff member we pass. Polkerris's distress about the end of his ten-year relationship is so well-hidden, he's like an actor rehearsing a new role. He seems to be skilled at concealment. It dawns on me that he could easily have used the fire exit to follow Sabine Bertans on the night she died. The man's a free agent now he's living alone.

'Shall I try Lily's phone again?' he asks.

'Do it while I search her room, please.'

Most of the girl's worldly possessions appear to be crammed into the confined space. A dozen photos are tacked to the wall above her bed, from the days before her family fell apart. There's a braided rug on the floor and a menagerie of toy animals strewn across her bed, as if she's yearning for the simplicity of childhood.

'She's not answering,' Polkerris says. 'Lily's never missed a shift before.'

I don't know whether the panic on the hotel manager's face is real or fake, after watching him camouflage his emotions so effectively. An object on the girl's bedside table gives me a jolt when I scan the room again; it's a bright pink phone with floral stickers on its case. I know immediately that it's Sabine's. But why is it in Lily's room, unless she's been hiding the truth? When I try to switch it on, the battery's dead. I'm searching for a charger when the hotel porter appears in the corridor.

'I've been looking for you, sir,' he says, before passing me a manila envelope. 'This was hand-delivered for you during the night.'

I can tell already that it's from the killer. Tom Polkerris is watching me, so I keep my expression neutral when I draw the Polaroid photo of Lily Jago from the envelope. The image is different this time. It's been taken from a distance, showing Lily by a window, gazing out from the hotel's restaurant. The killer must have stood in the grounds, taking the snap unseen. He's not in a rush with his new victim. He hasn't even begun turning her into a perfect bride, but someone has written a few words on the back of the photo: *with the bride in her glory, be she ever so fair.*

'Take me to Rhianna, Tom.'

Polkerris fumbles for his phone. 'Let me call her first.'

I seize the mobile from his hand. 'Now, or I'll arrest you for obstruction of justice.'

My threat has the desired effect; Polkerris sets off to find his ex at a rapid march.

48

Lily can tell that a new day has begun because grey light is filtering between cracks in the boarded-up window. Her mind feels groggy, but her senses are more acute. She can smell varnish on the shed's rough walls and hear seagulls bawling, but she's never felt more alone. Even the sea has deserted her. She can no longer hear waves shifting across the beach. It must be low tide, hours passing while she's drifted in and out of consciousness.

Lily strains her wrists, but her movements only tighten her constraints. She looks for a way to free herself, but can only rub her hands against the table's splintered edge, to loosen the binding. The rope chafes her skin yet she keeps on trying.

'I have to go home,' she mutters.

She doesn't want to die like Sabine, before her life's even begun. When her gaze catches on the mirror, she stares at the bridal costume again. She used to dream of walking down the aisle like a fairy-tale princess, but her mother warned her that white weddings don't always bring happiness. Thoughts flit through her mind as her pain increases. She can only hoid onto an idea for moments before it slips out of range. She recalls her mother's kindness, Harry walking her home from school, and the conflict on Tom Polkerris's face when he touched her cheek.

Lily's mind is still racing when footsteps crunch across gravel, then the lock clicks open and misty light floods inside. She's too afraid to breathe. Instinct makes her fight her restraints, trying to yank her hands free.

'Who are you?' The words emerge as a hoarse whisper, but there's no reply before a blindfold covers her eyes.

He's standing so close she can hear him singing to himself, under his breath. The words are unclear, apart from the chorus about a fair bride. His voice is high and reedy, almost feminine. When his singing ends Lily knows she's being examined, panic threatening to make her scream, but she swallows hard to silence it.

'Let me go, please. I'm so scared.'

A hand settles on her shoulder, the touch lighter than before, then a bottle of water is held to her lips. She gulps it down, thirsty after being denied liquid for hours. Someone is keeping her head upright so she can drink without choking. The gesture is so gentle, Lily can't believe it's the killer.

'Why are you doing this?' she asks. 'Is someone forcing you?'

The hand withdraws, making her hold her breath, waiting for a blow that never comes. She can hear someone weeping, the sound low and mournful.

'Tell me what's wrong,' Lily says, keeping her voice steady. 'Maybe I can help you.'

There's no reply, but the hands are still tender when they

skim her collarbone. Lily flinches as a piece of cold metal slithers around her neck; the killer takes his time fastening the clasp, the tears ending as rapidly as they began. His footsteps sound heavy on the wooden floor as he crosses the shed. When the killer touches her again, her heart thuds against her ribcage: he's gagging her with a wad of cotton, making it hard to breathe. Her hands are bound together even more tightly, before she's dragged outside.

Lily is shoved into a confined space, her knees pressed against her chest, unable to call for help. It's only when a car engine starts, its vibrations making her body shudder, that she realises she's being driven to a new location. Exhaustion is taking its toll, her thoughts cancelled out by fear.

49

I follow Tom Polkerris back inside the hotel, my thoughts buzzing as we climb the stairs. Why have the victims' photos been hand-delivered to me and Harry Jago? Is the killer flaunting his power, or proving that we face the same danger? I can only be sure of one thing: Paul Keast didn't deliver the photo, because he was locked inside a holding cell. He could be working with a partner. If I'm right, his sidekick will go on attacking victims, even though the farmer is locked away. Either that or I've blundered down the wrong path, destroying two friendships in the process.

Rhianna fails to open her door, so Polkerris uses his master key. The smell of cigarette smoke taints the air, despite notices inside every hotel room warning guests not to light up, proving that she's a rule-breaker at heart. Rhianna has chosen a bigger suite than the one she shared with Tom, and its contents are more organised. The clothes in her wardrobe are arranged by colour; her shoes stand in neat rows, many still wrapped in tissue paper. But her sitting room reveals a side of her personality that fills me with discomfort. Dozens of magazines are heaped on her sofa, all dedicated to the wedding industry, with items ringed in red felt tip. Brides and grooms gaze out from the glossy pages, improbably good-looking, with blue-white smiles.

'She's still obsessed by bloody weddings even though I wasted all my savings on ours,' Tom says. 'You wouldn't believe how long she took planning it.'

'Rhianna could have dropped an envelope through the letterbox last night.'

'What do you mean?'

'She may know something about the murders.'

Polkerris looks shocked, unable to believe his ex is involved, but I can see how the killer might have exploited her obsession until anger about her failed marriage simmered to the boil. Maybe she resents other women's chances of romance now her own relationship is broken. I put my thoughts about the hotel manager's motives aside to focus on practicalities, aware that time is running out to bring Lily Jago home alive.

It's 9 a.m., and the island's perfect summer has been interrupted. Strong gusts of wind slow my progress down to the station, drizzle spitting at my face. I usher everyone into Madron's office to share the news that Lily has been taken. She could have been targeted because the killer knows she's been hiding information, including her possession of Sabine's phone.

'Rhianna could be involved in some way, but we have to find Harry Jago too. If he knows the killer's identity, he'll talk when he hears Lily's in danger.'

'What do you want us to do?' Lawrie Deane asks. Tension resonates in his voice – another young woman of his daughter's age has been abducted from streets that have been safe for decades.

'Use trusted volunteers to check every building, shed and barn again, to look for Rhianna and Harry. I want boats docked in the harbour searched too. If the killer's following his usual pattern he'll keep Lily hidden until nightfall, then leave her body in a location that's used for wedding photos.'

'I still don't get why he picked her,' Isla says. 'She's different from the other victims. Maybe that's why the photo's nothing like the earlier ones.'

'Lily's less confident, but she wasn't born here and she's single. He seems to hate women who remain separate from men.' I study each face in turn. 'I want to know who's spent time with Harry Jago. Start with our suspect list, but remember it could be some pillar of the community we haven't considered until now, and it looks like someone's helping him. That would explain the touches of romance, alongside all that crude violence. I'm going to see Jeff Pendelow for some advice. The rest of you can divide the island into sections; keep a list of properties you search. I want Rhianna and Harry Jago brought in this morning.'

'What happens to Paul Keast?' Eddie asks.

'Gannick's at the farmhouse now, looking for proof. He could have taken Lily before his arrest, if he's got a helper. Let his lawyer have a preliminary meeting, but delay the interview until this afternoon. It's more important we find his accomplice.'

'That solicitor's high maintenance; I bet she puts in a complaint,' Deane mutters.

'Book her a table at St Mary's Hall for lunch and cover her expenses. A high-class meal and plenty of gin and tonic should keep her sweet. We can hold Keast until early tomorrow morning, and we may need her input again.'

Isla and Eddie look upbeat about our chances of success, but Deane's face remains sullen. The old-timer seems to doubt my approach, remaining silent when I leave the team to organise the search. There are less than five hundred dwellings on St Mary's, but the open farmland is littered with caves, byres and sheep barns, making our lives complicated. The weather is worsening too; rain pelts the back of my neck as I leave the station, the sky darker than before.

The motorbike's engine coughs out a protest when I kick the starter pedal, as if it's feeling the strain, like me. I remember the anxiety on Lily Jago's face when I questioned her. She looked like a schoolkid being told off by a brutal teacher. I've seen her tough side too, when she defended her brother. She'll need to rely on that reserve of courage in order to survive.

The five-minute journey to Old Town passes in a

flurry of low stone cottages and flower fields, the sea appearing and vanishing between stands of trees. I'll need all the help at my disposal to track the killer down, including the islanders' expertise. I park the bike outside Jeff Pendelow's house, by Old Town Bay. The view doesn't calm me today; the sea is battleship grey, breakers cresting as far as the eye can see. The psychologist doesn't answer his doorbell so I walk inside like last time, calling his name. I find him stretched out on his settee, his skin blanched with pain.

'Sorry to disturb you, Jeff. I'm after some advice.'

'You're soaked, Ben. Let's sit in the kitchen, it's warmer there.' When he hauls himself upright, his movements are laboured as we walk down the hallway. 'Forgive the mess. Bending down's tricky right now, which is a great excuse to let things slide. Val would be appalled by the state of the place.'

The psychologist's kitchen looks cluttered but tidier than his unruly garden; the shelves are packed with utensils, which must be a daily reminder of his wife's passion for cooking, before her illness advanced. Jeff seems more comfortable once we're seated, with a pot of coffee between us. His gaze is curious as he studies me over the top of his glasses, as if he expects me to outline my fears and phobias so he can make his diagnosis.

'Another girl's been taken, Jeff. It should be easy to track the killer down – he's following the same pattern, but I know we're missing something.'

'Give me a quick overview. It's details about his

315

methods that could expose him.' The psychologist nods thoughtfully while I describe the killer's MO, scribbling notes on a foolscap pad.

'He captures his victims at night, removing them from the scene in a vehicle we can't identify. We've received photos of the women dressed as perfect brides, apart from the one he failed to capture and his latest victim. The attacks have happened at Pulpit Rock, Halangy Beach and Holy Vale. He transforms the women into idealised brides then strangles them, before displaying their bodies at beauty spots that are often used in wedding portraits. He seems passionate about the region. Historic items of jewellery made of Cornish gold, called sailors' charms, have been found on the victims' bodies. He gets them to write a line from an old wedding song on the back of their photos.'

'What's the connection between the victims?'

'They're all unmarried and leading independent lives; that's where the similarity ends. One was a Latvian student trying to improve her English by working in Scilly, then a German journalist, a pilot, and now another worker from the Star Castle.'

Jeff's frowning with concentration when he scans his notes. 'You say there's no sexual element, but he seems to love rituals. He's not just claiming them for himself, but for the Scillies too, by using locally crafted jewellery. I'd say you're looking for someone with a dissociative personality disorder. He can cause pain without experiencing guilt, and he's likely to be a skilled congenital liar or you'd have spotted him by now. Part of his pleasure comes from deception. Most serial killers enjoy power as much as violence.'

'What about his method?'

'I'm still thinking about the locations. They're all on the ancient pilgrim trail that cuts through the heart of St Mary's, aren't they? That's how Holy Vale got its name.'

'I'll look into that.'

'Strangulation's a horribly intimate way to kill someone. The killer can stare into his victims' eyes as life drains from their bodies. I imagine that makes him feel all-powerful.'

'Is there a specific trigger for this type of killing spree?'

'It could be a sudden spike in psychotic symptoms, or a resurgence of past trauma. A buried memory may have resurfaced, but this kind of violence never comes unannounced. He'll have hurt people before.'

'The guy lives on the island. We've probably chatted to him in the Co-op.'

'That's sobering, but not unusual. Two per cent of the world population has psychopathic tendencies,' he replies. 'He may be hiding his illness behind a mask of respectability, doing a high-status job. People with personality disorders are great at concealment.'

'Do you think he could have recruited a helper?'

'Psychopaths often prey on the most vulnerable.' He peers at me over the top of his glasses again. 'The objects he's leaving could unlock it for you. He believes those sailors' charms are sacred in some way.'

'I've thought that right from the start.' Jeff's words remind me of Julian Power, and his passion for collecting.

'I'm worried about your safety, Ben. He's on a mission and you're in his way. Guard yourself and the people around you. All of you need high-level protection.'

'Rhianna may be in danger as well.'

'The manager from the Star Castle?'

I nod in reply. 'There's a chance she's involved.'

'You know she's Catholic, don't you? She comes to mass occasionally.'

'Is that relevant?'

'There could be a religious element to the murders. Has it occurred to you that he may see his victims as impure?'

'How do you mean?'

'The white gown symbolised virginity years ago, didn't it? His victims are all mature enough to have a sexual history.'

'That's really helpful, Jeff. Thanks for your time.'

'Come back if you want to talk again.' He gets up slowly, with a fresh tremor of pain crossing his face. 'You know where to find me until this bloody back mends, but don't take my suggestions too literally. I was just trying to interpret his mindset based on the facts you gave me.'

'It's made me see it from a different angle.'

When I get outside, rain forces me to shelter under a tree, where I fire off a text to Nina, warning her to stay at the hotel. Breakers hammer the shore, the sound thunderous while I check my messages. Eddie's voice is so jubilant I can hear it above the tumult, telling me that Rhianna has been found wandering across Porth Minick Beach and brought to the station.

My ride back to Hugh Town leaves me drenched. No one else is braving the storm, only a few huddled sheep observing my journey. I'm soaked to the skin when I get back to Hugh Town, and the hotel manager's appearance is less polished than normal too. Rhianna's elegant clothes have been replaced by jeans and a T-shirt, with sand clinging to her trainers, blonde hair hanging down in rats' tails.

'We've been looking for you, Rhianna.'

'I was planning to come here, but I needed a walk to sort my head out.'

'Can you tell us how you've been spending your spare time?'

'There hasn't been much lately. I've worked non-stop, but it was pointless.' She keeps her gaze on the door, like she's longing to escape.

'Tom mentioned you're getting a divorce.'

'He wanted it kept quiet, but I should have refused. It's been a strain, pretending everything's fine.' She frowns back at me. 'His ego can't handle me walking away.'

'It was your decision?'

She nods her head. 'A month ago I finally met someone who cares about me. I need to know why he's been arrested. There's no way Paul's involved in Sabine's death.'

'You've been seeing Paul Keast?' My thoughts spin in a hectic circle.

'I bumped into him on the beach when I was taking a quick break from that bloody hotel. We've seen each other or talked on the phone every day since. He's so kind and gentle, the opposite of Tom. We're not going public as a couple until I leave the castle.'

'Even Steve doesn't know.'

'It's no one's business but ours. We've been stealing minutes together, late at night or early in the morning.'

'What made you buy all those bridal magazines?'

'I'm setting up a website for couples organising their weddings on a tight budget. It's a business I can run from the farm in my spare time, when I move in with Paul.'

'Your marriage ended because of him?'

'He's not to blame,' she snaps, her expression turning sour. 'Tom brought this on himself.'

'How do you mean?'

'He was unfaithful. My self-respect's been on the floor, but Paul's been amazing.'

'When did you find out Tom was seeing other women?'

Rhianna no longer resembles a china doll. Her cheeks are flushed with emotion, eyes red from crying, like a normal human. 'He can give you the grubby details. I'm not reliving it again.'

'Did you tell Father Michael about the break-up?'

'I don't need anyone's blessing to start a new life.'

Rhianna's tears have dried, the determination on her face convincing me that she would be hard to brainwash. She's upset, but not broken. I can tell she's ready to move on, with no lasting damage.

'We found your fingerprints in Sabine's room. How do you account for that?'

Her face blanks. 'I keep an eye on the staff from abroad, to make sure they're not homesick. I dropped by the day before she was killed.'

The story sounds credible, and I can't arrest her for buying two dozen bridal magazines or having an affair, but discomfort nags at me after she leaves. I ask Eddie to track her movements until we find Lily Jago. No matter which way I twist the information, the killer's obsession with brides remains a mystery.

50

I'd like to interview Paul Keast straight away after hearing Rhianna's claims about their relationship, but Jeff Pendelow's words linger in my head. The killer believes the calling cards have a powerful symbolism, and the only islander with such a reverence for objects from the past is Julian Power. I need to strike his name off my list of suspects before doing anything else, but when I walk to the travel company's office, the quay is deserted apart from a few seagulls fighting a vicious turf war. I pause outside the building, sheltering from the gusty wind coming off the sea. The location of Power's office is ideal for the killer's purposes: it allows him to watch female visitors arriving every time the ferry disembarks.

Power is at home when I call at his property beside Tregarthen's Hotel. He looks irritated when I explain that a further search is needed.

'Your officers ransacked the place two days ago.'

'It won't take long, I promise. Then I'd like a quick word about the museum's records, please.'

'What if I refuse?'

'I'll arrange a warrant over the phone.'

He gives an irritable sigh. 'Every room holds items of great historic value. Many of them are fragile.'

'I understand, Mr Power. I won't break anything.'

The man seems to expect me to hurl his treasures across the room. He hovers by my shoulder, proving his reputation as an oddball, but I remind myself that he's always been law-abiding. His spiky, condescending manner doesn't make him a murderer.

The scale of Power's obsession with collecting comes into focus when I climb to the first floor. His spare bedrooms are piled high with cardboard boxes, but when I peer inside a couple, they only contain tarnished silverware, pieces of china and Art Deco lamps. Power has run out of space, but his appetite for antiques is unquenched.

I'd need weeks to conduct a full search, so I limit myself to hunting for spaces where a victim could be hidden, but Power's hoarding makes it unlikely. The master bedroom is so packed with items, he must have to clamber over boxes every night to reach his bed. He seems reluctant to meet my eye when we get back downstairs, anger or embarrassment making him look away.

'Are you absolutely sure there's no mention in the museum's records of the family that donated the stolen items, Mr Power?'

'I told you, I've checked the ledger twice.'

'Can I see it, please?'

He chunters under his breath before leading me to his office. My eyes linger on a wall display of quills and inkpots, until I see a dusty leather-bound book, held together with ribbon. Its bindings are falling apart from age and overuse.

'It took me hours to read it cover to cover,' he complains.

The scale of the challenge hits me when I look inside. The handwriting is so small, it takes me several minutes to decipher one entry, which describes a gift of carved whalebone to the museum in 1932.

'Can I borrow it for a while?'

Power looks horrified. 'That ledger's irreplaceable.'

'I'll take care of it. Sorry to trouble you again, I didn't realise you had such a large collection.'

His shoulders relax by a fraction. 'It will all go on show eventually; the museum is the sole beneficiary in my will.'

Power gives the first heartfelt smile I've ever seen him produce. The man's passion for his collection runs so deep, he seems to welcome the prospect of dying so it can be viewed by the public at last.

Lawrie Deane is placating the solicitor we invited from the mainland to advise Paul Keast when I return to the station. Mary Tunstall looks close to retirement age, and she's ignoring the islands' relaxed dress code. She's wearing a pinstripe suit, her dyed auburn hair scraped back to reveal a sour expression. Tunstall shares her frustration about the interview being delayed the minute I arrive. Apparently the Met Office are predicting record-breaking rainfall over the next twelve hours; she needs to get back to the mainland before the predicted deluge arrives. Her mood shifts from irritation to outrage when she hears that Liz Gannick is conducting a forensic search of the Keasts' farmhouse, even though the brothers signed a consent form.

When Paul is finally brought to Madron's office he looks more vulnerable than before. He's unshaven, the shadows under his eyes proving that his night in custody was sleepless. Tunstall looks pleased when he answers all my initial questions with a terse 'no comment'. His expression only changes when I ask about his relationship with Rhianna Polkerris.

'She believes in me,' he says. 'Steve can move to the mainland, and we'll stay together on the farm.'

'I found dozens of bridal magazines in her room. She could have helped you to hurt those women.'

'Tom Polkerris would do that, not me. He treats women like dirt; that idiot humiliated Rhianna for years.'

The contempt on my old friend's face could be for show, but his anger seems real. It could be because his killing spree has been halted, or that he's felt overlooked for years. Until now he's been eclipsed by his brother's confidence. Gannick has found no hard evidence at the farmhouse that he was involved, and his role in the murders is looking less certain.

Our meeting ends with a reminder from the solicitor that her client must be released after thirty-six hours in custody unless the CPS agrees a special dispensation, or the arresting officer will be in breach of the law.

Tunstall's high heels tap out a victory march on the lino as she leaves, reminding me that lawyers inhabit a strange moral universe. They will defend anyone for money, even when the counter-evidence is over-whelming. I look Paul in the eye before he's returned to his holding cell, but I can't tell whether he's glad or ashamed to have stonewalled most of my questions about the women's deaths. Madron's office has never felt emptier when I'm left alone by the window, watching rain clouds race across the sky.

51

Lily can't tell how long she's been locked in the boot of the car, her throat parched with thirst. She's exhausted when the killer hauls her into his arms again. He's panting for breath as he carries her down a flight of stairs, then lays her on a hard surface that's covered with plastic. It sounds like he's shifting furniture, something heavy dragging across the floor. When her gag is finally removed, she's too afraid to scream, her voice a dry whisper.

'If you let me go, I won't talk to anyone, I promise.'

He makes a hushing sound, but more words spill from her mouth.

'My brother needs me. Please, you can't do this—'

Suddenly a hand covers her nose and mouth. It presses down so hard, she can't breathe. Lily is on the verge of blacking out when the pressure finally lifts, allowing her to inhale. She's too terrified to speak when the hands touch her again: this time she's hauled into a chair. After lying down for so long, the sudden change of position makes her head spin. She can feel him loosening the bindings around her wrists, then a heavy chain tethers her ankles to the chair leg.

The footsteps retreat, followed by a door slamming, before she can breathe freely again. She's afraid to move, but the rope is so loose it only takes minutes to free her hands – the chafed skin on her wrists burns, yet she's too relieved to care. When she pulls back her blindfold a brilliant square of light sears her retinas. Lily gazes around at a huge vaulted room with brick walls and no windows. The only source of illumination comes from a mirror directly in front of her. It's circled by small lightbulbs that cast a savage glare, like in an actor's dressing room. A tray of make-up lies on the table, containing mascara, eye shadow and foundation. A young girl's photograph is propped against the mirror, her face unfamiliar. Lily normally avoids studying her own appearance; it's too homely to celebrate, but now she has no choice. Her face looks thinner than before, blanched by fear, with hollows under her eyes. She looks down at a sheet of paper that lies on the dressing table, to avoid staring at her own reflection.

It contains a single sentence, printed in bold handwriting.

IF YOU CAN BECOME THE GIRL IN THE PHOTO, I'LL LET YOU LIVE.

Lily's heart beats too fast when she read the words again. She has always hated the oily texture of make-up on her skin, but now she must learn how to use it. She must abandon her own image to stay alive.

52

It's 2 p.m. by the time I catch up with Eddie; the young sergeant's upbeat mood seems to have vanished.

'Gannick just called,' he says. 'There are no trainers matching the print in Holy Vale at the farmhouse, and the blood at Jade's house isn't Paul Keast's.'

'His arrest warrant will lapse by 10 p.m. tonight if no new evidence is found.' Paul may have hated Jade and Sabine for rejecting him, but there's no solid proof he hurt them, and the news about his new relationship undermines his motive for going on a killing spree.

I stare at our suspect list again, with Eddie at my shoulder. Tom Polkerris is still a suspect. He seemed to have a jaded view of white weddings, but his obsession may run even deeper than his ex's, and he had the perfect opportunity to watch Sabine and Lily at the hotel. The cruelty he showed as a boy may still be driving him.

'What do we do now, boss?' Eddie asks.

'Let's speak to Polkerris first.'

Isla stays behind, sifting through Liz Gannick's latest report. Lawrie Deane is still with the forensics chief at the Keasts' farm, but I'll need to bring the team together soon to plan tonight's safety arrangements. Everyone on St Mary's needs our protection, including Lily Jago. If the girl's still alive the killer will be preparing to display her body tomorrow morning.

There's no sign of Tom Polkerris in the Star Castle's reception area so Eddie and I march down the narrow corridor. I rap once on the door of his office, before barging inside to find the hotel manager kissing one of the hotel's waitresses, his hand inside her blouse. She blushes furiously, before scurrying away. I can hardly believe that we've found evidence of his infidelity so soon, but it may happen all the time. After she's gone, Polkerris stands by the window, glowering at us. The situation would be laughable under different circumstances, but my sense of humour has taken a nosedive.

'How old is she, Tom?' I ask. 'Seventeen?'

'Old enough to know her own mind,' he says. 'One minute we're having an appraisal meeting, the next she's all over me.'

'It must be nice, being irresistible,' Eddie mutters.

Polkerris shows us the palms of his hands. 'It was a mistake, all right? I've been under pressure. You can't arrest me for that.'

He lowers himself onto a plush sofa, his smooth facade back in place, no visible creases in his expensive suit.

'How many times has it happened?'

'What do you mean?

'You employ temporary staff, mostly female, young and easily impressed. It's an abuse of power.'

'I haven't broken any laws.'

'Your fingerprints are all over Sabine's bedroom. Did you sleep with Lily Jago too?'

'You're loving this, aren't you?' he sneers. 'It's a personal attack.'

'I bet your staff know all about your antics.'

Polkerris's body language is changing, his shoulders hunched in self-defence. 'I slept with Sabine once, that's all.'

'Hannah Weber was fascinated by the history of this place. She visited twice, describing the castle as "magical" in her journal. Is she another of your conquests?'

'We never even met.' The look on his face contains pure hatred. 'You can't forgive and forget, can you?'

'No one likes a bully; the only difference now is how it's described. We call it coercive control. If a female employees rejects you, she could lose her job. You'll get the sack when this goes public.'

'The owners won't believe you.'

'Trust me, they will.'

I take a good deal of pleasure from arresting Tom Polkerris. The solicitor is bound to advise her new client to answer every question with 'no comment', just like Paul Keast, but at least we can hold him overnight. If he's the killer, he can't harm Lily again, if she's still alive.

Lawrie Deane calls me soon after the paperwork is completed and Polkerris is placed in a holding cell at 4 p.m. The sergeant explains that he forgot to mention that the Rawles' house hasn't been fully searched. Frank was out during his visit, and Elaine claimed that her husband had the only key to the attic.

'I can't see why they'd lock it, when it's just those two living there.'

'I'll pay them a call, Lawrie. I should check on Leo Kernick anyway.'

I can't imagine the Rawles marring their respectable image, let alone going on a killing spree, but Jeff Pendelow's suggestion that the killer might be a pillar of the community is still ringing in my ears.

The rain is steady when I set off, but getting soaked again is the least of my worries. I'm digesting the clashes between Rhianna's story and Tom Polkerris's. It still seems possible that the killings sprang from the collapse of their marriage, but I need to carry on checking every detail, until evidence is confirmed.

Frank Rawle's appearance is pristine when I reach his house. The razor-sharp creases in his shirtsleeves contrast with my sopping-wet windcheater. His Labrador trots out to greet me once the door opens, begging to be stroked.

'I was about to call you, Ben. I'm afraid Leo's gone,' Rawle announces. 'We hoped he'd stay longer, but he left before we woke up.'

'Was he any calmer by the time he went to bed?'

'He's still in shock. It'll take him months to recover.'

'Could you drive to his studio later to check he's okay?'

'We sold our car years ago, but I can take a walk there now.'

'Thanks, Frank. Could we have a quick chat first?'

I send Lawrie a message on my phone to let him know that Kernick's on his own, before following Rawle inside. A grandfather clock ticks loudly as he leads me through to his living room. I'd like to fire out questions then hurry back to the station, but the situation requires delicacy. The man's shirtsleeve pulls back as he gestures for me to sit down, revealing a thick surgical bandage.

'How did you hurt your wrist, Frank?'

He looks embarrassed. 'I tripped in the back garden. Elaine insisted on dressing it for me as a precaution. It's just a sprain.'

'Your house has already been searched, but I hear you keep the attic locked. Would it be okay to look inside?'

I feel awkward hunting for evidence linking Rawle to the murders, when he's been a respected community member for decades, but his dominating personality singles him out. The rooms on the first floor have the same dark panelling as the hallway, making them feel claustrophobic. When I climb the final flight of stairs to the attic, Rawle takes his time producing a key.

'My wife would hate this,' he says. 'She treats this room as sacred territory.'

'I won't take long, I promise.'

Time shifts into reverse when the door finally swings open. The loft has never been modernised, with bare rafters overhead, the years receding to the late nineties. The musicians in Primal Scream, Nirvana and the Fugees look fresh-faced in the posters above the girl's narrow bed. The duvet cover has faded from red to pink, the musty smell proving that the window is rarely opened. Old-fashioned cans of hairspray and tubes of lipstick lie on the dressing table. Leah Rawle beams down at me from the wall. The young man beside her in the photo looks familiar; his arm is draped around her shoulder, a cigarette dangling from his lip. A guitar stands propped against the wall.

'It looks like your daughter was keen on music.'

'Leah dreamed of teaching it, once she qualified.' Frank Rawle is still standing in the doorway, reluctant to cross the threshold. 'We should have given everything to charity long ago, but Elaine won't hear of it.'

Leah's possessions have been treated like priceless artefacts. The air tastes of dust and old memories, my breath catching when I walk further inside. A wedding dress hangs from the wardrobe door, its lace turning yellow. Twenty years have passed, but there's still a dull sheen on the silk, the bodice covered in embroidery.

'Was your daughter due to get married?'

'The ceremony was just a week away. They'd booked the church and planned their honeymoon.'

'She was engaged to an islander?'

'Didn't anyone tell you the story? Her fiancé was Michael Trevellyan.'

'The priest?'

Rawle nods in reply. 'He was working on his parents' flower farm back then. They were far too young, but we relented in the end. It was obvious they were in love.'

I stare back at him. 'I had no idea.'

'Mike's life fell apart afterwards. I know his religion brings him solace, and his ministry's been exceptional, but his life would have been happier if Leah had survived.'

I'd like to know how the girl died, but the question seems insensitive. My old headmaster appears keen to escape his memories. Leah Rawle's death has impacted on everyone she knew down the years: her mother's spirit was broken, while her fiancé has allowed religion to replace love. It bothers me that the priest spoke to Hannah Weber just before she was attacked. It crosses my mind that he could be staying at her bedside to watch her die, rather then helping her survive, but the idea seems ridiculous. Why would a respected man of the cloth go on a killing spree, twenty years after his fiancé died? But anyone can commit violence under the right circumstances. I call the priest's mobile number straight after leaving the Rawles' home, but get no reply.

53

Lily's hips ache from spending so long in the same position, but it's impossible to stand. When she concentrates hard, voices whisper through the walls, the sound impossibly distant. She screams for help, but her throat is so dry she can only produce a guttural moan. Lily shouts louder the second time, but there's no response.

She stares at the photograph again, hands shaking as she lifts it closer to the light. The girl looks about her own age in the close-up, her features lovely. The breeze has swept back her hair as she smiles for the camera. The colours have faded, but her make-up still looks perfect, her lips frosted pink, grey shadow and mascara making her eyes look huge. Lily rubs foundation into her skin, but her freckles are still visible, scattered across the bridge of her nose. Sabine must have sat in the same chair, dazzled by the lights, hands shaking as she applied mascara.

'I won't do it,' Lily whispers out loud.

She wipes off the make-up, her decision restoring her calm. At least her reflection is one hundred per cent true, with a spark in her eyes that could signal hope or despair. She tugs at the chains around her legs, the metal's cold weight biting into her flesh. When she works her fingers between the links, the pressure makes her cry out in pain, but it's her only option. Sabine tried to follow the killer's instructions but died anyway. She must free herself before he returns, then run past him through the open door.

54

It's still raining in the late afternoon, when I head back to the station and start the motorbike, keen to reach Father Michael. It feels like the islands are trapped in a tropical storm, the atmosphere thick with humidity as I ride past Town Beach, where the shore is deserted. The sky looks like a length of pale grey cloth, smeared with charcoal. The priest takes a long time to answer my knock, his expression distracted. This time he's blocking the doorway, denying me entrance, despite the foul weather.

'I was just speaking to a parishioner, Ben. How can I help?'

'I'd like a quick talk, if possible.'

He lingers on the threshold. 'The hospital's expecting me.'

'This won't take long.'

Father Michael's pace is slow when he leads me into his living room. He takes the chair opposite, but our roles have been reversed. The priest looks weighed down by sins that need to be confessed.

'You had contact with all the victims, didn't you, Father?'

His body language is heavy with exhaustion. 'I knew you'd want this conversation sooner or later.'

'It's quite a coincidence that you spent time with each of the women.'

'I didn't know any of them well.'

'You heard Sabine's confession, you spoke to Hannah Weber, Jade Finbury sometimes attended mass, and then there's—'

He cuts through my speech. 'What are you saying, Ben?'

'It can't be easy living alone for so many years.'

'I'm human, like you. It gets lonely sometimes.'

'It's worse for priests. You have to carry out wedding ceremonies all summer long.'

'The ritual is a joyous union between people who love each other. Why would that cause me pain?'

'You keep saying your life's got a bigger purpose, but you've never recovered from Leah's death, have you?'

'My work gives me comfort.' The man's sadness echoes in his voice. 'I'd have lashed out years ago, when the grief was raw, if I wanted to get even. Why would anyone wait so long to punish other women just for being alive?'

'You tell me.'

'Leah made me see things differently. I felt trapped here, but she showed me the islands' beauty. She loved their history, and how the light refreshes the landscape every day so you never tire of it.' He stares down at his hands. 'I lost myself after she died, but that's part of the gift she left behind. I had to be tested to find my faith.'

'The victims are dressed in white, like nuns taking their vows. They call it taking the veil, don't they? Maybe you see them as novitiates, not brides.'

'This is nonsense.' He rises to his feet rapidly. 'Go ahead and turn this place over if you want. You can start upstairs.'

'I'll look down here first.'

The priest falls silent when I reach his kitchen. The back door hangs open, and his table holds evidence of a recent meal: two plates hold unfinished sandwiches, and a pair of water glasses only half drunk.

'Who was here just now, Father?'

'One of my parishioners, like I said. He missed lunch so I prepared some food.'

'Tell me his name.'

The priest appears to search his conscience before answering. 'Harry Jago. The boy was so terrified he ran off before I could stop him.'

'You let him get away, even though his sister's been taken?'

'Lily's missing?'

The priest sinks onto a chair while I call Eddie to inform him that Jago has escaped again, this time from the priest's house. Father Michael looks paler when I ask my next question.

'Explain your relationship with Harry for me, please.'

'His mother was a good, hard-working woman. She only made one mistake, which was marrying the wrong man. She arrived here with nothing except two kids to feed, so I paid her to clean this place and the church. I promised to keep watch over Harry and Lily before she died.'

'The boy seems afraid of you.'

'Only because I hold him to account. Harry knows I'm disappointed when he goes off the rails, but I support him anyway. I was far worse at that age.'

'I bet he'd do anything for you.'

The priest's eyes glitter with anger. 'Now you're accusing me of grooming a vulnerable young adult? I told him to report to the station, but only he can decide.'

'His sister's got hours to live, and Harry might know the killer's identity. I bet he told you everything.'

The priest makes no reply, but a history of violence shows in his face, and my accusations have triggered his fighting impulse. His hands form fists at his sides, even though he keeps his temper in check.

'Stay with me while I search your house, Michael.'

The priest's calm returns while I rummage through cupboards, looking for a Polaroid camera, a weapon, or anything to link him to the murders. He keeps quiet while I check each sparsely furnished room, where crucifixes hang over every doorway. I can't imagine contemplating my faith twenty-four hours a day. The pressure to avoid even the smallest transgression must be hard to bear. His face is expressionless when I climb the stairs to inspect his study, where a Bible lies open on his desk.

'I need to look in your cellar.'

'You're wasting your time.'

The priest takes so long prevaricating, I return downstairs alone. He's still grumbling as I descend into his basement, the air cool and dry, the walls freshly whitewashed. It's virtually empty, apart from a crate containing old photo albums from Michael's youth. The images show him sitting beside a field full of daffodils, but he looked troubled even then. I notice a wooden chest standing by the wall just before I leave; it's the size of a coffin, obscured by shadows. When I lift the lid a bride's veil is cocooned inside a muslin bag, with a delicate pair of white shoes. I'm still holding them when the priest appears behind me, his face tight with anger.

Father Michael removes the veil from my hands, like a parent handling a newborn child, then wraps the shoes in their original tissue paper. He's about to replace the items when I notice a piece of paper lying in the box, covered in black script. The priest gives a grudging nod when I ask to see it. The yellowing page matches the museum records I borrowed from Julian Power.

'Where did you get this, Father?'

His face remains blank. 'I don't know where it came from.'

342

'Why should I believe you? First you let Harry Jago escape, then I find bridal clothes in your cellar.'

'Let's go back upstairs, I'll explain everything.'

I reach out my hand. 'I need that sheet of paper first.'

He takes his time handing it over, then watches me place it in my pocket. The priest's gentleness only returns once we reach his living room. He gives me an encouraging smile, as if he's about to deliver a difficult sermon.

'I asked Leah's parents for some of her bridal clothes twenty years ago.' His gaze drifts to the window. 'I was on the mainland at a job interview when she died; I wasn't there when she needed me most. That's why I visit the hospital so often. I hate the idea of a human soul slipping from this world to the next, without any form of comfort.'

'How did Leah die, Michael?'

My question makes him flinch. 'Frank and Elaine asked the coroner to record a verdict of death by misadventure. They couldn't stand the idea of people gossiping.'

'She killed herself?'

The priest looks down at his hands. 'Leah had been diagnosed with depression. I thought loving her would help her through it. She kept her feelings hidden in the last few weeks, pretending to be excited about the wedding, while the illness took over. Leah's note said that she loved me more than anything, but couldn't see a way out. She didn't want to be a burden.'

'Who found her?'

'Frank, when he got back from school. He protected me from seeing her body, and all the ugly details. He and Elaine have treated me like a son since then. They never blamed me for pushing her deeper into that brutal illness.'

'But you blamed yourself.'

He wipes his hand across his face like he's cleaning a slate. 'None of this is relevant to Harry Jago. The boy needs good role models. I've been mentoring him, for his mother's sake.'

'Were you involved in the killings, Michael?'

'How could I be? I've barely left the hospital for the last three days.'

'People trust you. Your parishioners would do anything for you, especially if they're vulnerable.'

His jaw drops open. 'Do you honestly believe I've been brainwashing people?'

'Tell me exactly what Harry said. You hid details from Sabine's last confession too.'

'I took a vow of secrecy. When someone unburdens their soul to me, that trust is sacred. If I break the sacrament I can no longer serve God.'

'Harry Jago isn't a believer. There was nothing holy about your talk today.'

'He begged me not to say anything. That's a confession, isn't it?'

'Tell me where the boy's gone.'

He weakens at last. 'I told him to hide in the

fishermen's huts by Watermill Cove. He needs to examine his conscience until he's ready to talk.'

'Call him for me. He'll answer if he sees your number.'

The priest obliges, and Jago picks up instantly. When I seize the receiver, the boy's breathing is so ragged it sounds like he's run a marathon.

'Listen to me, Harry, it's DI Kitto. Your sister's been taken. If you know something, tell me, before it's too late.'

The boy gives a guttural cry before the line goes dead.

55

Lily's fingertips are raw when footsteps clatter outside. She has tried to loosen her chains until her skin bleeds, but she's still trapped. Her heart lurches in her chest when the door creaks open. She can hear the killer moving closer, but can't twist round far enough to meet his eye.

'I'm thirsty,' she whispers. 'I need water, please.'

He's dressed in dark clothes, a hood with narrow slits exposing eyes she can't recognise. Lily mumbles a quiet thank you when he places a bottle of water on the dressing table; she gulps the liquid down in a few rapid gulps. He has already retreated, but she can feel him assessing her.

'You haven't followed my instruction.' His voice sounds rough, as if he's just smoked a pack of cigarettes, but he could be trying to disguise it.

'There's no point. I can't become someone else with a few dabs of make-up.' The man stays quiet, as if her defiance has stunned him into silence. 'Who is the girl in the photo anyway?'

The killer's voice sounds plaintive when he begins to sing:

'The bride in her glory will ever be fair,
Come winter or summer, no queen can compare,
With the bride in her glory, be she ever so fair.'

Lily forces a smile. 'Did you write that song for her? She's special to you, isn't she?'

Lily's plan seems to be working. The man hasn't hurt her yet, and she can feel him listening, even though he's hidden by the dark air.

347

56

I burst outside without looking back at Father Michael, still uncertain of his role in the women's deaths, while he's spent most of his time at Hannah Weber's bedside. I push my confusion aside to call Eddie, telling him to meet me at the cove.

The rain is lighter when I ride through Trenoweth, but it's 6.30 p.m., the sky darkening as I pass the Long Rock. The standing stone looks like a needle on the horizon, pointing its accusing finger at the clouds. The facts of Leah Rawle's death are still registering, but I can't prove that it's influenced the recent killings. Eddie has arrived before me, the police van standing beside a cluster of ramshackle fishermen's sheds overlooking Watermill Cove. He's at my side when I fling open the doors of the first hut. It's empty, apart from the acrid smell of decaying fish, bait boxes and reels of twine. The next shed is the same, but the third looks different. Its interior has been scrubbed clean, and there's a table with a mirror beside it, lengths of rope abandoned on the floor. I can see brown stains on the fibres; one of the victims pulled so hard against her constraints, she made herself bleed. The killer kept one of his victims here, but my call to Jago has sent him running.

Eddie's enthusiasm takes a nosedive when he sees the killer's handiwork. He gives the table a vicious kick, but I'm still considering the props that surround us.

'It's a strange kind of torture,' I say. 'The killer wants to turn the women into brides, just before they die.'

'Tom Polkerris is screwed up enough to do that, isn't he? The bloke hated Rhianna's fixation with the perfect wedding and wasting their savings on it, even though their relationship was on the wane.'

'We're just guessing, Eddie. Let's review what we actually know about the killer.'

My deputy parks himself on a crate, while rain taps out a hectic rhythm on the thin roof above us. 'He's got access to a vehicle, and a warped idea about brides. The bloke likes the thrill of strangling women with his bare hands.'

'The guy's a control freak too. I bet he loved posting those photos through the station door, and to Harry Jago, showing us he's in control.' I rub my hand across the back of my neck. 'But look at this place. He's swept the floor and laid a clean sheet over the table; that mirror's been polished recently too. It's like a religious ceremony, but Father Michael's got an alibi for almost the whole time the killer's been at work.'

My deputy dips his hand inside a cardboard box,

producing a fistful of wilting flowers. 'Whoever did it picked these, to make a garland for her hair.'

'I still think two very different people might be working together.'

'We know Paul Keast and Rhianna Polkerris are secretive. They fell in love without anyone finding out.'

'But there's no hard evidence against them. We've still got a dozen male islanders with no alibis too.'

Eddie's face is full of yearning for a quick solution, but we're facing the same obstacles that have blocked us from day one.

57

Lily senses that she doesn't have long. She's still sitting by the mirror, her reflection paler than ever, but she doesn't regret her choice. If she dies, at least she'll be herself, not pretending to be someone else. The killer refused to answer her questions, then left her alone, but now he's back. The man is pacing the stone floor, ready to hurt her, unless she can make him talk.

'Tell me about the girl in the photo, please.'

Lily can only see a blurred outline reflected in the mirror. He's on the far side of the room, head bowed, face concealed by his hood.

'She was a pure spirit.' His words are choked with emotion, the voice suddenly so light in tone the speaker could be a woman. 'Holding her in my arms meant everything.'

'But you lost her?' The voice has faded into silence. 'I know how that feels. My mother died recently; I miss her every day.'

Lily is concentrating so hard, her fingernails are cutting the palms of her hands, the pain reminding her that she's still alive. People must be searching for her. They'll arrive soon, if she can only keep him talking.

'I can't bring her back. I've been fooling myself.'

'Hurting me won't help you.'

The killer's closer now, his tone growing shrill. 'You're like the others. None of you are loyal to the islands, or to me.'

The blow comes before Lily can brace herself, a hard punch to her ribcage, emptying her lungs of air. Pain travels through her core, but she forces herself not to scream. When her eyes open again, she's alone, the darkness around her thicker than before, until her gaze catches on a chink of silver. The door stands ajar by a few millimetres, keeping her hopes alive.

58

Hours slip by too quickly, time passing in a flurry of meetings, CPS evidence reviews and a brief interview with Tom Polkerris. It's 7 p.m. when the hotel manager is brought into Madron's room. The man's smugness has reduced, but his answers are useless. He's already admitted to sleeping with Sabine after a late shift in the hotel bar, but there's evidence he was working when Hannah Weber was attacked. If he's got an accomplice, he's a good liar. My old classmate looks bemused when I ask if anyone else is involved, continuing to deny any link to the attacks.

I release Paul Keast after the interview ends, even though the thirty-six hour cut-off hasn't arrived. There's little point in holding him when there's no hard evidence that he's guilty. He doesn't say a word when Eddie hands over his bag of possessions, slipping through the station doors to check on his livestock or see his new flame. Tom Polkerris is a different kind of prisoner. He grows angrier as the hours pass, battering his fists against the wall, then shouting curses through the hatch in the cell door.

Liz Gannick inspects me with her sharp glare when we meet in Madron's office, as evening gives way to night. Her crutches are propped against the wall, like she too wants a quick getaway.

'You're sending me back to that bloody hotel, aren't you?'

'Polkerris is a credible suspect, Liz. He mistreats women, he's a plausible liar, and he had easy access to Sabine and Lily. I need you to find proof. The bloke loves manipulating people and he's been edgy from the start.' I remember his agitation on hearing Sabine was dead. He may have been afraid of exposure, instead of regretting the girl's death.

'I'll start with his car,' Gannick says. 'If he's guilty, he's used it recently to capture his latest victim. There may even be fresh DNA.'

'It's too late to send samples to the lab. If Lily's still being held, she'll be dead by morning.'

'I can't work miracles, Ben.'

'Pity.'

Gannick's face looks anything but angelic when she grabs her crutches and swings back into motion. I'm so concerned about lone women being attacked that I tell Lawrie Deane to accompany her to the hotel, but at least I know Isla is safe. I've sent her out on a last foot patrol with Eddie, asking for sightings of Lily Jago, leaving me alone at the station.

I've only just turned on my computer when a call arrives on the landline. Frank Rawle is offering his help again. I decline politely; the man's desire to get involved still bothers me, but he takes a leadership role in every part of island life. He runs the parish council, the school's advisory board, and is a hospital trustee. The man's constant efforts to improve the quality of life on St Mary's make him an unlikely murderer.

I swallow my fear that we're acting too slowly to save Lily Jago. We spent the day searching every obscure shed and outbuilding, as well as interviewing suspects this evening. All I can do now is learn what the sailors' charms mean to the killer, even though I'd rather be outside hunting for the missing girl. The rain on the station's roof sounds like bullets from a scattergun, the brutal sound reminding me the girl may be dead already, her corpse battered by the elements.

I spend the next hour struggling to read the museum's records. The past twenty years' entries are easy because Elaine Rawle's handwriting is perfectly formed, but the sailors' charms may have been left to the museum decades ago. The previous manager ran the museum for fifty years, his minute scrawl growing illegible as he aged. I get no help from the extra sheet I found in Father Michael's basement, apart from confirming that it was torn so cleanly from the ledger, its absence is hard to spot. My gaze scans the list of items, certain I'm missing something, but none of the names jumps out at me.

There's a scratching sound outside, just as my eyes are straining from overuse. It's pitch dark when Shadow bounds through the door. He normally gives me a boisterous greeting, but his behaviour's changed. The dog lets out a series of barks, his pale eyes locked onto my face. There's nothing outside except darkness and rain, coursing down the windows, while the islanders shelter indoors.

'Where's Nina?'

The dog gives a pitiful whine, prompting me to call her number, but there's no reply. Now he's standing by the door, howling for release, and I know something's wrong. I told Nina to keep her phone switched on at all times, but when I call again, there's still no answer.

59

Lily is alone once more in the vaulted room, her ribs throbbing. She still can't guess where she's being held. The room is so huge it looks more like a crypt than someone's basement. She could try putting on make-up, but it won't save her life. No amount of camouflage will make her look like the girl in the photo.

She still can't move, despite trying to free herself. When she looks in the mirror the thread of light catches her eye again – that hairline crack in the darkness seems to beckon her towards it. She presses her feet hard against the stone floor, dragging her chair forwards, a few centimetres each time.

Lily can't tell how long it takes to cross the room, but it soon dawns on her that she has made a grave mistake. The hem of the wedding dress is black with dirt, the silk in tatters. If the killer sees the damage, her punishments will be worse than before.

When she manages to open the door, a steep staircase leads up to a small landing. The next door is covered in locks and bolts. It would be impossible to haul herself up so many stairs without falling, and the effort would be pointless. The killer is sure to have locked her only escape route from the outside.

60

I'm still clutching my phone when a text arrives. The message is from Eddie, saying that he and Isla have visited the hospital: Hannah Weber's condition is unchanged. The injured woman isn't the only one stuck in limbo. I need to find Nina before it's too late. The receptionist at the Star Castle sounds too cheerful when I make my call.

'Ms Jackson left earlier this evening. She went out on her own.'

'Isn't she back yet?'

'I don't think so, sir, but I can check her room.'

'No need, I'll do it myself.'

Instinct makes me grab the museum's record book then hurry outside, ignoring the downpour. I hang onto Shadow's leash so he can't bound off into the darkness, but he looks back every few seconds, frustrated by my slow running speed. It's only when we reach the entrance that his barking goes into overdrive. The dog is a few paces ahead when I chase down the corridor. Shadow reaches Nina's room first, howling for attention, but there's no reply when I hammer on the door.

'Where the hell are you?'

The book drops from my hands as shock takes hold. Nina is missing too, having ignored my advice to stay put. When I look through a narrow window, the hotel grounds are deserted, with lanterns casting their glow on flowerbeds that have been flattened by the relentless downpour. Nina is the killer's ideal victim: independent, solitary, with no intention of remaining on the islands. Shadow is losing patience now we've come to a standstill. He's whining at full volume, the sound ear-splitting.

'Shut up, can you? I can't think straight.'

My hands are shaking when I see that the record book has fallen open on the floor, at the point where I inserted the missing page. Someone must have used a sharp blade to cut the sheet from the ledger, leaving a tiny strip of paper, by the book's spine. I feel even more certain that there's a link between the stolen items and the murders, gazing down at the list of donors. This time a familiar name jumps out at me, my brain going into overdrive as I rush back outside.

I'm still not thinking clearly when I unclip Shadow's leash. He's free to do as he pleases, but seems determined to stay at my side. My dog races across the grass, as raindrops hit my face like shrapnel, carried by a hard wind. He tracked Nina across five miles to

Watermill Cove and now it's my turn to do the same, before it's too late.

My breathing's ragged by the time I reach Church Road. I'm about to head for the Rawles' home when a light inside the museum catches my eye, and I remember Frank saying that his wife often visits late at night to do a final security check. I rush through the entrance, calling her name, but there's no reply. The only light comes from behind the counter, illuminating a list of benefactors engraved on a brass plaque. How did I miss the Rawles' name, right at the bottom of the list?

Someone is moving around downstairs, their footsteps tracking slowly across the parquet. Elaine must be in the storeroom with the door closed, unable to hear me. I pull my phone from my pocket and call Eddie to get him to come to the museum while I wait for her to surface. He's at the far end of the island, paying house calls to check everyone's safe. My deputy's tone is shocked when he hears that Nina is missing: we're looking for two victims now instead of one. I can hear Isla speaking in the background, her tone brittle as I end the call.

The museum's lights must operate from a central system because nothing happens when I press a switch by the stairs. I use my phone as a torch to make my way downstairs, but the dog streaks ahead, his night vision more acute than mine. Objects loom towards me; a row of ships' figureheads ghostly in the dark. The lights flick on suddenly when Elaine Rawle emerges from the storeroom, her eyes glassy with fear.

'Thank God it's you,' she whispers. 'All that clatter-ing upstairs scared the living daylights out of me.'

'The door was unlocked. That's a bad idea with a killer roaming around.'

'It's still hard to believe.' The woman's voice sounds weaker than before. 'Did you come here looking for something?'

'Just your help, when you've got your breath back.'

'It's okay, I'm feeling calmer already.'

Shadow's behaviour changes when she approaches. He snaps at her, teeth bared, as she reaches down to stroke him.

'Ignore him. He's bad-tempered, but he won't bite.'

'There's nothing to frighten him here.' Elaine's gaze is fixed on the Victorian sailing gig that's been the museum's pride and joy for decades.

'What do you know about the families that donated items to the museum years ago, Elaine?'

'Not a great deal. Why do you ask?'

'Did you ring anyone about those sailors' charms?'

She looks apologetic. 'I'm afraid no one had any information.'

'You're lying.'

Her eyes blink rapidly. 'What do you mean?'

'I found the missing page from the record book, with Leah's veil. You can stop pretending.'

Her face distorts with anger. 'I can't believe Michael let you open the box. How dare you touch my daugh-ter's things?'

'The sailors' charms are from your family. You donated them to the museum, but regretted it after Leah died, so you cut the page from the ledger and hid it with her veil. Did you make an excuse to visit Michael's recently, to leave it there?'

Her eyes have glazed over. 'My grandmother began collecting the charms after her husband was lost at sea.'

'No wonder Julian Power couldn't find any record. You hid the jewellery you stole for a whole year.'

Her voice is cold when she speaks again. 'It was mine by right.'

'Where are Lily and Nina?'

Elaine starts to back away, but Shadow jumps up at her, jaws snapping. I realise now why Frank Rawle was so keen to get involved in the case.

'You can't hide in a place this small, Elaine. It's time to face what you've done.' Shadow's barking goes into overdrive.

'Keep that bloody dog away from me.'

'Sacrificing those lives didn't bring your daughter back.' Tears roll down Elaine's cheeks, but I don't care how much she's suffered. 'Where's Frank? I bet he planned all this with you.'

'He's at home in bed.'

'That's another lie.' I reach forward to grab her arm.

'You're hurting me,' Elaine's voice rings out. 'I didn't do anything.'

I'm still holding onto her when footsteps shuffle

behind me, but my reactions are too slow. Shadow jumps up to defend me, but Elaine delivers a vicious kick to his chest that sends him sprawling. There's a sudden pain between my shoulders and I'm on my knees, my attacker shoving me to the floor.

61

Lily is still sitting near the bottom of the stairs. She lacks the strength to drag her chair back to the mirror. It's been so long since she ate anything, her vision is blurred, but her thoughts clear when raised voices drift down the stairwell. The fury behind each word is terrifying. She's certain the killer would rather die than be taken prisoner. Fear and lack of sleep have left her exhausted, but she tries to imagine herself bold and confident like Sabine, strong enough to win any battle.

The voices stop suddenly, the quiet more ominous than before. Lily concentrates hard, but can only hear her own rapid breathing, the cavernous room filled with silent ghosts. Tension rises in her stomach when the door at the top of the stairs is wrenched open. Instinct tells her that she's about to die. The killer's tread is faster than before, then a new voice cries out, bitter with anger. When her eyes open again a man is tumbling down the stairs, arms braced to protect himself, but all she can do is watch.

62

My face batters against the last three steps before I land in a crumpled heap. I catch sight of Lily Jago a few metres away, swathed in white, her expression terrified. Both our lives depend on me recovering fast, but my limbs aren't working, a burning pain searing my cheek. I'm still lying on the stone floor when Elaine Rawle lunges out of the dark. She grabs my phone from my shirt pocket, then hurls it at the wall, the plastic shattering.

'I wanted to keep the girls here, on St Mary's. Can't you understand that? They made beautiful brides, like Leah. It was their destiny.' Her voice is mournful when she stands over me.

'Let us go, Elaine. You can plead insanity.'

'I've never felt saner. This is for my daughter, not me.'

'I know she killed herself. I bet you found Leah, not Frank.'

'Don't say her name! She was beautiful, even when she hung herself from the rafters in her wedding dress. My daughter was perfect then and she's perfect now.'

There's a mad certainty in her eyes when she binds my wrists with a short rope. Now that the shock is easing, the pain from my fall hits my system. Elaine is gathering more rope from the corner of the room and my last chance of freedom is vanishing.

I wait until she's kneeling over me then kick her in the face, a fitting revenge for the lives she's taken. My foot lands a glancing blow on her temple, sending her sprawling. There's no sign of the headmaster's elegant wife now. Grey hair tumbles witch-like down her back when she flies at me again, but my second kick lands right between her eyes. She falls like a deadweight, and it's hard to believe that such a genteel woman could cause so much damage. Old-fashioned lavender perfume cloys in my mouth as I check she's not faking being unconscious. Right now I don't care if she lives or dies, but she can't have acted alone. Elaine lacks the physical strength to abduct the victims. Her husband must have cudgelled me from behind then pushed me down the stairs.

'Get down here, you bastard,' I yell out. 'What are you waiting for?'

Lily has dragged her chair closer when I pull myself into a sitting position. The pain from my fall makes my head spin, but the girl's touch is comforting when she unties my ropes.

'Have you seen the other one's face, Lily?'

'He always wears a hood.' Her voice is shaky, but she's holding it together.

'It must be Frank Rawle. Don't worry, help's on its way.'

Lily is too busy undoing the knot to answer, and I'm more concerned about finding Nina than guessing the second killer's identity. Once my hands are free I root through Elaine's pockets, hunting for a key to unlock the girl's chains, but I only find a pocket-knife, which won't help at all. The door hangs open at the top of the stairs, and I keep hoping Eddie will guess I'm down here, but there's no sign of him.

A man's tall form thunders down the stairs before I can speak to Lily again. He's brandishing a crow-bar as he charges straight at me. I put my hands out to defend myself, but his first blow lands on my hip, making me shout out in pain. His mask covers his face, apart from narrow eye slits. I lash out with Elaine's knife, but my injuries make me clumsy. He lands a second blow on my ribcage then steps aside as I run at him again, leaving me stabbing at thin air. I'm losing the fight when new footsteps resonate on the floor above. I'm praying that Eddie and Isla have arrived at last.

When another figure races down the stairs, his form is lost in shadows as I sidestep the killer's blows. I feel a flood or relief when Harry Jago leaps onto my attacker's back, his weight making him collapse forwards. The boy sits on his shoulders, pressing his masked face into the dirt.

'How did you find us, Harry?'

Jago is panting for breath. 'I followed him here. I knew it was him who'd done it.'

There's relief on the boy's face when he spots his sister, still in chains but definitely alive. Harry helps me roll the man onto his back, banding his arms at his sides.

'Where's Nina?' I hiss at his masked face. 'What have you done to her?'

I'm expecting to see Frank Rawle's craggy features, but the picture blurs when I push back the hood. Jeff Pendelow stares up at me, a line of blood trailing from his nose. The shock is so powerful my voice falls to a murmur.

'What made you hurt those women, Jeff?'

The psychologist lies completely still, with tears seeping from his closed eyes. Harry Jago is gripping his arms to stop him escaping, even though I can see he's given up the fight. Pendelow's shirt is torn, and the wound Jade Finbury inflicted on his ribcage is covered by a strip of dressing. When I think about him attacking her, anger floods my system again. Jade would still be alive if her blow had landed in the centre of his chest. Pendelow makes no attempt to resist arrest, and shame crosses his face when I tell him his rights. His eyes close once more, blinding himself to the punishments he's facing.

63

Lily focuses on her brother's face. Harry crouches beside her to undo the padlock, then puts his arm around her shoulders.

'Are you okay?' He scans her face for signs of injury.

'Don't let them take me to hospital.' She reaches for his hand. 'I know you didn't hurt anyone.'

He shakes his head. 'I couldn't tell who was driving the car by Pulpit Rock, the night Sabine died. I only found out it belonged to Jeff's wife when I broke into his garage, looking for a place to hide. The garden's so overgrown the building's almost hidden.'

'So you followed him here. You saved my life, Harry.'

'I should have worked it out sooner. What did those bastards do to you?'

'They scared me, that's all.'

The boy is crying tears that should have been released long ago. Pride has forced him to suppress his misery until now. When Lily puts her arms around him, time slips backwards. He's the brother she used to adore, brave enough to scare the bullies away when he walked her back from school.

'Take me home,' she whispers.

Exhaustion topples her at last. Harry lifts her from her seat after her eyes close, with another woman's wedding gown trailing along the ground. Lily is fast asleep when he carries her upstairs, into the light.

64

Eddie is the first person I see after hauling myself back upstairs, the museum's strip lights dazzling me after too long in darkness. Harry Jago has taken his sister home and Tom Polkerris will be sent back to the hotel with his tail between his legs. The killers are being kept separate, but soon they'll be safely locked in holding cells, contemplating long prison sentences. My deputy is fizzing with excitement when he rushes towards me.

'Nina's fine, boss, Isla's with her now. She took a taxi to Watermill Cottage to meet the owners.'

'Why didn't she answer her bloody phone?'

'She didn't say.'

The fear I've been carrying loosens its grip, until Eddie's smile vanishes. 'Something else is wrong. Is it Hannah Weber?'

'The other news can wait. Let's get you checked over first.'

'Tell me now.'

'It's Shadow, boss.' He stares down at his hands. 'I'm

sorry, but I couldn't do much for him in the end, except hold him and keep him calm. They kicked the life out of him. He was so badly injured, perhaps it's for the best.' His apology fades into silence.

'Where is he?'

I push him aside, looking for my dog. Shadow's body lies motionless on the floor and my own pain is forgotten when I drop to my knees. A coat has been draped over him, but there's no sign of life when I say his name. No animal could survive the brutal kick Elaine Rawle delivered to his chest; the assault must have stopped his heart in its tracks.

'The evil bitch,' I mutter the words under my breath.

The horror of the case catches up with me at last. A dog's death shouldn't compare to two human fatalities, and a third victim whose life hangs in the balance, but I'll never forget his wayward intelligence, or his bravery. I pull the coat back to look at him for the last time. His flesh feels cold when I touch his side, until a dull rhythm vibrates under my hand. It's slow and erratic, barely perceptible, but it's better than nothing.

'Call the vet, Eddie,' I yell out. 'His heart's still beating.'

It only takes ten minutes for the islands' vet, Sam Nancarrow, to arrive. He's my godmother's oldest son, newly returned to the islands, and a childhood friend of mine. I can tell he's horrified by Shadow's injuries; he examines the dog carefully before administering an injection, then carries him out to his car.

My strength leeches out of me once the door closes, making my legs buckle. I slump on the floor, my back propped against one of the museum's cabinets. Tonight's events will soon be enshrined in local folklore, but whatever happens now, the island is safe. St Mary's inhabitants can wander across its beaches all night long without fear of danger. The day's tension is still flooding from my body when Eddie crouches in front of me.

'Your face is a mess, boss. I'm taking you to the hospital.'

'Not till we've seen Frank Rawle.'

My old headmaster is dressed in pyjamas and a dressing gown, his eyes cloudy with sleep when he opens his door. He seems bemused to hear that his wife is at the station, and I sense that Elaine's exploits come as a shock. His wife has spent many late evenings at the museum; this time he fell asleep before she returned. When I ask about her relationship with Jeff Pendelow, he explains that she's been having informal counselling sessions with the psychologist all year. Frank begged her to see him because she remains obsessed by their daughter's death, despite the passage of time. He looks appalled when I explain that Elaine has been arrested as an accessory to murder. He must come to the station tomorrow morning to give a statement.

My deputy insists on waiting in the hospital corridor while Ginny Tremayne applies an ice pack to my cheek to bring the swelling down. When my reflection appears in the mirror above the sink, I see a frowning black-haired giant, littered with bruises, but at least no bones have been broken. The medic looks relieved to hear that the killers have been caught, five days after Sabine Bertans' body was hung from Pulpit Rock. Her face glows with pride when she learns that her daughter's hard work helped track the killers down.

Once my treatment is over, I walk down the corridor to Hannah Weber's room. It's dark inside, apart from the flashing light of a heart-rate monitor. The woman appears to be sleeping peacefully, instead of gravely ill, when I settle on a chair beside her bed.

'We caught them,' I tell her. 'They'll never hurt anyone again.'

Her eyelids flutter as she shifts in her sleep. I wait another ten minutes, hoping for signs that she's regaining consciousness, but none come, so I leave her in peace.

Eddie offers to drive me back to the hotel, but I choose to walk. The deluge has passed, leaving the night air dry with salt as the tide loosens its grip on Hugh Town harbour. When I cross the sand towards Garrison Hill, floodlights are casting their glare on the Star Castle's ancient walls, and I wish with every fibre in my being that Sabine Bertans had chosen a different island for her working holiday. If I could turn back time, Jade could carry on flying her plane, and Hannah Weber would be safe at home in Germany. I stand on the shoreline until waves break over my feet, telling me it's time to leave.

65

Saturday 10 August

Sunlight floods into Lily's room when her eyes open. The pain in her side is easing, and Harry is at the end of her bed, watching her stretch.

'What time is it?' she asks.

'Lunchtime. You've been asleep for hours.'

She pulls herself upright. 'Have you spoken to the police?'

Harry nods. 'They said I was wrong to go looking for the car I saw when Sabine was taken, but I'm a victim too. They won't be pressing charges. That Kitto bloke wants to see me every week till I find permanent work.'

'I knew you'd be okay.'

'How did you keep it together, Lily?'

'I thought about everything I want to do before I die.'

He manages a smile. 'You're too young for a bucket list.'

'I'm old enough to have ambitions.' When Lily looks at him again, his hands are trembling. 'You're feeling rough, aren't you?'

'A beer would sort it, but it's time I let that go.'

'We both need to make changes. I love the islands, but we should move back to the mainland.'

'Why?'

'Some good has to come out of all this,' she replies. 'I want to go to university, and you'd have a better choice of work.'

'Don't worry about that yet.' He rises to his feet. 'Are you hungry?'

'Starving.'

'Have a shower then get back into bed. I'll bring you some food.'

When Lily eases onto her feet the pain in her back reminds her that she survived a nightmare. She could have died, like Sabine and Jade. Her body shudders as she releases a fresh wave of tears. Then she stands under the shower, her face tipped back, letting the hot water remove the last traces of another girl's make-up from her skin.

66

I've been at the station all morning. I could have stayed at the hotel nursing my bruises and let Eddie hear Jeff Pendelow's and Elaine Rawle's confessions, but my curiosity wouldn't allow it. Lawrie Deane looks exhausted when he comes to find me. He kept guard here last night, checking on our two prisoners every fifteen minutes, but I can tell that something worse than sleeplessness is bothering him.

'Jeff was a mate of mine. I went fishing with him loads of times,' he mutters. 'He hasn't said a word since being caught.'

'How about Elaine?'

'The woman keeps babbling about how she wanted to keep the girls here on the islands, so they wouldn't desert her. They had to atone for her daughter's death.' Deane hesitates for a moment. 'I can understand why she lost the plot. If one of my girls died, I'd go crazy too. No parent should have to lose a child.'

'Thanks for keeping watch, Lawrie. Go home and get some sleep.'

'Not until you've interviewed that bastard,' the sergeant replies, with a grim smile. 'I wouldn't miss it for the world.'

'They're both to blame, not just him. Is the solicitor attending both interviews?'

'She won't stop moaning,' he replies. 'Mary Tunstall's acting for him, but she'll be present at Elaine's interview until another brief arrives from the mainland.'

'Let's get started.'

I shuffle my documents into a pile, but Eddie's shout goes up before I can lift them from the desk. When I reach the holding cells it looks like Jeff Pendelow may have claimed his third bride after all. Elaine Rawle's body is on the floor, blocking the entrance to her cell, forcing me to shunt her aside. The woman has torn strips of fabric from her dress, using them as a noose. She must have acted fast. The wall chart shows that only ten minutes have elapsed since Eddie's last safety check.

It's a relief when Elaine comes round, gagging for breath. The woman may have committed two murders, but enough blood has been spilled already. I want the victims' families to see both killers sentenced. We'll have to keep her under constant surveillance until she's taken to the mainland. The woman's appearance has changed when I leave her slumped in her cell. Her clothes are in tatters, grey hair hanging down in limp curls, like a broken rag doll. Lawrie Deane stations himself outside her cell, with the hatch open, to prevent another suicide bid.

It's early afternoon before Jeff Pendelow is brought to Madron's office. His solicitor looks aggrieved, but he seems calm. The psychologist is just as I remember him, white hair swept back from his face as he studies me and Eddie over the rim of his glasses. Only the flatness of his gaze seems different. Maybe I never noticed it before, or he's an accomplished actor. There's no emotion on his face when I explain the terms of his arrest.

'Your sciatica was make-believe, wasn't it, Jeff? You wanted to seem too weak to harm anyone.'

'That's not true. I've been in pain for weeks.'

I shake my head in disbelief. 'Why not start at the beginning? Tell us why you killed Sabine Bertans and Jade Finbury, and attacked the other two victims.'

'No comment.'

'Our chief forensics officer has spent the morning at your home. She's found traces of blood in your kitchen and a trainer matching a footprint from Jade's murder scene. We've already got enough evidence to put you away, but the details interest me.'

'No comment.'

Pendelow seems to relish his last opportunity to exert control. I'll have to use my trump card to crack his defences.

'Your wife will hear about your antics.' A flicker of shock crosses his face. 'It'll break her heart. Even someone with memory problems would recall something that terrible forever.'

'That would be an act of monstrous cruelty.'

'Worse than murdering two women and assaulting two more?' Tunstall whispers to her client, instructing him to keep quiet, but anger has lowered his defences. 'You'll feel better if you get it off your chest, Jeff.'

His gaze fixes on the window. 'Elaine's been mentally ill for years. She believes that Leah inherited her depressive tendencies, resulting in her death. It's guilt that made her break down. I started listening to her outpourings a year ago, when I was caring for Val, and she helped me in return.' His shoulders hunch as he holds back tears. 'She showed my wife so much kindness, I fell for her. I'd have done anything she asked.'

'Including murder?'

'Elaine asked to borrow Val's car, so I let her take it. I didn't ask why, even though her behaviour had become erratic. She'd started telling Frank she was going to the museum late at night, then coming to my house, but there was nothing joyous about her visits. She was plagued by terrible dreams about Leah begging for release. She killed the first girl on August the third, the date her daughter was due to get married. Elaine believed it would free Leah's spirit.'

'Tell me what happened, the night she borrowed the car.'

He leans forward, his face bowed over his knees. 'She'd been tracking the girl for weeks. Elaine followed her from the hotel out to Pulpit Rock. She used a rock to beat her unconscious, then dragged her into the car. It descended into madness after that.'

'What do you mean?'

'Her psychosis fascinated me. She could be perfectly lucid one minute, then deranged and incoherent the next.'

'She's not one of your patients, Jeff. Tell me what happened.'

'Elaine used to talk about longing to keep young girls here, wedded to the islands forever, but I thought she was fantasising until I saw Sabine's body in the boot of Val's car that night. Elaine was terrified because Harry Jago had appeared out of nowhere. She was convinced he'd seen her.' He rubs his hand across his face, like he's wiping words from a blackboard. 'She had everything ready in the vault under the museum. A mirror, rope and a chair. She wanted each girl to look just like Leah. She took Polaroid photos, before strangling them, even though her victims pleaded for their life.'

'You must have helped her hang Sabine's body from Pulpit Rock. She couldn't have done it alone.'

'She threatened to tell everyone it was my idea if I refused.'

'You could have stopped it at any stage. Instead you helped her hang Sabine's body from a cliff. You might have got away with it if you'd quit there, but you helped her attack three more women.'

'Maybe my own mind fractured when Val grew ill; it was easy for Elaine's ideas to slip through the cracks.'

'Come on, Jeff. You're the sanest man I know. You got something from it, or you wouldn't have killed again. What made you choose Hannah and Jade?'

'Elaine selected them, not me. Leah wanted to stay here forever until illness stole her dream of getting married, teaching music and raising a family. Elaine hated the young women that fly away so casually, too independent to settle on the islands.'

'So you deny responsibility, apart from helping her display the bodies?'

He looks exasperated, like I'm missing his superior logic. 'Val was beautiful when we got married, but I watched her fade, like a flower in the hedgerow. Once she'd gone, right and wrong grew blurred. Religion, politics, morality – none of it mattered anymore.'

'Those women paid a high price for your loss of faith.'

The interview lasts another twenty minutes, but he reveals nothing about his own motives. He claims it was Elaine's idea to add a line from one of the island's old wedding songs to each victim's photo, to honour her daughter's memory. Leah Rawle loved ancient folk songs; she had been collecting lyrics and melodies from St Mary's oldest inhabitants when she died.

I'm still processing the information when I leave the interview at five o'clock, to find DCI Madron in the corridor outside. My boss looks as dapper as ever, his pepper and salt hair combed into place, tie knotted tight around his throat. I've been so busy with the case, I'd forgotten he was due home. His expression is solemn when he asks me to step inside his office. He casts his gaze over the papers heaped on his table and the incident board plastered with photos, my jacket slung over his chair.

'I see you've commandeered the place, Kitto.'

'Sorry, sir. We needed the biggest room for briefings.'

He bats my apology away with a wave of his hand. 'Eddie and Isla have given me the details already, but I want it from the horse's mouth.'

It takes me half an hour to share the full story. My boss listens in silence, hands clutching the arms of his chair like he's riding a runaway train.

'It's not quite the disaster I feared,' he says. 'No one could have guessed it was Jeff and Elaine. They seemed like decent, upstanding citizens.'

'Thank you, sir.'

'It wasn't a compliment.'

'It sounds like one.'

'If you hadn't pursued the evidence, Lily Jago would be dead too.' His smile lasts for a nanosecond. 'I'll review the case file before writing my overview report for the Cornish Constabulary.'

'The team worked like troopers. If you don't give them a commendation, I'll resign.'

DCI Madron's frown returns. 'Those types of threats are unacceptable, Kitto. You always want things your own way.'

'Who doesn't?'

The air between us hums with frustration. 'At least Hannah Weber's recovering.'

'How did you know?'

'She said a few words this morning. Apparently that's a good sign with head injuries. Her boyfriend's on his way from Heidelberg, then she'll be airlifted to Penzance hospital. They've got a good neurology department, so let's keep our fingers crossed.'

'That's a relief, sir,' I say, rising to my feet. 'I need to interview Elaine Rawle.'

He fixes me with a stern gaze. 'You're not calling the shots any longer, Kitto. I'll take over now, and don't come back until your face heals. You look like you've lost a boxing match with Tyson Fury.'

67

I don't follow my boss's instructions to the letter; there are tasks I need to finish before sailing home to Bryher. I buy a dozen of Shadow's favourite snacks from the Co-op, then collect my wetsuit from the hotel and walk down to Porthcressa Beach. Now that the Atlantic squall is over, summer has returned, the sun still hot enough to burn. Islanders pass by on the pavement but don't bother me with questions, and I can guess why. News travels fast here. Everyone will know already about two senior community members being arrested for murder. People stare at me from across the street, assessing my injuries from a safe distance, before continuing their journeys. I'll be the main topic of conversation in the pubs tonight: DI Benesek Kitto and his team caught the murderers in the end, but he took one hell of a pasting along the way.

I drop my towel on the sand then wade into the sea, letting the brine lift me off my feet. The ocean's chill works like an anaesthetic when I ease into a steady crawl. My injuries don't hurt while the waves sing in my ears, their saline taste filling my mouth. I need to start training again tomorrow. The swimathon is only a week away, and I'm determined to win, in memory of Sabine.

It doesn't take me long to reach Pulpit Rock, but no one could climb the cliff face now. The tide is roaring home too fast; I'd be battered against the rocks if I swam any closer. When I stare up at the rock forma-tion, the huge stone preacher is still addressing his watery congregation. I remember the bizarre sight of a bride with veil billowing from the cliff, and think about all the mistakes I made. Tomorrow I'll have to apol-ogise to everyone I wrongly accused. Father Michael only wanted to comfort a sick woman and support a damaged young boy. The case has cost me at least two friendships. The Keast brothers will never forgive my betrayal: I'd feel the same, if someone accused me of cold-blooded murder.

The sun is weakening when the current washes me south again to Porthcressa. The beach is emptier now, just a few couples heading to Dibble and Grub for an early glass of wine, and a dark-haired woman in a yellow bikini paddling at the water's edge. Nina raises her hand when she sees me wading ashore, but I don't like farewells. She'll fly back to Bristol tomorrow, for-cing me to forget her all over again.

'What happened to your face, Ben?'

'Just a slight disagreement with a flight of stairs.'

'The concrete won.' When she touches my jaw part of me wants to drag her back to the hotel, while the rest wants to avoid any more damage. 'Congratulations. I hear the killers are behind bars.'

'I should have caught them sooner, but they were well camouflaged.'

My eyes fix on the horizon, the light fading over the off-islands, but I can see Nina from the corner of my eye, wearing the smile I've never really understood. She knows how to pull me close and push me away at the same time. The tide's in full spate now, the waves racing further up the shore.

'We can have that farewell drink now, if you like,' I tell her. 'But there's something I have to do first. Shadow had an operation earlier, I want to check he's okay.'

She rises to her feet, slipping on her sandals. 'I'd like to see him too. Then I need to ring the owners of Watermill Cottage.'

'How come?'

'They're letting me stay another six weeks.'

'What about your exam?'

'I can fly back for a few days to take it.'

Nina keeps step as we cross the beach. Her amber-coloured gaze is assessing my reactions; there's no escaping her direct stare.

'I thought you only came back to say a proper goodbye.'

'You should pay more attention,' she says, laughing at me. 'I had to find out why you stuck in my head.'

'Shadow's the real draw, isn't he?'

'You could be right. I need to get dressed before we visit him.'

'No, please, stay in the bikini.'

Her smile widens. 'I can put it on again later; give me five minutes.'

She rests her head on my shoulder, then flits away. Now she's running across the beach, leaving me to watch the sea's spume trailing across the sand, like a bride's veil.

Author's Note

I always end my books by asking readers not to use them as guidebooks, and *Pulpit Rock* is no exception. It's set on the beautiful island of St Mary's, the biggest and most densely populated island in Scilly, but I have taken liberties with its geography to build an exciting story. There's a heavy pinch of imagination sprinkled all over the island's ancient terrain. Pulpit Rock does stand at the tip of Peninnis Head as I have described, but its scale has been exaggerated, which is just one example of dozens where I have stretched the truth. What matters to me is staying true to the spirit of the landscape, because I've loved St Mary's for years. It's a glorious place, and I would hate to upset the locals, in case they exclude me from their great pubs and hotels.

The idea for this book came from a walk I took last summer, from Hugh Town to the north of the island. A bride and groom were having their photo taken against the backdrop of Pulpit Rock. It was such a striking image, with the bride's veil floating on the breeze, that

I had to include it in my story. I hope this dark tale won't put any couples off using the same setting for a photoshoot in the future.

I can heartily recommend St Mary's to anyone who enjoys a rocky, unspoilt coastline, studded with quiet, sandy beaches. You'll find archaeological sites galore, and the chance to ply back and forth between the islands on a network of tiny ferries. The place feels like the land that time forgot. Visitors trundle around on golf buggies and rented bicycles, instead of cars, and no one gets upset if there's a long queue at the Co-op. I always keep a few pebbles from Porthcressa Beach on my desk, to remind myself of the island's beauty while I work.

Acknowledgements

I would like to thank everyone on St Mary's for being so welcoming over the years. Particular thanks are due to my friends Linda Thomas at Porthcressa Library, talented YA author Rachel Greenlaw, Clive and Avril Mumford and Victoria Hitchens. I owe a big debt to Jeremy Brown and his multi-talented partner Kate, for inviting me to take part in the islands' brilliant Creative Scilly Festival. Thank you also to St Mary's Creative Writing Group for inviting me to join them in a workshop and giving me their lovely anthology, which proves just how many talented writers live in Scilly.

I am grateful to Five Islands School for letting me spend time with their boisterous and brilliant pupils, encouraging them to consider writing as a career. Thanks to the very helpful staff at the Star Castle Hotel, for allowing me to include the building in my book. The managers are nothing like those described in *Pulpit Rock*; the hotel is a special, luxurious place to stay.

Thanks to Teresa Chris, my agent, to whom this book is dedicated. She keeps me writing, even when gin and chocolate fail, and always leads me to the best garments when we go clothes shopping. Thank you so much to everyone at Simon and Schuster for your support, particularly my brilliant editor Bec Farrell and my kind and thoughtful publicist Jess Barratt.

My writer friends Penny Hancock, Mel McGrath, Louise Millar and everyone in Killer Women also deserve my gratitude. Thanks for picking me up whenever my confidence flags. My Twitter pals have also supported me beautifully over the years. Janet Fearnley, Peggy Breckin, Polly Dymock, Hazel Wright, Julie Boon, Jenny Blackwell, Louise Marley, Christine South, Angela Barnes, Rachel Medlock, Sarah LP and hundreds more – you are all brilliant. It's your passion for my stories that carries me to my desk every morning, determined to write more.

Finally, thanks to my lovely sister Honor, and my long-suffering husband Dave for believing in me, right from the start.

Loved *Pulpit Rock*?
Read on for an exclusive extract
from the new thriller by Kate Rhodes,
coming soon …

DEVIL'S
TABLE

1

Sunday 19 December

The twins wait until the house falls silent. Outside their bed-room window the storm is gathering force, whirls of sea mist racing past.

'Let's go,' Jade whispers. 'We can't be late.'

Ethan knows he should refuse. Their father's punishments will be harsh if he discovers their actions, but his sister is already zipping up her windcheater. When Jade opens the window to jump onto the flat roof below, Ethan knows he must follow, even though he'd rather stay warm in bed.

The boy's anxiety is soon replaced by excitement. Mist swirls around him as he chases ahead, but nothing can slow him down. He learned to walk on this path; each bump and tree root is imprinted on his memory. There's a break in the fog when the twins pause beside a field of narcissi. The flowers' odour is heady tonight, the blooms yielding their sweetness to the dark. St Martin's is bathed in moonlight, turning the flower fields silver, until a new wave of fog rushes inland, blurring the horizon.

'Race you to the beach,' his sister yells.

'Stay on the path, Jade. Dad'll kill us for spoiling the flowers!'

She ignores his warning, never afraid of tomorrow's punishments. Ethan watches her trample through knee-high blooms, with broken petals sticking to her jeans, before she disappears into the white air. Instinct tells him to go home, but he was born second, destined to play catch-up forever.

Ethan is halfway across the field when Jade gives a high-pitched scream. The noise is soon replaced by the dry sound of wind attacking the tamarisk hedges that surround the fields. There's no reply when he calls Jade's name. His sister loves spooking him, but Ethan is already afraid. Ghosts dance before his eyes when a fresh wave of mist rushes inland.

'Where are you?' he shouts. 'Stop messing around.'

A hand settles on Ethan's shoulder, the grip so harsh each finger leaves a bruise. Someone kicks the backs of his knees, dropping him to the ground, and it can't be Jade: his sister isn't that strong. Ethan yells for help, but his attacker grabs him from behind, tainting the air with booze and cigarettes. He hears Jade scream again, the sound weaker than before, but Ethan can only see a wall of fog that's hiding the stars. He tries to shout to his sister, telling her to run, but his voice has stopped working. The arm locked around his waist is too powerful to fight, even when he lashes out. It's only when he bites his attacker's hand that its grip weakens.

The boy seizes his chance to escape. Fear makes him sprint home, tripping over the rutted ground. He tries to shout Jade's name again, but no sound emerges. He can only hope that she's found a safe place to hide. His eyes are wide with panic when he clambers back up the drainpipe. Ethan gazes down from the window, searching for his sister, but tendrils of fog have smothered the glass once more, hiding the fields from view.

2

My grandfather valued beauty over safety. He could have built his home anywhere in Scilly, but he chose Hell Bay on Bryher's western coast, at the mercy of every Atlantic squall. My girlfriend, Nina, seems oblivious to tonight's storm, calmly writing Christmas cards at my kitchen table. The view from the window consists of rain pouring down the glass and breakers hammering the shore fifty metres away. My dog, Shadow, gambols at my feet, begging for a final walk.

'No chance, mate. It's pissing down out there.'

'Don't be mean, Ben,' Nina tells me. 'He deserves a run.'

When I open the front door the wind rocks me back on my feet, but Shadow is overjoyed. He streaks outside at top speed like he's seeking the eye of the storm, leaving me shaking my head. Four months ago he was so badly injured, it took two operations to stem the internal bleeding, followed by weeks of pain as his wounds healed, yet he never came close to giving up. The vet said that wolfdogs are a tough breed, and he must be right. The only difference in Shadow's behaviour since his near-death experience is his tendency to stay close to my side, apart from occasional forays across the island. I can see him chasing the tideline, tail wagging, while he looks for something foul to drag home.

'He's better, but still not a hundred percent.'

'PTSD,' Nina replies. 'He needs time to recover.'

'Do dogs get depressed, like humans?'

'They have emotions, that's for sure: dogs cry when they're upset, like us.' A gust of wind rushes inside, blowing her envelopes from the table. 'Shut the door, for God's sake. My stuff's going everywhere.'

I can tell she's only pretending to be angry. She moved to Scilly in August, and it's taken me four months to second-guess her moods. Nina's serenity masks the sadness of losing her husband three years ago; her shield of mystery is still so impenetrable, I'd need an X-ray machine to discover what else lies beneath. She's spent every weekend here for months, but values her own company too highly to compromise. I asked her to move in with me weeks ago, and I'm still waiting for an answer. Tomorrow she will return to St Martin's, a thirty-minute boat ride away, where she's house-sitting for a local couple who are spending the winter abroad. The arrangement suits her perfectly.

She can study for her counselling diploma, do gardening duties, and keep me at arm's length. Nina is busy collecting her cards into an orderly pile, giving me time to study her. I can't explain why she's stuck in my head like a tune I can't stop humming. She never fusses over her appearance, apart from running a comb through her hair each morning; she's dressed in old Levis and a plain blue T-shirt. Her chocolate brown hair hangs to her shoulders in a neat line, the olive skin she inherited from her Italian mother a shade darker than mine.

'Don't stare, Ben. It's distracting me.'

'Why are you writing cards at midnight? They won't get there in time.'

'It's the thought that counts. Why aren't you sending any?'

'Christmas is a marketing conspiracy. When's the last time anyone gave you something you actually need?'

'What a narrow, bloke-ish thing to say.' Nina rolls her eyes. 'Stop bugging me and play the piano instead.'

'Is my conversation that bad?'

'I'd prefer music tonight.'

I haul myself upright with a show of reluctance. Nina handles her violin like it's an extension of her body, while I make constant mistakes on the piano my dad inherited from the island's pub. I taught myself to play out of boredom as a kid, copying songs I heard on the radio, because my parents refused to buy a TV. I can still pick out a few tunes, but conjuring one from memory is harder. I play the first notes of 'Someone to Watch over Me' in the wrong tempo, then muscle memory kicks in and life gets easier. Before long I'm following the storm's music instead, echoing the wind's high notes and the waves' slow heartbeat.

When I finally stop, Nina is curled up on the settee, smiling. 'Not bad, for a man who never practises.'

'They offered me lessons at school, but rugby got in the way.'

'You're a natural then.'

'Flatterer,' I say, closing the lid of the piano. 'You want a lift to St Martin's tomorrow, don't you?'

She shakes her head. 'Ray's cooking me breakfast, then we're going in his speedboat.'

'The old boy's sweet on you. Don't break his heart, will you?'

My uncle Ray is a hard man to impress; a lifelong bachelor, who returned to Bryher after years at sea, to build boats. He's famous for enjoying his own company, yet Nina can spend hours pottering around his boatyard, without any complaint.

'Are you jealous, Benesek Kitto?' She only uses my full name to mock.

'I've got a three stone weight advantage if he wants to fight it out.'

Nina stands up abruptly. 'Stop boasting, will you? It's time for bed.'

'Is that your idea of seduction?'

'It's the best you'll get.'

'Maybe I should play the piano more often.'

I don't put up a fight when she leads me to the bedroom. The sex between us is less frantic these days, but I still want her badly enough to grit my teeth while she peels off her clothes. My hefty, carthorse build embarrassed me as a kid, but the way she looks at me removes self-doubt. She takes her time undoing the buttons of my shirt, stripping away layers of fabric, until nothing separates us, except the overhead light that exposes every detail. I love watching her move, and the emotions flowing across her face. It takes effort to hold my shattered senses together, but when she finally lets go, it's worth the wait.

Her eyes are still cloudy when we collapse back into the pillows, her amber gaze softer than before. 'That's clinched it,' she murmurs.

'About what?'

'I choose you, not Ray.'

'Lucky me.'

'But it was a tough call.'

I stand up to turn off the light, her eyes closing when I slip back under the covers. Nina's hunger for sleep still amazes me; she can remain unconscious for twelve hours at a stretch without moving a muscle. She shifts towards me, mumbling something under her breath.

'Changes are coming, Ben. You have to be ready.'

'How do you mean?'

I wait for a reply but hear only her slow breathing and the gale rattling roof tiles overhead. Her oval face is as calm as a statue in the moonlight that sifts through the curtains. I'm still digesting her words when Shadow scratches at the front door, the sound reminding me of the squealing car brakes that often woke me in London. His fur is soaked when I get him inside, so I rub him dry with an old towel, then he lies at my feet, warming himself by the embers of the fire. When I look around, Nina's belongings are scattered around my living room. A copy of *Persuasion* lies on my coffee table, her red scarf hanging by the door, and the violin her husband gave her the year before he died is propped against the wall. She's even begun leaving clothes in my wardrobe, which must signal progress. When I finally get to meet her parents I'll know she means business.

Shadow doesn't complain about being left alone for once, content to stay warm by the hearth. My girl-friend's pronouncement is half-forgotten; things have already changed beyond recognition. I slept alone for five years, but now Nina's here, and I'm not prepared to let her go. When I peer out of the window for a final time the storm is getting worse – fog is rushing inland, blindfolding my house with thick white air.

**Don't miss out – *Devil's Table* is available
to order now.**

Don't miss the other atmospheric locked-island thrillers featuring DI Ben Kitto from highly-acclaimed author, Kate Rhodes

'An absolute master of pace, plotting and character'
ELLY GRIFFITHS

'A vividly realised protagonist whose complex and harrowing history rivals the central crime storyline'
SOPHIE HANNAH

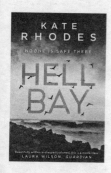 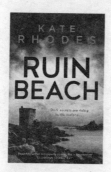 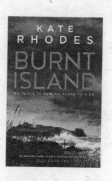

'Gripping, clever and impossible to put down' **ERIN KELLY**

'Beautifully written and expertly plotted; this is a masterclass' *GUARDIAN*

SIMON & SCHUSTER